ATLANTIA

Also by Ally Condie:

Matched
Crossed
Reached

ATLANTIA

A Novel

ALLY
CONDIE

DUTTON BOOKS

AN IMPRINT OF PENGUIN GROUP (USA) LLC

DUTTON BOOKS
Published by the Penguin Group
Penguin Group (USA) LLC
375 Hudson Street
New York, New York 10014

USA * Canada * UK * Ireland * Australia
New Zealand * India * South Africa * China

penguin.com

A Penguin Random House Company

LIBRARY OF CONGRESS CATALOGING-IN-PUBLICATION DATA
Condie, Allyson Braithwaite.
Atlantia : a novel / by Ally Condie.
pages cm
Summary: "Rio has always dreamed of leaving the underwater city of Atlantia for life in the Above; however, when her twin sister, Bay, makes an unexpected decision, Rio is left stranded below where she must find a way to unlock the secrets of the siren voice she has long hidden and save Atlantia from destruction"— Provided by publisher.
ISBN 978-0-525-42644-8 (hardback)
[1. Fantasy. 2. Twins—Fiction. 3. Sisters—Fiction.] I. Title.

PZ7.C7586At 2014
[Fic]--dc23 2014020665

Printed in the United States of America

1 3 5 7 9 10 8 6 4 2

For Truman,
who is a creator and a maker

CHAPTER 1

$\mathcal{M}$y twin sister, Bay, and I pass underneath the brown-and-turquoise banners hanging from the ceiling of the temple. Dignitaries perch on their chairs in the gallery, watching, and people crowd the pews in the nave. Statues of the gods adorn the walls and ceiling, and it seems as if they watch us, too. The temple's largest and most beautiful window, the rose window, has been lit from behind to simulate the effect of sunlight through the panes. The glass shines like a blessing—amber, green, blue, pink, purple. The colors of flower petals Above, of coral formations Below.

The Minister stands at the altar, which is made of precious wood carved in an intricate pattern of straight lines and swirls, of waves that turn into trees. Two bowls rest on top of the altar—one filled with salt water from the ocean that envelops our city, one filled with dark dirt brought down from Above.

Bay and I wait in line with the other youth our age. I feel sorry for everyone else because they don't have a brother or a sister to wait with them. Twins aren't very common in Atlantia.

"Do you hear the city breathing?" Bay whispers. I know she wants me to say that I do, but I shake my head. What

we hear isn't breathing. It is the never-ending sound of air pumping through the walls and out into the city so that we can survive.

Bay knows that, but she's always been a little crazy about Atlantia. She's not the only one who loves our underwater city or refers to it as alive. And Atlantia does resemble a giant sea creature sprawled out in the ocean. The tentacles of our streets and thoroughfares web out from the larger round hubs of the neighborhoods and marketplaces. Everything is enclosed, of course. We live underwater, but we're still human; we need walls and air to protect us.

The Minister raises his hand, and we all fall silent.

Bay presses her lips together. She is usually calm and serene, but today she seems tense. Is she afraid that I'll go back on my word? I won't. I promised her.

We stand side by side and hand in hand, our brown hair threaded with blue ribbons and braided in intricate plaits. We both have blue eyes. We are both tall and carry ourselves the same way. But we're fraternal twins, not identical, and no one has ever had any trouble telling us apart.

Though Bay and I are not mirrors of each other, we're still as near to the same person as two completely different people can be. We have always been close, and since my mother's death, we have drawn even more tightly together.

"Today will be hard," Bay says.

I nod. *Today* will *be hard,* I think, *because I won't be doing what I always wanted to do.* But I know that's not what Bay means.

"Because it used to be her," I say.

Bay nods.

Before my mother died six months ago, *she* was the Minister of the temple and she presided over this ceremony, one of several held to mark the anniversary of the Divide. Bay and I watched each year as our mother gave the opening speech and blessed the youth of the year with water or dirt, depending on what each person chose.

"Do you think Maire is here?" Bay asks.

"No," I say. Bay is referring to our aunt, our only living relative. I keep my voice flat but use the most cutting words I can. "She doesn't belong here." The temple is our mother's place, and she and her sister, Maire, were estranged for as long as I can remember. Although, when my mother died—

Don't think about it.

The Minister begins the ritual, and I close my eyes and picture my mother conducting this service instead. In my mind, she stands straight and small behind the altar. She wears her brown-and-blue robes and the Minister's insignia, the silver necklace that mimics the carving on the pulpit. She opens her arms wide, and it makes her look like one of the rays that swim through the sea gardens sometimes.

"What are the gifts given to we who live Below?" the new Minister asks.

"*Long life, health, strength, and happiness.*" I chant the words with everyone else, but, for my family, at least, the first part has not been true. Both of my parents died young—my father of a disease called water-lung back when Bay and I were babies, and my mother more recently. Of course, they still lived longer than they would have Above, but their lives were far shorter than most of the people who live in Atlantia.

Then again, our family has never been like most families in Atlantia. It used to be that we were different in ways that made people turn green with jealousy, but lately Bay and I are different in ways that make people pity us. Their envy has been washed away by our misfortunes. Bay and I used to walk the halls of the temple school and everyone respected us, because we were the daughters of Oceana, the Minister. Now we are objects of pity, the orphaned children of parents who died too soon.

"What is the curse of those who live Above?" the Minister asks.

"Short life, illness, weakness, and misery."

Bay squeezes my hand, comforting me. She knows that I'm going to keep my promise, and that in doing so I'll have to make a choice opposite to the one I'd always planned.

"Is this fair?"

"It is fair. It is as the gods decreed at the time of the Divide. Some have to stay Above so that humanity might survive Below."

"Then give thanks."

"Thanks to the gods for the sea where we live, for the air we breathe, for our lives in the Below."

"And have mercy on us."

"And on those who live Above."

"This," the Minister says, "is the way the gods have decreed it must be since the Divide took place. The air was polluted, and people could no longer survive for long Above. To save humanity, they built Atlantia. Many chose to stay Above so that their loved ones could live Below.

"Those of us underwater in the Below have long, beautiful lives. We work hard, but not nearly as hard as those on land. We have time for leisure. We don't have to breathe ruined air or have cancer eat our lungs.

"Those Above work all their lives to support us Below. Their lungs decay, and their bodies feel tremendous pain. But they will be rewarded later, in the life after this one.

"The choice to save our world in this way was made by the gods and by our ancestors. We accept their choice every day of our lives, except for today, when we make our own. Though we believe the gods have sent us Below for a reason, we also have the chance to go Above if we wish, to dedicate our lives to sacrifice."

The Minister has finished the speech. I open my eyes.

The new Minister is a tall man named Nevio. I still haven't gotten used to seeing the Minister's insignia hanging around his neck. I still think of it as belonging to my mother.

Why would anyone *choose to go Above if you die so young and have to work so hard?* the children of the Below used to ask each other when we were smaller. And I never answered, but I kept a long list at home of all the reasons I could think of to go Above. *You could see the stars. You could feel the sun on your face. You could touch a tree that had roots in the ground. You could walk for miles and never come across the edge of your world.*

"Come forward," Nevio says to the first person.

"I accept my fate Below," the girl says. A murmur of approval goes up from the crowd. For all the grand speeches about the virtue of sacrifice, the people of Atlantia like it when the youth validate their own choice to stay Below. Nevio the Minister nods and dips his fingers into the bowl of seawater and sprinkles it over the girl, speckling her face with drops too small to be tears. I wonder if it stings.

The first person to choose the Above is surrounded by the peacekeepers and swept away to a secure location. There is no opportunity to say good-bye to friends and family. Once the ceremony concludes, the peacekeepers load everyone who has chosen the Above onto a transport and send them up to the surface. The finality of the decision always appealed to me—no loose ends, only leaving. I knew it would be hard to see my mother's face when I made my choice, but she would have Bay. They wouldn't be alone, and I would—at last—be Above.

But when my mother died, everything changed.

Another boy goes up for his turn. I know him by sight—Fen Cardiff, handsome and charismatic, with blond hair and dangerous, laughing eyes. There's an irreverent, ironic note in his voice even as he speaks the sacred words. "I choose sacrifice in the Above."

I think I hear a woman cry out. She sounds surprised and wounded. His mother? Didn't he tell her what he was going to choose? He doesn't glance up into the stands—instead, he turns around to look back at the rest of us in line, as if searching for something or someone.

In the moment before the peacekeepers take him away, I find myself staring right into his eyes, eyes that will soon see the Above. I am so jealous of him I can hardly breathe. But I promised Bay I wouldn't do it, that I'd stay here with her. My palms feel sweaty. *I promised Bay.*

She is the only person I've ever told that I want to go Above. That I dream about it every night, that when I see the immense glass jar of dirt on the altar in the temple I can picture exactly how it would feel to touch it and smell it, to have it under my feet and all around. And in the years before my mother died, Bay promised that, when the time came, she'd let me go. She herself couldn't bear to leave Atlantia—she loved the city and my mother too much—but Bay assured me that she would keep my wish a secret so that no one could try to stop me. Once I declared it in front of the crowd at the temple, my mother would have no choice but to let me leave.

Even the Minister and the Council cannot override the decision of each individual person regarding the Above and the Below.

I love my mother and my sister but, for as long as I can remember, I've always known that I need to see the Above.

But I can't go.

On the day my mother died, Bay cried so much that the water from her tears streamed down into her hair, and I had the fleeting thought that my sister might turn into a mermaid, with seaweed hair and salt always on her face. "Promise me," she said when she could finally speak, "that you won't leave me alone."

I knew Bay was right. I couldn't leave her, now that my mother was gone. *"I promise,"* I whispered to Bay.

The only way for Bay and me to stay together is to remain Below. While we can both choose to stay, both of us cannot choose to go because we are the only two children in our family. One person from each gene line must always remain in Atlantia.

A few more people, and it's my turn.

Nevio the Minister knows me, of course, but his expression when I come to the front remains impassive, the way it has for everyone else. My mother would have been the same way—she was always different in her Minister robes, more removed and regal. But would she have kept her composure if I'd said I wanted to go Above?

I will never know.

The salt water is in a blue bowl; the dirt in a brown one. I close my eyes and will myself to speak in the right voice—the flat, false one my mother always insisted that I use, the one that hides the curse and gift that is my real voice.

"I accept my fate Below," I say.

The Minister flecks salt water onto my face, blessing me, and it is done.

I turn back to watch Bay come past the altar. She is moments younger than I am, or she would have gone first. Watching my sister is a bit like watching myself make the choice. The processed air of the temple moves over us as if Atlantia truly breathes.

Bay has a soft voice, but I have no trouble hearing her.

"I choose sacrifice in the Above," she says.

No. Bay. She said the wrong line. She was nervous and made a mistake.

I move to help her. There must be a way—

"Wait," I say. "Bay." I look at Nevio the Minister to see if he can stop this, but he stares at Bay, an expression of surprise flickering across his face. It's only a moment that I glance at him, but it's too long. Peacekeepers surround Bay, as they have the others who chose the Above.

"Wait." No one hears me or pays attention. That's the purpose of the voice I use.

"Bay," I say again, and this time there's a tiny hint of my real voice in my tone, and so she turns to look at me, almost as if in spite of herself.

I am stunned at the sadness in her eyes, but not as much as I am at the purpose I see there.

She meant to do this.

In the seconds that it takes to wrap my mind around the impossible—*This is no mistake, Bay* wants *to leave*—they pull my sister out of reach.

I push through the crowd quickly and quietly, trying not to cause a scene because a scene will be stopped. The priests all know me, and they know that Bay and I are inseparable. Already some of them move in my direction to block my path, sympathetic expressions on their faces.

Why would Bay do this?

Justus, one of the kinder priests, comes closer and reaches out to me.

"No," I say, my real voice, my real pain and anger cutting and coming out, and Justus drops his arm down to his side. I look up and see his face—shocked, stunned, slapped with the sound of me speaking.

I've done what I always promised I wouldn't. I've used my true voice in public. And it is as my mother always warned me it would be—there's no way to take it back. I can't bear to look at the horror on Justus's face. Justus, who has known me all my life. I don't dare glance back at the crowd to see who else has heard.

Though my feet are firmly on the ground of Atlantia, I'm dissolving.

My sister's gone.

She decided to go Above.

She would never do this.

She did.

Bay asked me if I heard the city breathing.

I hear my own breathing now, in and out and in and out. I live here. I will die here.

I am never going to leave.

CHAPTER 2

*D*own in the deepmarket, the sellers call out, nudging their carts into people's backs and bodies to get attention.

"Pure air!" someone shouts. "All flavors and scents. Cinnamon, cayenne, rose! Cedar, lilac, saffron!"

"Something new to wear!" another cries. There are shops up closer to the surface, near the temple, but down here the wares are much more varied—a jumbled flotsam and jetsam of junk and treasures. The goods are tumbled out in carts and stalls instead of arranged precisely behind glass windows. The selling stalls are dilapidated but utilitarian, pieced together out of old metal pilings and plastic slats.

Bay and I used to go everywhere together, and, after the temple, the deepmarket was the place we came most often after our mother died. I haven't found any clues in the temple as to why Bay left, so I've come here to look for something. Anything. A message. A note. Any sign from her at all.

After the peacekeepers released me on the day Bay left, I went back to the room the two of us shared and tore it apart.

I had to find *something* that could explain what she'd done. *Maybe,* I thought, *there would be a letter, labeled in her neat handwriting, explaining everything, bringing her motives to light.*

I turned out the pockets of all of her clothes. I pulled off the bedspread, blankets, and sheets from her bed, heaved the mattress from the springs and looked underneath. I went through all of my own belongings, just in case. I even steeled myself and opened the box in the closet where we kept the last of my mother's things, but everything was exactly as it had been when we packed it away. No note.

Nothing.

To go so suddenly, without any explanation, was cruel, and Bay was never cruel. She could be annoyed and sharp when she was tired or under stress. But those qualities in her were never as strong as they were in me—she was the gentler sister, quicker to laugh, certainly better suited to follow in my mother's footsteps. I never resented it when people said that, because I knew it was true.

In the days since Bay left, I've done everything I can think of to get to her. I fought through the crowd at the temple until the peacekeepers pulled me back and put me in a holding area with other family members who'd shown signs of causing a scene. After they released us, I went to see the transport go to the surface, but of course it had already left. I stood there, trying to think of a way to follow, but the Council keeps a close watch on the transports and the locks that take them up. That is the only safe way for the living to go Above. Most of the transports are not pressurized for human survival. They're meant for the transfer of goods and food between the Above and the Below.

And even in my most desperate imaginings, I know the Council won't let me join my sister Above. They'll never permit me to go and I can't think of a viable way to escape.

As I walk past a stall in the deepmarket, I see brocades embroidered by someone well-skilled, and I almost reach out to touch the fabric, to linger looking over the designs. But I keep moving, pacing the length of the market way, leaving behind the crawl of stalls and coming out into the area at the edge of the deepmarket where the races take place.

In spite of the crush of people, it gets very cold in the deepmarket. The market's hours are limited. Closing time coincides with the dimming time in order to conserve the energy it takes to heat this part of the city and keep the air going. We are deep down here. I shiver, though the walls of Atlantia have never been breached or broken in any significant way.

When the people prepared for the Divide long ago, they asked for inspiration in designing Atlantia. The story is that the Minister at the time had a dream, in which the gods told him that our city should be patterned after the grand cities of old. The Minister saw Atlantia clearly in his dream—a beautiful place of temples and churches set on plazas. He saw colorful buildings with shops on the ground floor and apartments rising above them, and boulevards and streets connecting everything together.

But, of course, it all had to be underwater.

And so Atlantia was conceived as a series of enormous enclosed bubbles, some higher than others, some lower, connected by canals and walkways. The engineers discovered that it was better to make smaller habitats and join them together than to create one large bubble for everything. The centermost sphere is the most desirable part of Atlantia. It holds the temple, the Council buildings, the upmarket, and several living areas. Other, smaller enclosures encompass the lesser churches, markets, and neighborhoods. Some of the deepest bubbles of all are the areas that encompass the machineries of Atlantia, the bays where the mining drones come in for repair and storage, and the deepmarket.

The engineers spent years designing all of this. Some of the original blueprints are on display in a special glass case in one of the antechambers of the temple. There are rusty stains and splatters on the diagrams. The rumor is that, as the engineers were dying, they sometimes coughed blood onto the papers. They couldn't stop in their task or humankind would have perished, so they kept on at their sacred, consecrated work. When I mentioned the rumor about the spots on the paper being blood to my mother, she did not debunk it or say the stains were something else. "So many sacrificed for us to live," she said, and her eyes were very sad.

The destruction Above meant that there were few natural materials left for use Below. Our city's underpinnings are made mostly of manufactured goods, with some precious overlays of old materials like the wooden pulpit in the temple and the stones covering a few of the best streets. But Atlantia is still beautiful. One of the things we Atlantians are most proud of is our trees—made of steel trunks and individual, shimmering metallic leaves, they are as lovely as anything that ever existed Above.

So people say.

The engineers used the transportation from one of those old cities—a romantic system of canals and boats called gondolas—as a model for our public transit down here. Of course, our gondolas are modernized—they have engines and run on tracks through dry concrete canals. The people of Atlantia love the gondolas although they require constant maintenance. Even though workers repair the gondolas each night after curfew, it's not uncommon to see a boat beached off its track during the day, machinists swarming around like mermaids gathering about the hulls of shipwrecks in pre-Divide illustrations.

My mother found the architecture of Atlantia fascinating, and she loved the trees and the gondolas almost as much as she loved the temple. "Flourishes in the face of death," she told Bay and me once as we looked at the diagrams. "The engineers left their signature in every working of Atlantia. They made the city useful *and* beautiful."

"It's a second kind of immortality," Bay said. "They live on in heaven, and in Atlantia herself."

My mother looked over at Bay, and their love of the city was so palpable that I felt left out. I loved Atlantia, but not the way they did.

These lower areas have less embellishment and look more utilitarian than some of the other parts of Atlantia. Here, the rivets are clearly visible on the walls, and the sky is lower. Up at the temple, the soaring rises inside the building echo the high arches of the false sky outside.

I pass by one of the stalls that sells masks. They aren't the air masks we carry strapped over our backs—the ones we're told to keep with us at all times in case of a breach in Atlantia's walls. The masks sold in the deepmarket are designed to be worn for fun, so you can pretend to be someone else. I feign interest in them, touching the faces of fantastic creatures that used to live in the Above—lions, tigers, horses—all of them known to me only from pictures in books. There are also more fanciful masks—a variety of sea witches, some with green faces, some blue.

Children delight in telling one another stories about the sea witches. We talked about them at school and when we played together in the plazas. Once, when my mother wanted me to come with her to the temple for a late service and I didn't want to go, I tried to use what I'd heard as an excuse. "If I go out near the dimming time a sea witch might get me," I told my mother. "Or a siren."

"Sea witches are an old superstition," my mother said. She didn't deny the existence of sirens—people, usually women, who can use their voices to convince others to do their bidding—because everyone knows sirens exist. They were the first miracle that came about after the Divide. They were born to the younger generation of those who came Below, and they have been serving Atlantia ever since.

I am a siren.

It is a secret my mother decided to keep because sirens' lives are consecrated to the service of Atlantia, and siren children are given to the Council to raise. My mother didn't want to give me up.

"Sea witches *are* real," I told my mother. "They have names." *Maybe,* I thought, *people know when they're sea witches, but they keep it a secret, the way I keep* my *secret about being a siren.* The thought thrilled me.

"And what are the witches' names?" my mother asked in the amused voice I loved, the one that meant she was willing to go along with my game.

"Maire," I said, thinking of a story I'd heard the day before at school. "One of them is named Maire."

"What did you say?" My mother sounded shocked.

"Maire," I said. "She's a sea witch *and* a siren. She has magic, more than just her voice. She gets what she wants from you and then she turns you into sea foam before your family even has a chance to bring your body to the floodgates." One of the girls at school told me that Maire *drank* the foam, but I decided to spare my mother this gory detail since her hands had gone to her mouth and her eyes were wide. Too wide. She wasn't pretending to be horrified. She *was* horrified, and my mother was not easily shocked.

"Don't tell that story anymore," she said. Her voice trembled and I felt sorry. Perhaps I'd used too much of my voice in telling the story. I hadn't meant to frighten her.

"I won't," I said. "I promise."

Some people said that sirens didn't have souls, and so I asked my mother if that were true of Maire. "No," my mother said. "Every living thing has a soul. Maire has a soul." And of course, my mother knew what I was really asking. "You have a soul, Rio," she told me. "Never doubt that."

It wasn't until later that our mother told us the truth—that the siren Maire was her sister. Our aunt. "But we no longer speak to each other," my mother said, a great sorrow in her voice, and Bay and I looked at each other, terrified. How could sisters grow so far apart?

"Don't worry," my mother said, seeing our expressions. "It won't happen to you. They came and took Maire away when they found out she was a siren, and we weren't raised together. We grew apart. You see? It's one of the reasons we have to keep Rio's secret. We don't want her to be separated from us. We don't want to lose her."

Bay and I nodded. We understood perfectly.

And this was an enormous secret for my mother to keep from the Council, especially later when she became Minister.

She was supposed to report to the other Council members and work with them closely. She was not supposed to have secrets from them.

But she did have secrets. At least one, and maybe more.

It was on Maire's doorstep that they found my mother the night she died. She went to see her sister, but I don't know why.

———

I've made it to the edge of the deepmarket, where they keep the swimming lanes—several heavy cement canals once used for the gondolas. Years ago, some enterprising group hauled the lanes down here and set them up for racing. It must have been difficult to move something so heavy.

Aldo, the man who organizes the races, nods to me as I approach. "I heard your sister went Above," he calls out. "I'm sorry to hear that." Aldo is a few years older than Bay and me. Even though his blue eyes and dark curly hair and smooth features should make him handsome, they don't.

"Thank you." Those two words are all I can manage to say without emotion when people offer me their condolences.

Aldo's moment of civility has already ended. "I'm going to have to redo all the race brackets for this weekend now that she won't be swimming."

"Did she leave anything here for me?" I ask.

"What would she leave?"

"A note," I say. "Or something else. I'm not sure."

"No," Aldo says. "She always took her gear with her. We don't have room to store much down here. You know that."

I do. The racing lanes themselves use most of the available space, and the spectator stands take up what's left. There is a small bank of rent-by-the-hour lockers pushed up near the wall where Aldo posts the brackets; we can keep our things there while we race.

"Could there be anything in the lockers?" I ask.

"No," Aldo says. "I went through them last night. They were all empty."

He says it in a disinterested tone, and I believe that he tells the truth. My heart sinks.

So. She didn't leave anything here, either. Aldo turns and walks away.

The water slaps against the walls of the cement canals. Steely thin bleachers rise up on either side, calling to mind the seats in the temple. The priests knew Bay began racing here after my mother's death, and they turned a blind eye to it. We needed the money. The temple takes care of all of its students' room and board, of course, but all our work there is considered consecrated and we receive no coin in return. Almost everyone else had two parents to watch over them, to give them pocket money and pay for books and buy new clothes. But the Minister also takes no money for her work, only room and board and clothing. Our mother looked out for us by selling her personal possessions when we needed something new. However, she'd gone through most of those items by the time she died.

So Bay set out to earn money. It was surprising, how clearly she knew exactly what to do. After I promised to stay, she still grieved deeply, but she was back to her old self in other ways— calm and collected, thinking things through.

"They have races in the deepmarket," she told me. "Swimming ones. People bet on them."

I knew about the races, even though up until then Bay and I rarely watched them. The priests discouraged it. "But those people have been swimming for years," I said.

"We can learn fast," she said. "It's in our genes."

Bay and I both take after my father physically—we are tall and strong, while my mother was small and delicate. When we were twelve, we passed her in height and kept on growing; she laughed that she had to look up to the two of us.

My father was a racer, back when it was an approved sport and they had fancy sleek swimming lanes erected in the plazas on weekends. That's how my mother met him. She was attending one of the races, and he came out of the water after finishing and looked up and saw her. In a crowd of people stirring and shouting there was one spot of stillness: my mother. She stood up because that's what everyone else was doing, but she kept on reading the book she'd brought with her. That intrigued him. What was so interesting that she couldn't even be bothered to watch the race? So he climbed up in the stands and found her and asked her to go to one of the cafés with him. She agreed. That was the beginning.

"But racing is what might have given him water-lung," I protested.

"They've never proven the link," Bay said.

She sold one of my mother's few remaining personal possessions—a tiger god statue—and used the coin to buy each of us a training suit and practice time in the lanes.

"I feel naked," I told Bay the day we first tried on the suits.

"You shouldn't," she said. "These things are almost as modest as our temple robes. We're covered from stem to stern."

That made me laugh, which I hadn't done often since my mother died, and Bay smiled. We went out to the lanes together, and the teacher shook his head. "Aldo didn't tell me you were so old," he said. "It's no use for me to teach you."

"We're only fifteen," Bay said.

"Still too old," the man said. "You have to start younger than this."

"We paid you to teach us," Bay said. "It's no concern to you how fast we are as long as you have your coin."

Of course, when we both picked up swimming fairly quickly, he acted as though he'd predicted it all along. "It's in your genes, of course," he said. "You'll never be as good as you could have been, if you'd started younger. But I suppose your mother wanted to keep you up at the temple. I can't say I blame her."

"It doesn't matter if I'm not in the faster brackets," Bay said to me quietly. "I only have to be good enough to enter and win some of the races."

"Wait," I said. She'd said I, not we. "What about me?"

"No," Bay said. "It's too dangerous."

Because of my voice. I knew that was the reason. It always was, for everything. But this time, I didn't see why.

"It's like everything else," Bay said. "Anything you do in public runs the risk of exposure. It's better if you watch. You can tell me if anyone tries to cheat. You can keep an eye on the clock and see if Aldo tries to rig the results."

I fumed. "If I'm not going to race, why did I bother learning to swim?"

"It's part of who we are," she said. "Our father knew how. And doesn't it seem stupid that most of us don't know how to swim? When we live underwater?"

"Not really," I said. "If there's ever a breach, we'll all die anyway."

"Don't think like that," Bay said. So we kept training together, day after day, but I never raced.

Aldo comes back out with more papers to post on the wall. The rustling of the pages brings me back to the present.

"I could swim in her bracket," I say. Racing would be a connection to Bay. A way to burn off some of the restlessness eating me up inside.

Aldo raises his eyebrows. I can tell that he likes this idea, because he is both sharp and lazy and this will save him some work. "When the two of you trained side by side, you always kept up with her."

"Yes," I say. "I did."

"I don't have a problem with it," he says. "But the other racers will have to agree with the substitution. And I'll need to let the bettors know."

I nod.

"Come again tomorrow and I'll tell you what they say," Aldo says. He heads back in the direction of the stall where he takes the bets.

I stand there for a moment more, watching the smooth turquoise water wash against the sides of the racing lane. Aldo colors the water artificially so that it looks more enticing. For the first time since Bay left I feel a tiny bit better. If I make my body tired, maybe my mind can rest, even if only for the moments when I swim and stare down at the line on the bottom of the lane and think about nothing but pushing through my own fatigue.

"*Rio*," a voice says behind me.

And in one heartbeat my thoughts go from blue to black.

I know that voice, though I haven't heard it in a long time, not since my mother's funeral.

She's here.

Maire.

My mother's sister.

The siren woman some people call a witch.

The one I think might have killed my mother.

How else to explain her crumpled figure on Maire's doorstep? Or why Maire never said anything, never offered a single word of explanation as to why my mother might have come to her?

"Maire wouldn't have killed her," Bay said, when I told her about my suspicions. "A sister couldn't do that."

I turn around and look back at the throngs in the deepmarket, but I can't find Maire among the moving cloaks and banners and faces. Still, I feel her watching me, even if I can't see exactly where she is. Does she expect me to answer her?

Maire doesn't know about my voice. My mother took great care to keep that part of me hidden from everyone, even her own sister.

"But if Maire has a voice like mine, won't people expect me to have one, too?" I asked once, when I was small.

"No," my mother said. "There have never been two sirens in the same family line. We've always believed that the siren voices are a gift from the gods, not simple genetics."

"Then why don't you treat it like a gift?"

Her eyes softened. "I'm sorry," she said. "I wish we could. But it is a gift, just not one you can use right now."

"When?" I asked.

She had no answer for me, but I had one for myself. After I went Above. My mother was always so pleased with my self-control. She didn't know that the reason I could manage it was because I never planned to do it forever. I thought I would go Above and speak at last.

"Maire is your greatest protection," my mother said. "Because she has a siren voice, people aren't looking for any of us to have one as well."

Rio. I hear my name again now, a single, clear word meant for me.

I start walking, fast, away from the rows of sellers and stalls and back up toward the lower reaches of Atlantia's neighborhoods.

I think I feel Maire following me, and I think I hear her, too. It's almost as though she's whispering to me, sentences I can't quite make out, hiding an undercurrent of words in the sound of the air channeling through the walls of the city. And I can't help myself. I wonder, *Could I do that, too?*

If I use my voice, I'll be like Maire. I'll be marked as a siren and people will fear me.

Every time I see Justus, the priest, he won't meet my gaze. Even though he heard me speak only a single word in my real voice, it was enough to make him keep his distance. That's the safest response for me, and I should be glad. But I'm sad about it. He was my mother's best friend, the gentlest priest, the one Bay and I hoped the others would choose as Minister after she died.

But they didn't. They chose Nevio.

A group of teenagers push past, laughing and talking together. They glance over at me and then look away. For a minute I'm tempted to call to them in my real voice. I could play upon the boys; I could make the girls feel jealous, wish they'd never ignored me.

"Hello," a voice says, persuasive, delicious, and for a moment I think I've done it, I've spoken. But I haven't.

Maire stands in front of me in her black robes, with her disheveled hair. Her face is at once too sharp to be anything like my mother's and yet too intelligent to be dissimilar. I have never seen her so close before.

"I need to speak to you," Maire says. "About your mother. And your sister."

You do not, I almost say, in my true voice, but I have been so long silent that it seems a pity to speak now. To ruin anything for an aunt who cares nothing for me.

I walk past her. She follows. I hear her boots on the street behind me. I feel the dark of my losses in those words *mother* and *sister*, in the way she said them so they would echo in my mind, cold as a cathedral with no candles.

I have always known that if I stayed Below I would be made small, and I feel it happening.

"Rio?" Maire says. "I was there at the temple the day Bay left. And I heard you speak."

I stop.

It wasn't only Justus who heard me.

"I always wondered if you were a siren, too," Maire says, a ring of happiness in her voice, and I flinch in spite of myself.

"If," Maire says, "there is ever *anything* you want, or need, I can help you. I helped your mother, you know. Even Oceana the Minister needed *me.*"

That's a lie. And my mother would be proud of how my voice comes out even and flat, although I want to scream. "My mother didn't need you," I say. "She had us. Her daughters."

"There are some things you only tell a sister," Maire says. "And some things you only ask of a sister." Now her voice sounds soft and sad, faraway, even though she stands close to me. It's unnerving. "You think that I am the evil sister, and that your mother was good," she says. "But Oceana did need me. And Bay needed me, too."

Bay didn't need Maire. Bay had me.

"She left something for you," Maire says. "Come along and I'll give it to you."

I'm caught between two things I know to be true.

Bay wouldn't have gone Above without leaving me some kind of message or explanation.

She also would never have left that message or explanation with Maire.

Would she?

Maire's voice is tangling things, confusing me.

A gondola comes behind us, slipping along in its cement canal. I want to get away from Maire and back to the temple. I break into a run.

"We need to talk, you and I." Maire's voice follows me. "I can help you get what you want, your deepest desire."

Does she even know my deepest desire? To go Above?

I have the terrible feeling that she might. That she might know my whole heart and mind.

"I can help you get Above," Maire says, her voice fading, haunting. "But it has to be soon. We are running out of time. Can't you hear the way the city is breathing?"

CHAPTER 3

$\mathcal{I}$ sit down in a pew in the temple and let the familiar scents of candle wax, stone and water, and old cloth settle over me. I take a deep breath and wait for my racing heart to slow down. It's been pounding since my encounter with Maire.

The priests move through the nave, their robes brushing the ground and making hushing sounds. I keep my head bowed in order to avoid eye contact. I don't want any more condolences about Bay leaving.

I should be safe from my aunt here. Those known to be sirens are not allowed in the temple. They have their own place of worship, somewhere among the tight restricted maze of Council buildings. But it wasn't always that way. In fact, in the beginning, many sirens were priests, using their voices to cry out warnings about pride and sin and to call people to sacrifice. But then some became intoxicated with their own power, and started using their voices to hurt or manipulate, and the Council began taking the siren children to raise so that they couldn't use their voices for ill, only for the good of Atlantia.

A woman at the front of the nave lights a candle. People sit in almost every pew. I wonder if anyone else is mourning someone who left for the Above. I'm certainly not alone in seeking solace here tonight. The temple never closes. It is the one place you are always allowed to stay once the curfew call has sounded.

My mother sometimes worked late at night, hearing the prayers and pleas of those who came with their crises of faith, their screamings of doubt, their whimpers and roars of sin. She believed it was important to listen to people, so much so that she kept working the occasional late shift even after she became the Minister.

She also believed that sirens should be allowed inside the temple, but she could never get enough priests to vote in favor of changing the rule. She saw the temple as the house of the gods *and* the people, the place where they could come together, and she thought it wrong that some were excluded from that opportunity. "They say that the sirens are miracles, not people," she told Bay and me once, in a rare moment of frustration with her work. "Can you imagine believing such a thing? People can be miracles."

I look up at the stone carvings above me, the buttresses and the gallery and the grim gargoyle gods watching us.

The gods are shown as different animals of the Above. On the pillar nearest me is the god Efram, who, because he is fierce and cunning, is represented by a tiger carving. There are many tiger gods, but if you know what you are looking for, it is easy to tell them apart. Efram, for example, has the largest eyes. He sees the most.

"The gods know everything," my mother used to say when I had a hard time hiding my voice. "They know how difficult this is. And they are pleased with you, Rio."

Are they pleased with me for being a siren—or for hiding it? I wanted to ask. But I never did.

When I was small, I realized I could make Bay do what I wanted with the way I said something. But I could never control my mother. Even when I cried my hardest or pleaded fervently, she could resist me. It wasn't always easy. When I wept or begged or tried to manipulate her, she closed her eyes, and I knew she prayed for strength to overcome me. The gods always granted it to her. It was a sign of their favor. Ministers cannot be swayed by sirens. They are chosen, in part, for their ability to resist.

I remember the day when we were five and I made Bay cry so hard she could barely breathe. I did it on purpose. I liked it when I was doing it—I felt hot and cruel and clever and powerful—but afterward, I broke down in remorse. My mother held me tight. She was crying, too. "You are a good girl, Rio," she said. She sounded relieved.

"I hurt Bay," I said. "And I wanted to."

"But you were sorry after," my mother said, "and you don't want to do it again."

I nodded. She was right.

"That is the difference," my mother said, almost as if she were no longer speaking to me. "That is the difference."

She put her hands on either side of my face and looked at me with love. "Rio," she said, "everyone wants to hurt someone else at some time in his or her life. It is part of being human. But you were born with more power to do it than most. That is why you have to keep your voice under control." And, of course, there was the other, equally important reason. We didn't want the Council to take me away.

My mother knew I was a siren very early on, from when I began to babble as a baby. She had to take leave from her work—she couldn't allow anyone else to take care of Bay and me until I was old enough to learn how to mask my voice. She gave the excuse that I was sickly.

Some of my earliest memories are of my mother coaching me, telling me how to speak safely, and of Bay helping me practice. I tried to make my voice like hers, soft and quiet, but it never sounded quite the same. Still, the voice I use now is one I learned from trying to be like Bay.

In my dreams, I always speak in my real voice, and so I looked forward to going to sleep. After my mother died, I often found Bay next to me when I awoke, burrowed close for warmth, her hands cold and the smell of salt water on her. I never knew when she climbed in with me, but I was glad she came to me for comfort.

I don't sleep well now. I don't care about hearing my voice any longer. I want to hear Bay's.

I'm weeping now, and I try to hide that fact. I know the priests are concerned about how profoundly I mourn my sister. At some point they will tell me to accept her choice and return to work full-time instead of keeping these irregular hours. But for now, they extend me grace. They loved her, too.

I run my hand along the varnished wood of the pew in front of me. The pews are carved out of old trees, like the pulpit, and they are extremely valuable, since there are not many wooden seats in Atlantia. But anyone and everyone can sit on the pews, can touch them. When my mother was Minister, she let me touch the pulpit, too, feel the curls of the waves and the leaves of the trees with my fingers, and I knew my religion better in those moments than I have before or since. I felt a reverence mixed with resignation and righteousness that I thought must be faith, must be the way Bay and my mother felt all of the time.

Someone sits down at the edge of my bench, and I slide a little farther in the other direction. There are plenty of empty pews, and I am annoyed that someone has chosen this one under Efram. *Find another god,* I whisper in my mind. *Try one of the lion gods, like Cale. Ask him to roar your prayer to the heavens.* Instead, the person slides closer and reaches out to take a hymnal from the shelf in front of us. Under the clean scent of soap, I detect the faint but unmistakable smell of machinery oil. His hands are work worn and his fingers careful and sure, and I think I know what his trade must be. A machinist, someone who repairs broken things.

"I heard you," he says. "I thought I should see if you were all right."

I wipe my sleeve across my face. "There's no shame in crying," I say flatly, though it feels like there is.

"Of course not," he says. Then there's a moment of quiet, when even the priests seem to have stopped rustling about in the temple and Atlantia does not breathe. Then. "My name is True Beck," he says. I still don't look at his face, though his voice sounds kind and deep. He turns the pages of the hymnal, and I wonder if he's looking at them or at me. "I know your sister left to go Above. My best friend did, too."

I don't say anything. I don't think much of ties that aren't blood. No bond is the same as that between sisters.

"His name was Fen Cardiff," True says. That's the name of the boy who left right before Bay, and in spite of myself I look at True. When I do, my first thought is: brown and blue. Brown hair, brown eyes, blue shirt, blue shadows under his eyes. I've seen him before. Atlantia is a small enough place that we see each face in passing at one time or another, but large enough that we don't know every name.

"I didn't know he was going," True says.

He is handsome, the type of boy who looks as though he might once have had sun on his skin, though that's impossible this far down. He has intelligent eyes and the kind of strength that isn't bulky and belligerent but streamlined and swift instead. I notice all of this and it means nothing to me. Since Bay left, I haven't felt anything but loss.

"Are you older or younger than Fen?" I ask. Because if True is younger, then what does he have to complain about? All he has to do is wait, choose to go Above, and find his friend.

He doesn't answer me. "Listen," he says. "I think you and I should talk. Maybe not here."

"About what?"

"*Them,*" he says. "Bay and Fen." His voice has a hint of urgency in it, and the way he pairs their names seems significant. As if they go together: Bay and Fen. And a dark cold spill of doubt curls through my heart. Did Bay leave because of that boy? A boy I never even knew was important to her?

"I saw them together," True says, as if he knows what I'm thinking. "More than once."

"That can't be," I say. "Bay never told me anything about him."

"I think we can help each other."

"What do you need my help with?" I ask. "You seem to know everything already."

"I don't know *anything,*" True says, and the despair in his voice sounds something like the sorrow I've been holding in my heart, that I haven't even been able to speak to myself because it would overwhelm me. True leans closer, gripping the hymnal very tightly, bending the thick cover. "I don't know why he left. You don't know why she left. You and I have the same question. Maybe we could come to an answer together."

Justus walks past, his head turned away as if he's searching the pews for someone, but he's not, he's trying to avoid someone he's already seen. Me. Because he heard my real voice that day when Bay left. He's a good man and was a friend to my mother, so he doesn't ask me any questions, he leaves me alone. He hasn't told anyone, or I wouldn't be allowed in the temple. His reaction to my voice has been the best one that I could hope for, and yet it still hurts.

"Bay and Fen are gone," I say to True. "We're here. There's nothing to talk about."

"You don't know that," True says. "Someone might know something. *I* might know something. You can't decide not to talk to people."

He's so urgent, so earnest, and I have to bend my head so that he won't be able to tell that I'm trying not to laugh. He has no idea what he's saying. He has no idea that he's speaking to someone who never *could* talk to people. To someone who only two people ever really knew. And now those two people are gone.

True draws in his breath. I wonder if I've offended him. "If you change your mind," he says, "I go to the deepmarket most evenings."

I can't go back to the deepmarket. That's where Maire found me.

Up at the altar, candle wax drips. Cale and Efram and all the rest stare down at us. Someone rustles hymnal pages, a priest speaks softly in another pew, and the city breathes. Ever since Bay left, I haven't been able to stop listening to Atlantia.

Sometimes I could swear that the city *is* a person—breathing easily in some moments, wheezing and laboring in others.

Can't you hear the way the city is breathing? Maire asked.

And in that moment, I have my answer about what I must do, and I want to laugh because it's so obvious. I've wasted my time in the few days since Bay left trying to find out why she left. But the best way to learn why is to go Above and ask her. There has to be a way, in spite of all the obstacles.

Bay has set me free. All I have to hold me here is gone. Just because no one has ever managed to escape to the Above before doesn't mean that I can't be the first. If I die trying to get there, at least I didn't die locked down here in Atlantia. At least I died trying to get to my sister and the world I've always wanted to see.

I stand up and walk to the altar and take one of the candles and light it. Our candles don't last long so that we can conserve our precious air. I kneel and act like I'm praying for a few minutes, until my candle drips and the wick begins to blacken and fall apart on itself. When it finishes burning, I stand up.

True is gone.

———

Back in my room, I lie down on my bed and stare up at the ceiling.

I wish more than anything that I could hear Bay laugh. Even before she left, her laughter had gone.

Sometimes, to tease me, Bay would make a list of all the reasons to stay Below as a sort of companion for my list of reasons I wanted to go Above. She wrote down things like:

The sea gardens are full of color. The cafés are alive with laughter. The leaves on the metal trees catch the light. The plazas have wishing pools where we can toss our gold coins to send to the needy Above. The water changes as much as the sky. She and I compared notes, whispering so that no one else could hear us.

I roll over onto my side, feeling my braid underneath my head as I do. I haven't undone it since Bay left. It's wound with those blue ribbons, a complicated, beautiful style, and though I know I look rough and that pieces are coming out, flyaway bits escaping, I don't want to undo it. I braided her hair this way that morning, but it's much easier to do on someone else than it is to do for yourself. Once I take it out, I won't be able to put it back.

Is Bay having the same trouble Above? Did she throw away the blue ribbons? Do they prefer to wear other colors where she is now?

Maybe if I talked to Maire, she could help me. She could teach me how to use and manipulate my voice to get what I need. And she said she knew what I wanted.

But has using her voice really worked for my aunt, the sea witch? There are stories about her, and people are afraid of her, but has *she* ever gotten what she wanted? What good has it done her, in the end?

Look what happened when I said one little word, *no*. Now Justus can't look at me and Maire won't leave me alone. What if someone else, a stranger, had heard me?

I hear Maire in my mind again. *You think I'm the evil sister, and that your mother was good.*

Must there always be one of each? That's what I've always secretly wondered. If so, I know which sister I am. Bay is not perfect, but she is good. She believes in the gods. She loves our city and our people. She meant to stay Below and serve them all her life.

So if everything is reversed, if she's gone Above and I'm trapped Below, then perhaps *I* am the good sister after all.

I don't feel it. And if I use my voice on purpose, I will have crossed a line, and there will be no coming back.

Maire is not the answer.

I know I need to go Above. I don't yet know how. The wave of hope I felt in the temple has spent itself on the shore of exhaustion and loss.

The pillow is wet from my tears. Perhaps I should try to catch them in a bowl and give them to the priests to use for those who decide to spend their lives down here in the dark Below. We'll all weep and bless one another, those of us too scared or stupid or late to try a life Above.

CHAPTER 4

$\mathcal{I}$ cried so long that I slept in, and I'm tardy for work. I dress in my robes and snatch up my air mask by the strap and sling it over my shoulder. When I glance in the mirror, I see that my hair looks unkempt like Maire's and that I have the same blue smudges under my eyes that I saw under True's last night.

I know his pain was real. But I can't care about anyone's pain but my own. I am an aching, raw, walking nerve. Summoning enough restraint to keep my voice back is the most I can manage.

My classmate Hali notices the shadows. She and Bay were friends, and in the days since my sister left, Hali has been protective, providing a buffer between the rest of the temple acolytes and me at prayers and in the dining hall. I'm grateful to her, especially at mealtime, when we give thanks for those Above who sacrificed to provide our food and I can't help but think of Bay.

I wonder if we are always with the people who live Above the way they are always with us Below. We think of them when we eat the food they provide, knowing that each sweet or savory bite cost them some of their limited time on earth to produce. Do they resent us? I would.

"Maybe you should rest," Hali says. "You seem more and more tired every day since . . ." Hali trails off, as if waiting for permission to say Bay's name. I can't seem to find it in myself to give, so I stand there, unhelpful and unbending.

"It's good for me to work," I say. "We lose ourselves in service." It's a parroted, pet phrase of the priests in the temple. "Bay would have wanted it this way."

Now *I've* said my sister's name, and it hangs over us, pressing down. She weighs on us the way the water weighs on the city. She is everywhere and all around.

"Oh," Hali says, "of course." She holds out a pack for me. "I brought you your work kit."

"Thank you," I say. She's saved me a trip down into the workroom with all the other acolytes so I don't have to face more questions.

Hali nods, and before I can overthink it, I ask her something. "Were *you* surprised when she left?"

Hali holds her work kit on her hip, the way I've seen her balance her baby brothers and sisters when they come during visiting hours. "Yes," Hali says. "Bay loved Atlantia. She loved the temple. I never thought she'd leave. Some of us thought that she might be Minister someday."

I nod. I knew that people whispered about Bay following in my mother's footsteps. Bay knew it, too. But she never wanted to be the Minister. "Too much pressure, too many eyes watching," she always said. "I'd rather be a priest and serve the people and the gods that way." Bay always thought she'd like to teach in the temple school or administer at the floodgates. "I want to help people when they have to let their loved ones go," she said. That was before we had to prepare our own mother's body to go up through the floodgates. The memory washes around the edges of my mind, but I refuse to look at that dark place.

"But I can also understand Bay wanting to live a life of sacrifice," Hali says. "And the best way to do that is to go Above."

"So that's why you think she left?"

"Of course," Hali says. "Bay is one of the few people I know who *could* live a life of sacrifice."

Hali's argument isn't without logic. But why wouldn't Bay tell me that she wanted to serve in the Above? Why did she ask me to promise to stay, and then leave?

Why trick me?

Was she afraid I'd be angry?

"She didn't tell you she was going, did she?" Hali asks.

"No."

"She must not have wanted to hurt you," Hali says gently.

But Bay *knew* her leaving would hurt me. I move suddenly with the pain of that, and Hali takes a step back. "I'd better get to work now," I say.

"I'll see you later," Hali says.

I go down the hall from our living quarters and through the temple school. I know these rooms and hallways as well as I know the temple itself. I know who lives behind each door in the students' living quarters. I know the smells of the classrooms and workrooms, the scuff marks on the floors, the way the chairs cut into your back so that you are uncomfortable unless you sit with perfect posture. The walls are tiled in green and blue and white, sea colors, but the grout in between them is dirty brown from so many years of wear, even though the acolytes clean it constantly. That's what we spend most of our time doing, when we're not learning about the gods and the Divide. Later we get promoted to cleaning the temple itself, but that's not much easier. It's hard work balancing on the ladders while carrying soap and water. And the gods do not seem alive when you clean them. You have to take extra care as you wash their claws and paws, their hooked little hands, because those are the most delicate parts of the sculptures.

I bite my lip, trying to keep that other memory at bay, but pieces keep coming back—the way my mother's hands and feet were cold and still when we washed them as we prepared her for burial, how dry her hair felt when we braided it. How I kept trying not to look at her eyes.

⌒

Outside at last, I walk under the trees in the temple plaza. The leaves make a sound like chimes in the movement of the city's air currents. When the morning light comes in through the glittering metal of the trees, it is one of the most beautiful sights in Atlantia. This much loveliness requires constant maintenance—cleaning and repairing the thousands of leaves.

And the temple trees are different from the other trees in Atlantia—there are statues of the gods up there, high in the branches, looking down and watching us, as if each tree is a small temple. These gods are made of metal, not stone, but they are still sacred. Because of them the maintenance crews that take care of the other trees in Atlantia can't take care of the ones at the temple. The priests and acolytes have to do it. Or, rather, one acolyte has to do it. I've proven so efficient that now the task is entirely up to me. I can't say that I'm sorry, because I would much rather work out here.

ALLY CONDIE

I shrug the air-mask equipment off my back, which is against the rules. Most people seem to be accustomed to the mask's constant presence, but I take it off every chance I can. I hate the way it catches on the leaves—I already have to carry my repair equipment up with me, so bringing the mask as well makes everything unnecessarily bulky. I climb up into one of the trees and find Efram sitting in his spot at the top, his sharp metal teeth bared as he squats on his haunches. Sure enough, one of his paws has come loose, a common problem. "Efram," I say, talking to him as if he's alive. "What have you been grabbing at? What could be out of the reach of a god?"

Efram glares at me as I pull down my visor and fire up the torch from my kit to weld him back together. It seems as if he's saying *You know as well as I do that this isn't my fault.*

The problem is the temple bats. During the day, they sleep in their roosts inside the temple's bell tower. At night, when they're free to fly, they like to come settle in these trees, and they are especially fond of sitting on the gods and leaving guano like offerings.

But no one is allowed to harm the bats. They are the second of the three miracles that we were told would happen after the Divide if the gods were pleased with us. As miracles, they have our protection.

At the time of the Divide, no one brought any animals Below. The leaders thought that the animals would use up too much precious air. They also believed that the creatures of the Above and the Below should remain where they were. To keep us mindful of one another's worlds, they assigned land-animal faces and bodies to the gods for those of us who worship Below, and sea forms for those Above. It's strange to me to think that Efram looks entirely different to worshippers outside Atlantia.

When the bats were first seen, they were brown. It took years to catch the animals as they darted around Atlantia's skies, but finally our ancestors succeeded.

And they were shocked at what they found. Over time, faster than should be scientifically possible, the bats' wings had changed from pinkish in color to a beautiful translucent blue, as if to mirror the sea that had become their sky. Someone remarked upon how much they resembled certain gargoyles of the temple, and the priests saw that it was true. It became clear that the bats were not a nuisance but were, in fact, the second miracle. The sirens had been the first.

We are still waiting for the third.

Justus is the one in charge of taking care of the bats and the roosts where they come home to sleep during the day. It is one of the most sacred offices a priest can hold. Bay and I used to love it when our singing in the temple would wake some of the bats and they would fly in front of the rose window. The wings of blue were every bit as beautiful and maybe more so than the stained glass.

The bats aren't as common here as they once were Above, perhaps in response to their new environment. We rarely see them. But it is nice to know that we are not alone down in this city, that they skim around after the dimming time. And I know they *are* here because I see the evidence in the trees.

After I get Efram's leg back on, I climb down to the bottom of the tree and pick up a scatter of silver leaves that came off during the night. With small spurts of fire from my torch, I carefully weld them back on the way Justus taught me, attaching them to the branches by their ends so that they have full range of motion when the wind comes through.

"These repetitive tasks are symbols," Justus told me, "of the vigilance we must keep in order to remain righteous and content with the lot we've been given."

I have tried to be righteous all my life. Yet I have never been content.

When I get back to the temple, Justus waits for me. "The Minister would like to see you," he says.

"Me?" I ask. "Why?"

"I don't know," Justus says. He reaches out to take my work kit from me and I hand it to him. He looks sad. He does know what Nevio wants. Before, I would have asked Justus to tell me. But now I don't dare push him.

"When?"

"Now," Justus says.

Nevio's office used to be my mother's. I spent many hours in here watching her work. The room has a small stained-glass window. I know its colors as well as I know the claws and the teeth of the gods in the trees. Some of the reference books on the shelves are ones my mother used. The desk, made from solid mahogany, is carved with the Minister's insignia. That is also the same.

But the rest is different.

I sit down across from him on a chair made of glass and steel and I fold my hands.

"You have suffered two great losses in the past year," Nevio says. "First your mother, and now your sister."

I nod.

"Your profound grief is understandable," Nevio says, "and it also helps us face some of the realities of your situation." He sounds almost kind, and he leans forward across the desk to look into my eyes. "Rio," he says, "the temple has never been the right fit for you. Your mother and Bay belonged here, but this is never where you imagined yourself. Is it?"

I don't like Nevio, but he's right. I never had the faith that Bay and my mother did. A life alone in the temple was never what I imagined for myself. I thought I would go Above, and then when I promised Bay that I would stay, I thought I would be living and working in the temple *with* her.

"Where would you like to go?" Nevio asks.

I want to go Above so much that I think, for one short moment, about telling him. But even if Nevio could bend the rules, even if he could get the Council to agree, I don't trust him.

A flicker of annoyance and impatience crosses Nevio's face. I'm taking too much of his time. "Let's try another question," he says. "What do you like to do?"

"I like to fix things," I say, in a voice as stupid as he expects.

"Yes," he says. "Justus tells me that you are the one who has kept the temple trees in such good repair."

I open my mouth to thank him, because I assume that's what he wants, but before I can say anything he speaks again.

"Still, I'm sure we can teach another acolyte to perform your tasks here," Nevio says. "And I know they're always in need of good workers down in the mining bays where they repair the drones. That seems like a perfect fit for you."

The mining bays are down in the deepest reaches of the city, as far away from the temple as possible. It's the lowest you can physically go in Atlantia, as close as you can get to the seafloor, where the drones mine for magnesium and copper, cobalt and gold.

Is Nevio doing this on purpose? Has he sensed, in some way, how much I want to be Above so he's sinking me deeper?

It's clear that he wants me gone.

"When my mother died," I say, "I was assured that the temple would always be my home."

"Of course," Nevio says. "It will always be your *spiritual* home. And for now you can keep the room you shared with your sister. The machinists' quarters are full, I'm told."

At least I won't have to move out of the room where Bay and I lived. But I still can't believe Nevio is making me leave the temple. Can he do this? I suppose he can, since he's the Minister, but it feels wrong. Should I talk to some of the priests? Then I remember Justus's expression when he told me Nevio needed to see me. Justus knows, and even he isn't going to help me.

"I saved one of the pages your mother wrote," Nevio says. "I thought you would like to see it." He holds out the paper and I snatch it away. I can't help myself. He shouldn't have the things she's touched.

Rio is not intended for a life as a priest, my mother wrote, and I stop, a sudden sharp ache pinpointing the center of my chest, as if I've experienced a physical injury. My mother didn't write that. She couldn't have. But there it is, right in front of me, her handwriting as neat and measured as always. *Rio doesn't often think of the collective good, which comes innately to Bay. I'm not sure that's something that can be taught. I don't think that Rio is cold or strange—few people can care about the group as a whole the way a Minister or a priest must. But sometimes I reproach myself. I worry that it is my fault, that I've stunted her growth. But I cannot see her suffer, and in that I am a hypocrite. For that feeling has nothing to do with the collective good, and everything to do with one specific child. My child.*

"This must hurt you to read," Nevio says.

Yes. It does.

"You've gone through her journal?" I ask.

"Every page," he says smoothly.

"These were her *personal* papers," I say. "They should have been given to me and my sister, not kept here."

"We have the right to any of Oceana's papers that relate to her work as the Minister," Nevio says. "As you can see, the rest of the page consists of notes for a sermon she delivered, so this belongs to the temple's archives."

I turn over the paper. The other side is filled with notes, the kind of jottings-down she made as she planned out what she would say. I'd seen her do it hundreds of times, in this very office. There were so many occasions that required her to address the citizens of Atlantia—sermons for the congregation on Sundays, and speeches for the monthly Wednesday broadcasts, when she spoke about matters the Council wanted her to address.

One of our greatest fears is to be gone, she wrote.

We hope to observe, not inhabit, the moment of our own deaths.

The song of the sirens used to help us forget. And now we cannot remember.

And then the last two words on the page.

Ask Maire.

She wrote her sister's name.

That's as far as I get before Nevio takes the paper from me. "The notes on that side of the paper aren't relevant to your situation," he says. "The other side, the part that is specifically about *you*, is what matters. Having read it, you must understand why we can't keep you as an acolyte in the temple. Even your own mother would have advised against it, were she strong enough to recommend the truth instead of trying to keep you with her."

Nevio stands up and walks to the door. He opens it. Our interview is over. "Don't worry, Rio," he says. "I don't think it will take very long for you to see that this is a better fit for you."

I might not have believed as fiercely as Bay and my mother, but the temple has been my home for years. I know the smell of the candles late at night and the sound of the bats' wings coming home in the early morning. I sat in pools of colored light coming in through this office window and watched my mother write in the journal that Nevio has taken for his own. I used to belong here.

After losing my mother and my sister, I didn't think I had anything left to lose, but I do. You always have something left to lose. Until, of course, you die.

CHAPTER 5

I always thought the temple robes were heavy, but they're much lighter than the protective suits that machinists wear. One similarity between my old uniform and my new one is that the visor reminds me of the one I wore to fix the leaves and the gods in the temple trees. I resist the urge to pull it down and hide my face. The room is filled with workers; many of them sneak glances at me.

The supervisor, a middle-aged man named Josiah, shows me around the large room where the machinists work. It's very easy to hear Atlantia breathe down here. Bay would love that. And to my surprise, the workroom is extremely beautiful. The workstations are well-lit and the smell of oil and salt water is strong and pleasant. The low ceilings have been hung with little chips and bits of metal, probably scraps left over from repairs, and they catch the light in a way that reminds me of Atlantia's trees. "We call this the sky room because of the stars on the ceiling," Josiah says, pointing to the scraps as they glint above us.

"It's a beautiful workplace," I say.

"We all take pride in what we do," Josiah says. "Justus told me you have impressive skills, and he showed me a sample of your work. It was excellent. But everyone begins in here."

I nod. Because I'm new, my job will be the easiest task of all—quick fixes and polishes for mining drones that have suffered less substantial damage. The drones are steel-strong and complicated, and they often need repair thanks to the difficult nature of their task of extracting ore. I can't help but feel a little bit of interest in the drones.

"Word spreads quickly," Josiah says in a low voice. "Everyone here knows that you're Oceana the Minister's daughter, but I've asked them not to talk to you about her."

Of course. It's as Nevio insinuated yesterday in his office. My mother is no longer a leader. He wants everyone to let her go.

Josiah pauses near another room full of well-lit workstations. I see a heavy, round portal door at the opposite end. "We call that the ocean room," he says. "It's where we do the more difficult repairs. That door is where the drones come inside." That's why everything smells like salt. This is one of the few places where Atlantia opens up, and we are very, very close to the ocean.

I have to hide a smile. Maybe this is a way to get to the Above.

I've never been so deep, or so close to the sea.

"I can tell you're itching to work in the ocean room," Josiah says, laughing, and I realize that I've forgotten myself and I'm staring at the portal. "Don't worry. You'll move in there quickly if you're as talented as you seem to be."

"Thank you," I say.

Josiah's expression grows serious. "The most important part of the tour happens right now," he says. "I need to tell you about the mines."

I wonder why. We don't actually work in the mines or see any of the metals harvested there. That's what the drones are for. They're programmed to take their payloads somewhere else, some other part of Atlantia. They only report to this bay if they're in need of repair.

My face must register my confusion, because Josiah begins to speak more slowly to me. Already he's forgotten how good I supposedly am at metalwork. This always happens after people have heard me speak.

"There are two kinds of mines out there," he says. "There are the mines where the drones get the ore, and then there are the *other* mines—the floating bombs—between the walls of Atlantia and the ocean floor where the drones work. That's how the drones get so beat-up."

"I assumed it was from working," I say.

"That's what most people think," he says. "But if you're down here, you need to know the truth. In fact, *all* of the water around Atlantia is mined, not just the water down here."

"But why would we do that?" I ask. "Why would we put mines out there if it results in damage to our drones?"

"The drones can be fixed," Josiah says. "People can't. The mines are here to make sure that no one tries to leave."

When Justus told Josiah what a good worker I am, did he also say something about Bay? Did he tell Josiah that I tried to follow my sister the day she left?

"I tell this to every new machinist," Josiah says, watching me intently, "because now and then we get someone who thinks this is a way to get Above. They want to find someone who chose to leave, or sometimes they want to go themselves because they feel like they can't live down here any longer. They buy some of that illegal canned air in the deepmarket and strap it on and go up. But we're down so deep your lungs could explode the second you get out there. The mines exist to keep anyone from trying a route that would lead to death."

"I would never have thought of trying to leave," I say, and my voice is so plain and bland that I am quite sure Josiah will believe me. But, in spite of everything he's said, I still see a way out. I'll have to learn more to decide if it's at all viable, but I'm not ready to give up yet.

"Well," Josiah says. "That's everything. Let's get you started." He pulls down his visor and I follow his lead, glad for the layer of smoky-colored plastic that hides my face.

⌒

I work all day next to a girl named Bien, who is efficient and caustic, and a woman named Elinor, who is quiet and kind. We smooth out metal that has been scraped or bumped and put a protective sealant over the repairs. There is a brief moment of unpleasantness when one of the other workers begins humming to herself in an off-key tone and Bien makes a snide remark about the tune being as painful as a siren's song.

"The sirens are miracles," Elinor says, a gentle warning in her voice. "We should be careful how we speak of them."

"They're no more special than the bats," Bien says.

But the bats are *special,* I think. Even though I had to clean up after them, it was worth it for those rare glimpses when they soared past the window in the temple, completely out of place and yet perfectly at home in our world.

When we finish our shift, Elinor falls into step with me as I leave the building. "You did well today," she says.

"Thank you," I say, and I slide up the visor because it would be strange not to, since we've finished and are walking to the gondola stop together. I pull my helmet all the way off and feel the breeze against my hair, sweaty and still-braided.

Elinor stares at me. "Oh my," she says. "You look like her. Oceana the Minister." Then she puts her hand over her mouth as if remembering that she's not supposed to discuss this with me.

But I *want* to talk about my mother. "No," I say. "She was small. I'm tall. Our coloring is completely different."

"No, really," Elinor says. "Something about your eyes. How you're seeing everything. That's how she looked at people." Then she leans closer, glancing around to make sure no one can hear. "I know we're not to bother you about it," she says. "But I have to tell you how much she meant to me. I loved her sermons. I looked forward to them all week. And, once, I brought my sick child to the temple and your mother came past and touched my son's hand and he was better the very next day."

"She never claimed to perform miracles," I say, but I'm thrilled at what Elinor thinks of my mother, how she remembers her. "It's blasphemy to say that she could."

Elinor reaches into her pocket and pulls out something. At first I can't tell what it is—I think it might be a piece of stone— and then she brings it into the light and I see that it's a metal figurine, one of the tiger gods, the kind of token they sell in the deepmarket stalls for cheap. This Efram has the same snarling mouth and curved tiny claws as on the totems I've seen before, but in one of his paws he holds a trident, which is a symbol of the sea.

Another thrill goes through me. The gods of Above and Below are not supposed to mix. We have tiger and lion gods with fur and claws, the Above has sharp-toothed sharks and bulbous-eyed fish. We have scepters and swords; they have tridents and nets. This little amalgam is another blasphemy.

"I want you to have this," Elinor says.

"Why?" I ask. "I'm not my mother." I didn't preach the sermons that Elinor loved. I didn't help her sick child.

"Because you're what's left of her," she says.

After I ride the gondola back up into the city proper, I walk right through the door of the temple itself instead of going to my sleeping quarters. I want to light a candle again tonight and sit for a while under the stone gods and stained glass. I feel as though I need to show Nevio I'm not afraid to come back, that I am what is left of my mother and that she will always have a place here.

With one hand, I pick up the candle, a circle of ivory wax that looks like the round cakes of soap we use to clean the gods. That makes me smile for a moment, remembering a time when, dreaming of the Above, I picked up a candle from the storage room instead of soap. I smeared one of the gods' faces with wax before I realized my mistake. Bay laughed so hard she cried.

The pain comes so soon after the memory that it hurts to breathe. It hurts even to *be*. But there is nothing else to do. Not if I want to see her again. I have to keep going.

I keep my other hand in my pocket, closed around the figure of Efram that Elinor gave me. The three prongs of the trident poke into my palm and I think, *Three ways to get to the Above: The Council transports. Maire. Through the mining bay.*

Right now the last one appeals to me the most, in spite of what Josiah said. Maybe it's because I can picture how it might feel. The dark water. The floating mines. Me, swimming around them, fast and strong.

Someone comes up next to me at the altar.

She wears a head covering and nondescript clothes, to keep the priests from recognizing her immediately. But I know who she is. I don't even have to hear her speak.

"Sirens are not supposed to be in the temple," I say.

That makes Maire laugh softly. Her hands are steady as she lights a candle, and they are smooth and fine, the hands of someone who doesn't have to do hard work. "Oh," she says, "the way you can say that, with a complete lack of irony in your voice. You're something, Rio. You really are."

"I'll tell everyone you're here," I say. "I'll make a scene."

"Don't do that," Maire says. "I'm not going to stay long. But I need to give you something. Under the middle of the third pew back, on the side of the temple nearest the priests' door, you'll find what your sister left for you. And if you ever decide you want to speak with me after all, go and sit under Efram's tree in the temple plaza. I will find you. I am always here if you need me."

"I won't need you," I say.

She nods her head in either mock reverence or assent and slips away. I'm surprised at how easily I'm rid of her, and I wonder how many times sirens have stolen into the temple. I come here daily, of course, and the Council doesn't seem to have as much control over Maire as they should.

I'm not sure whether the thought thrills or frightens me.

I tell myself that after the candle burns out, I'll go right back up the nave and leave the temple, but of course I don't. I make my way to the third pew and sit down. I bow my head as if in prayer and reach a hand underneath the seat. At first I feel nothing, and then there it is, a thick cloth bag taped to the bottom of the pew. It's heavy. I think I know what's inside by the feel of it. Lots of small, solid pieces.

Money.

Bay left me money?

Is there a note inside, too?

I stand up holding the bag—it's a simple one, the kind that many of us in Atlantia have for shopping or carrying books—and walk out of the temple. I hope no one notices that I'm leaving with more than I had when I came in, but I don't think anyone has really paid attention to me this entire time. I have the uncanny feeling that Maire may have told them all not to see me, that she whispered some incantation when I first came inside. That would, of course, be illegal, as is the little god of Efram that sits inside my pocket.

When I get to my room, I open up the bag and dump the contents on the table. I was right—Bay's given me money. And something else wrapped in brown tissue paper.

I count the money first. Disk after disk of golden coin. There are five hundred and seven of them altogether, a small fortune.

If this *is* from Bay, where did she get all of it? She couldn't have won so much money in the deepmarket—could she? If so, was she racing when I didn't know?

Is this enough to buy an air tank that could get me to the surface? I didn't know they sold such things until Josiah mentioned it earlier. I've known about the vials of flavored air, of course, but do those sellers have other, more secret wares?

I take care not to rip the brown tissue paper surrounding the second part of the gift, just in case Bay has sent me a message, but there isn't any of her neat, careful writing on the paper. Instead the wrapping holds a smooth shell. A seashell, rare and hard to come by, even in the deepmarket, something that belongs to both the Above and the Below. The animals that make and wear these shells walk along our ocean floors and the Above's sandy shores. The shell's colors are beautiful—dappled greenish-blue and brown like the colors of the Divide.

"You're the only person in the world whose favorite color is brown," Bay used to tease me.

"That can't be true," I said. "It's mathematically impossible."

"Well, I don't know a single other person whose favorite color is brown," Bay said.

"Maybe not in Atlantia," I said. She understood what I meant.

"Maybe Above," she said.

There's no note with any of it—not tucked among the coin, not hidden in the shell.

Is this really from my sister? Or is Maire trying to trick me?

I pack away most of the coin but put some of it into a small pouch to take with me to the deepmarket tomorrow. Whether or not Bay gave me the money, it's going to come in handy.

Then I hold the shell up to my ear to listen for the sound of wind in the trees Above. They say that when people Above find shells on the shore, *they* try to hear the sounds of the sea.

And I swear I hear her breathing inside the shell. My sister. Breathing for me.

I match my breath to hers; I curl up tight on the bed. This was the sound I fell asleep to every night—her breathing, and mine. And I feel myself slipping, at last, back into dreams where it is safe for me to speak.

CHAPTER 6

When my shift at work ends the next day, I find myself caught up in a group with the rest of the workers, all walking together to the nearby plaza. When I try to slip away on my own, Bien notices.

"I've been promoted to the ocean room," she says. "Don't you want to throw a coin into the wishing pool for me?"

"Of course," I say. I don't want to waste a coin on someone I don't even know, but it seems ungracious not to participate. Apparently this is some kind of tradition among the workers, and I want to fit in.

"Do you think coins can really bring people luck?" Bien asks as she watches me toss the circle of gold into the dark pool. There's a hard glint in her eyes, like she's waiting or wanting for something to happen

I'm not sure what she expects me to say, but I tell her, "You're talented and you work hard, and those things are even better than luck."

"That sounds like something your mother would say," Elinor tells me, patting my arm.

"So we're allowed to talk about Rio's mother now?" Bien asks.

"Bien," Elinor says, a warning note in her voice.

"I don't see why not," Bien says. "If Rio doesn't mind . . ." She waits for me.

I say nothing. I have been bullied before, especially in the years before I moved to the temple school. The students at my first school laughed openly at my dull voice and unusual height. I've learned that sometimes answering the questions satiates the person bullying. Sometimes it doesn't.

"I just want to know what it was like living with someone so *famous,*" Bien says, and now I hear a definite tone of malice in her voice.

"Bien, stop," Elinor says. "This is not kind."

"We didn't live with her after she became the Minister," I say, though Bien already knows all of this. Everyone does. "The Minister has to have his or her own quarters in the temple."

"Did that make you feel bad?" Bien asks. "That your mother chose her work over you?"

I'm not sure *why* Bien doesn't like me, unless it's the usual reason, the one that made those children tease me: I'm different.

"We never saw it like that," I say.

"Of course you didn't," Elinor says, finally getting a word in edgewise. She seems furious with Bien.

"I don't know why I'm asking questions about your mother's life," Bien says, "when the most interesting thing about her is how she died. Do you know who killed her?"

Though I hate Bien for doing this, and my hands are tight in fists that could hurt her, push her down, pin her there and tell her to take it back—I know I could, I am that strong and stronger—there is a strange relief in hearing it said out loud.

In knowing that it's not only Bay and I who have thought of the possibility of murder.

Still, I have to wait a moment before I have the control to speak. Next to me, Elinor sputters in outrage, tells Bien that she is cruel, sacrilegious.

"I don't know," I say at last. "I don't know who killed her or how she died. Her heart just stopped."

"Do you want to know who *I* think did it?" Bien asks.

I will not give her the pleasure of nodding. But, actually, I do want to know. I want to know what people are saying. And of course Bien wants to tell me.

"Maire," Bien says. She has an expression of perverse pleasure on her face. She enjoys making me miserable. Does she do this to other people? I haven't seen it, but I haven't known her long. I can't tell if it is me in particular she wants to torment, or if she is a narrow-minded person who rejoices in broad, cutting strokes of cruelty that encompass as many people as possible. "Most of us think that Oceana was killed by her own sister."

"Not everyone thinks that," Elinor says.

Someone calls to Bien, and Bien, her work done, gives us a wave and sets off to join another group. I hear a burst of laughter as she joins them.

"I'm so sorry," Elinor says. "Bien is a troublemaker. She shouldn't have said such a thing about your aunt. I've heard people say that Bien's own brother was a siren and made her do terrible things before the Council took him away to raise, so she is especially poisonous where sirens are concerned. She thinks they should all be eliminated."

"Do you believe that, too?"

"No," Elinor says. "Of course not."

But do you think we should be locked up and contained? I want to ask her this, but of course I don't.

"That explains why Bien hates my aunt," I say, "but why does she hate me? And my mother?"

"I don't know," Elinor says.

"Who do *you* think killed my mother?"

Elinor shakes her head. "I don't think anyone did kill her. Her grand, generous heart simply stopped. Perhaps she was taken up by the gods. If so, it would be the third miracle."

But though I love my mother and am glad to hear that others do, too, I can't believe her a miracle. Just a human, one gone too soon.

"At least that money gets sent to the people Above," Elinor says, her voice almost fierce. "Still, I hate to think that you wasted a wish on Bien."

But I didn't. When I threw the gold coin into the pool, I made the same selfish, wonderful wish I've made ever since I was a child. *I wish that I could see the Above.*

Perhaps I should have wished for something else. Perhaps I should have wished to know the truth.

Could Maire have killed my mother?

I don't believe a sister could do such a thing.

But I also never would have believed that Bay could leave me, and she did. I saw her go.

～

It is agony to cry when you can't make a sound, when you have to stuff your pillow into your mouth, almost choking yourself so that no one will hear the timbre of your real voice. No one knows how much that hurts, not even the loved ones who want to keep you safe.

I miss Bay so much, and I am so angry with her. If she were here, I would cry out at her. I wouldn't care who heard. *How could you leave me?* My throat aches as if I've already screamed myself hoarse.

When was the last time Bay and I fought? I wonder. Before our mother's death, we used to fight all the time, because we were sisters in a shared, small world—room, temple, city—and because we were different and the same.

But I could never *really* fight because of my voice. I couldn't ever tell her how angry I was at her.

And so now I wonder if she also never knew how much I love her. Because I do.

There are two things that I've always known for certain: that I have to see the Above and that I love my sister.

Do I honestly believe I'm going to be able to do this? That I can swim through the mines? And buy an air tank to get Above? It's a ridiculous plan. I know it. There are countless things that could go wrong.

The impossibility of everything overcomes me.

In desperation I look around for something, anything to help. And I see the shell again. I seize it and hold it up against my ear. My own breathing is the only sound.

Then I hear something else.

My sister, singing a lullaby from our childhood, one that our mother used to sing to us when we were small.

Under star-dark seas and skies of gold
Live those Above, and those Below

They sing and weep, both high and deep
While over and under the ocean rolls

She sings it again, and again. The song is calming, lulling, sad and gentle, true. I close my eyes and listen.

CHAPTER 7

I sit down under Efram's tree, the one I repaired not long ago. I miss working here, with the shivering leaves and the sullen gods. I wonder why Maire picked this as a meeting place and how long it will take before she comes. I wonder why I'm here. Is it because my mother wrote Maire's name in her notes? *Ask Maire.* Or because it seems that Bay did trust Maire to give me the money and the shell?

Or am I here because I want to talk to another siren? The conversations I've had with Maire have been the only times I've spoken with someone who has the same power that I do.

She's all the family I have left.

Silver leaves scatter over the ground. I lean down to pick one up and *tsk* to myself when I see the heavy-handedness of the soldering work. Despite what Nevio said, they haven't found someone to take my place repairing the trees. Not someone as skilled as I am, anyway.

And then I see a splay of blue wing and brown fur on the ground.

One of the temple bats.

The bat's tiny body looks fine, nothing broken, but it's certainly dead. Its eye stares back up at me with nothing there. Against the ground, its wings are dark as the deep instead of blue as glass and sea. I hear people gathering near me.

"It's like seeing Efram himself fallen and broken," a man says, but he is quickly quieted. What he's said sounds too much like sacrilege. We are not supposed to believe that Efram, or any of the gods, could fall or break.

At least the gods are easy to fix. This animal is beyond any help we can give. "Find Justus at the temple," I say, and someone goes running.

It takes Justus only moments to arrive, but there's nothing he can do. He tells the others to move along. I stay behind.

"What do you think killed it?" I ask.

Justus shakes his head. "I don't know," he says. "I suppose it could be a natural death. There are a few tests I can conduct back at the temple to try and find out more." He lifts the bat carefully in his hands. There's a clean linen cloth in the bottom of the container and he places the bat gently inside, as if it weren't past all feeling.

"What was it doing out in the day?" I ask.

"It might have died in the night," Justus says. "It's not the first. They're not immortal."

Of course not. I know that. But it's very odd to see one of the bats dead.

Justus straightens up, careful not to step on the hem of his robe, and holds the box in his hands. "They're dying more quickly, though," he says, "since we lost your mother."

He leaves me there alone, and as soon as he has gone back inside the temple, I hear her.

Maire.

She walks softly. She doesn't step on any of the leaves or say a single word, but I still know she's here, just as I did that day in the temple.

"The trees sing," Maire says. "They told me you were here. And I've been listening and hoping that you would come."

It's unsettling to hear her say that about the trees. They're mine, not hers.

I say, flatly, not giving her even a hint of my real voice: "What do you want?"

"It's not about what I want," Maire says. "You know that. It's about what *you* want. To go Above and find your sister."

"And you think you can help me."

"Yes," she says. "I can. I helped your sister and your mother, and I can help you."

As if we've agreed to do so beforehand, the two of us start walking together. Across the courtyard, people wave to one another and call out to friends passing by in gondolas. A peace-keeper blows his whistle to warn a group of youth gathered too near the canal and they move away. I feel a sudden fierce love for my city.

"I can help you," Maire says, after we've walked in silence for a time, "if you let me. I won't make you do anything."

"You don't know that you *could* make me do anything," I say.

"That's true," she agrees, in a flat tone that sounds exactly like mine. I hate her for mimicking me.

She stops, and I realize that we've come to the back entrance of the temple compound, the part that leads to the floodgates and the morgue.

I haven't been here since my mother died. Bay and I had to go down through this entrance to prepare our mother's body. When we finished, we had to leave her there and climb the stairs to the floodgates' viewing area, where we sat in our reserved seats to witness her body going up. We were daughters of the Minister that day, one last time.

Maire strides right up to the guards at the floodgate entrance. "We'd like to go inside," she says.

"That's not allowed," one says. "You don't have Council and temple permission."

"I understand," Maire says, and the resignation in her voice convinces even me for a second. I'm turning away when she speaks again.

"Now," she says, just a single word.

It's cold and hot, a slice, a knife through one's brain and body. I step forward involuntarily.

The guards have already started to open the doors, as if they began to obey her before she finished speaking. Is that possible? Is her power so strong?

"Stay," Maire tells them.

And then, to me, she says, "Come."

I follow. I'm not sure whether I'm following her voice or my own strong, strange desire to go inside.

⟶

"I think," Maire says, "that we should go down."

Down. Into the floodgate chamber itself, not up to the viewing area. This is strictly forbidden unless you're a priest or have come with one to prepare a body, but Maire acts as if she has every right to be here.

We go through narrow, dank hallways, the ones that eventually lead to the morgue farther down. The guards don't follow us. They're likely calling for reinforcements, who will arrive in a matter of moments. But will it matter? How many people can Maire command?

"Not an army," she says, as if she's heard my question, "so our time is limited. They'll send guards who are immune to the sound of my voice, and they'll take me away. The Council will find it necessary to reprimand me and lock me up for a few days, so you and I should accomplish as much as we can at this meeting."

I can't get over the sound of that *Now*. My heart pounds. And I realize how silly my thoughts were earlier, about being a match for Maire in some way. Her voice has been honed and cultivated for years. It is a weapon, a beautiful one.

"Ah," Maire says. "Here we are."

She puts her hand on the door in front of us. It is metal and heavy, pressurized for when the water comes in. Somehow Maire opens it easily.

"Come along," Maire says, stepping across the threshold. There's no command in her voice, but I'm not sure I trust the invitation. I pause for a moment before I follow her inside.

The floodgate chamber is tall, many stories high. Along the carved buttresses supporting the ceiling sit ancient stone figures representing the gods. Like the ones in the temple, they were taken from churches Above long ago. I look up at the screaming tiger and dragon and lion mouths and at the glaring eyes. The floor is damp in places.

It took the engineers years to perfect the technology of the floodgates, to make walls strong enough that they could let the water in to this chamber alone without the pressure breaking the city wide open. It's a little terrifying to watch a body go up—it feels as though, at any moment, the water will break through into the viewing area. But of course that has never happened.

The water of the sea pushes against the top of the gates, presses down all around us. I think I hear the metal sigh and the stone moan.

Bay and I were together here at the floodgates, and we were together before that when the priests and representatives of the Council asked us their many questions after they found our mother's body: *Had she been unwell? Did she tell you of any chronic illnesses in your family, ones we don't have here in our medical records?* Bay and I sat side by side, saying no over and over again.

"What do you think happens when the dead reach the surface?" Maire asks. "Do you believe that their bodies become foam and their souls fly free?"

"I don't know," I say.

"I don't know about the souls part of it," Maire says. "But if a body makes it through the mines in the water and washes to the shore, the people Above take what they want from it. Clothing. Jewelry."

With that word it all comes back, the whole memory of that day, the one I've tried to keep locked away, pushed down in my mind.

<hr />

"I forgot to bring her ring," Bay said. "She always wanted to wear her ring when she went to the surface. How could I forget?"

"It's all right," I told Bay, but I didn't look at her, because they were bringing our mother's body into the floodgate chamber. We sat high up in the viewing area. Our mother looked small in their arms.

They set our mother down on the floor and chanted the prayers. I willed myself not to cry. I didn't look at Bay. And then, when the priests were finished with the prayers, they left the room, sealed it shut, and left our mother alone. Hundreds of us were watching—some of us in the viewing area, some on screens set up in the plazas throughout Atlantia—but she was alone.

I heard a creaking sound in the walls. It was the sound of water coming in.

The open mouths of the gods began to stream. The water cascaded to the floor, and soon our mother was wet, her clothes clinging to her legs, her hair swirling around her.

Far, far above was the exit of the floodgates, an enormous opening modeled after the rose window in the temple.

The water filled the chamber, and the body lifted up. The speed of the water increased, filling the chamber faster and faster.

The water rose above the level of the viewing area, and I gasped in air. It seemed as if we were going to drown as the water went past our windows. But of course, we were safe.

Our mother's body went up, up, up, toward the exit of the floodgates, and I thought I could see the sun for a moment, that it was shining all the way down on Atlantia.

When the chamber was nearly full, and I could barely see my mother anymore, the window began to spin. It looked like a flower opening.

And then she was gone.

When we came home that night, I found the ring and pressed it into Bay's hand. "I think she would have changed her mind anyway," I said. "I think she would have wanted you to keep this."

"Once they've taken what they need Above," Maire says to me now, "they dump the body in a pit. They don't want it any more than we do Below."

Maire is saying *a body*, but I think of *her body*. My mother's. I can picture it all exactly: her clothes in a tangle, her limp form slumped against the shore, pushed again and again by the waves. Someone from the Above coming down to find her. Taking what they can.

"The dead are not the only ones who leave Atlantia," Maire says, her voice a whisper, even though there is no one here but me. "Of course there are those who choose to go Above, like Bay." Maire pauses. "But there are others. The Council, when occasion requires it."

I already know this. Sometimes the Council takes their transports up through the locks—the series of compression and decompression chambers that lead to the surface. It's part of their work. The Council must negotiate with the people who live Above, to make sure everything runs smoothly. But the Minister never goes. The Minister's safety is too precious to put at risk, and his or her place is in the Below.

"Did you know that this time they're planning to take the sirens, too?" Maire asks. "Rumor has it that we'll leave very soon. If you let me, I could take you with us. Above."

Remember, I tell myself, *you can't believe what she says.* But I can't help it. I could go up with them and perhaps, once I was Above, I could find a way to escape.

"Sirens are miracles," Maire says. "Remember that."

"Then why are you all at the mercy of the Council?" I ask.

"Because we are human miracles," Maire says. "And so there are people we love, and the Council can hold that over us. Remember the time of the Divide? How they were able to get people to agree to stay Above by sending one of their loved ones to live safely Below? That manipulation is very like what the Council does with the sirens. It's how they control us. We do what they ask, and our loved ones have better lives. If we don't do what they want, they can make things difficult for those we love."

"Who do you love?" I ask Maire, because I cannot picture her loving anyone. Especially now that my mother is gone.

Maire laughs. "I love myself," she says. "I do what they ask because I want to live."

I understand her.

She and I are alike.

I love Bay, and my mother, but I also want to survive. Perhaps that is what I want more than anything else. If I'm honest with myself, how much of my desire has to do with seeing my sister again and how much of it has to do with my increasing certainty that, if I don't get Above, something in me will die?

Maire and I are two sides of the same dark coin.

"And of course I loved your mother," Maire says. She walks out into the middle of the floodgate chamber. "She was in this chamber years before her death, you know. All potential Ministers come here. The Council and the priests close off the public viewing area. One by one, each candidate for Minister lies down in the middle of the floor, in the same spot where their bodies will be placed when they die. Did you know this?"

No. My mother never told me.

"*I* know this," Maire says, her voice growing, pushing, pulling on me, "because I was there."

"You couldn't have been there," I say. "They would never consider you for Minister, and you're not part of the Council."

"That's true," Maire says. "But as you know, a Minister has to prove that he or she is either immune to the sirens or powerful enough to resist them. So the candidates for Minister come here, during the night, while the rest of Atlantia sleeps. The priests and Council watch as witnesses. And then the sirens come in. We take turns talking. The other priests and the Council don't hear what we say. They watch our lips, of course, they see the words, but they stay safe from our voices."

"What do you say?" I ask.

"Oh," Maire says, "it's different for each person. Of course. The point is to see who screams and breaks, and who can resist."

"They'd never let you talk to my mother," I say. "The two of you are sisters. They'd think you'd go easy on her."

"On the contrary," Maire says, "they thought I might know exactly what to say. And they knew those things might be even more difficult to hear, coming from a sister."

I don't ask her what she said to my mother, but Maire tells me anyway.

"I told her that her husband never loved her, that her children were going to die young," Maire says, closing her eyes. She seems like she tastes each word as she says it. "I told her that she wanted to be Minister for all the wrong reasons—for power, for gain. I told her about terrible things, evil things that

people do to one another. I told her that I did not love her."
Maire opens her eyes and there is a darkness in them that I
have never seen before, one so deep it shocks me, even coming
from Maire.

"I held nothing back," Maire says. "And it worked. Oceana's
ability to resist impressed the other priests and the Council.
She was the only one able to withstand every single siren,
including her own sister. And she wasn't born immune, the
way some people are. So she has me to thank for her excellent
control. Those few years we grew up together taught her resistance." Then she smiles at me. "Though perhaps I should
credit you with some of that, too. It's rather impressive she
trained herself to hold out against her own child."

That hurts, as Maire knew it would. But I refuse to let her
manipulate me. I remember how my mother did not resist me
when the need was real, how she always told me who I really
was even as she tried to shelter me.

"Without me, your mother never would have been the Minister," Maire says. "I helped make her into what she'd always
dreamed of becoming."

I don't believe Maire. My mother was the Minister because
of what *she* did.

"Of course, it hurt her," Maire says. "She knew it would, but
she didn't understand how hard it would be to hear me say
those things. She thought less of me after that day. She was
afraid. But there was no way around it. If I hadn't done what
I did, she would never have been the Minister, and she *had* to
be the Minister."

"You make her sound selfish," I say. "As if that's all she cared
about."

"No," Maire says. "She loved the city, but she had to be the
Minister because Atlantia *needed* her to be the Minister."

"Do *you* love Atlantia?"

"I love it and I hate it," Maire says.

When she says that, I feel it, too.

"I won't force you to do anything, Rio." Maire makes my name sound beautiful. She makes me sound beautiful. "But you can choose to come to the Above with us."

I close my eyes with the pleasure of that thought. If I say yes to Maire, maybe I could taste real air. I could walk across a sandy beach to a town with real trees and talk to my sister. Even if we were tasked with burying garbage while breathing in pollution for the rest of our lives, we would be together *and* Above, a circumstance I never thought possible.

"You can't get Above on your own," Maire says. "The transports they use to move goods between the Above and the Below aren't pressurized for human survival. The transports they use for taking people to the surface are guarded too closely by the Council. Even if you used your voice to get past those who guard them, the Council would know the minute you tried to ascend. They'd cut off your air and bring the transport back. You'd be dead in minutes. I've seen it happen."

I open my eyes.

"Even if you somehow scrape together the money to buy an air tank and attempt an escape through the mining bay," Maire says, "you'll be blown to bits by the mines before you exhale the last of the air you breathed in Atlantia. This is the best way. I'm your safest chance for the Above."

I hear something outside. The guards are at the door. It won't hold for long.

"You think you don't know me," Maire says, "but you do. I sang you some of your first lullabies."

And I don't know if it's her voice or the truth or both, but I think I do remember her singing a song long ago.

Under star-dark seas and skies of gold
Live those Above, and those Below
They sing and weep, both high and deep
While over and under the ocean rolls

"You see," Maire says, her voice sad. "You remember."

"I'm not sure that I do."

"Your mother cut me off from you when you were very small," Maire says. "And I always thought I knew why. When I heard you speak in the temple the day Bay left, I knew for certain."

"She wanted to protect me from you."

"She was right," Maire says. "She knew I'd want to talk to you, to teach you about your gift. I wouldn't have been able to resist. But I would never have hurt you intentionally." She looks up at the floodgates. "I wonder if that was what she was coming to tell me, the day she died. I wonder if she meant to tell me about you. Or if it was something else entirely."

My mother's last act was to go to her sister's house. What was she trying to do? Was she trying to tell Maire something? Give her a warning? Ask her a question? And did she die before her message was given, as Maire asserts? Or was she able to deliver it and then struck down? By whose hand? My aunt's?

My mother and my sister trusted Maire, but I'm not certain she repaid their trust.

The clamor outside is growing. They're about to break open the doors.

"I won't be able to control them for long once they get inside," Maire says. "There will be too many. You should go. Slip out the door as they come in, and I will make sure they don't see you. But take this." She presses another shell into my hand. It is ridged in black and white, mostly black, and rough to the touch. "This one holds *my* voice. This is how I will teach you about what you can do, since it will be difficult for us to be together in person very often. All you have to do is ask a question into that shell and then listen for the answer to come back to you."

"How can that work?" I ask. "How will you hear me?" If this is real, and not some kind of trick, then Maire's is a terrific, terrible power, and she can do things I've never heard of or imagined. I always thought my mother was the most powerful woman in Atlantia, but now I am not so sure.

"It's part of my magic," Maire says. "Your mother and I discovered it by accident. We used to do that child's trick of holding a shell to your ear to listen for the wind in the trees, and one day I whispered something into the shell for Oceana, and when she held it to her ear, she could hear my voice saying the words again. When Bay decided to leave, I saved some of her voice in the other shell so that you could have it later."

Does this mean that if I whispered questions into the other shell, Bay would answer them?

"No," Maire says. Once again she knows what I'm thinking without my saying it. "With other voices, I can just capture their sound. Mine is the only one that can communicate and change. The rest are echoes of what was already said."

My heart sinks with disappointment. "Can any other sirens do this?" I ask.

"None that I know of," Maire says. "And this isn't perfect. I can answer a few questions at a time before I've expended all my strength carrying my voice so far. And it will only work when you ask. I can't say anything unless it is an answer to your spoken question. I ordered it this way to help you feel that you can trust me, so that you will have a measure of control over our conversations."

Then her voice becomes brisk, and she sounds almost like one of my teachers back at school, except there is an edge of danger and urgency to Maire's voice. "Being a siren is more than simply using your voice," she says. "It's practicing how to control it, how and when to save it, when to let your voice soar. And all of that is scarcely the half of it."

She sounds sad again. Are the emotions real or is she manipulating me? It's not the sorrow in her voice that pulls on me—it's the sorrow in my own heart, that I can never fully speak. I've always wondered if I could, Above.

I'm wavering. And weak. Maire knows it.

What other hope do I have? Maire could help me get Above.

"The things you told my mother were not true," I say to Maire. "My father did love her. She wanted to be Minister for reasons that were pure." My mother loved helping people.

"I know," Maire said. "But I could make them sound true. It was a gift to her. I wanted to help her become the Minister." And I can't tell if it is reflected light or tears that I see in Maire's eyes. "I hoped she would love me for it. I think she did. And of course she hated me for it, too. Even *she* couldn't help that."

I swallow. "How do I know you're not lying to me now about helping me get to the Above? How do I know that you won't lie to me in the shell?"

"You don't," Maire says.

I'm out of time. The guards burst through the door. "Go," Maire says to me, and she starts calling to them, her voice so strange, a laugh and a cry and a song.

The guards all stare at her. Though some of them are supposed to be immune, none of them look my way.

As I slip away, I can't stop listening to Maire. She's singing that lullaby again, but this time Maire has turned it angry, into an attack. *"They sing and weep,"* she says, and I suddenly realize that line could be about the sirens.

And then Maire goes silent. Caught. What did they do to make her stop? Or did she know I was gone?

I hurry through the back hallways. Why did Maire tell me all of this at the floodgates? She knew she'd be imprisoned this way—did she want it like that? Certainly there were hundreds of places where we could have met where we'd be much less likely to get caught.

Why teach me this way, instead of in person? Why get herself locked away so that we have to trust the shell, so that she can only answer the questions I ask?

Does she not entirely trust herself, her own eagerness to have her sister's daughter as a pupil?

Or is there another reason, one so dark and deep I can't even begin to fathom it?

My mother and my sister trusted Maire. But they are both gone. Neither of them can tell me if that trust turned out to be justified.

It is entirely possible that they were both betrayed.

As I come back out into the plaza, I lift my eyes to the sky and to the stone-and-glass version of the floodgate exit—the temple's rose window, high and colorful against the daylight.

Maire took me to the floodgates to talk about my mother. But she also took me there to remind me of what death looks like. Bodies laid out on the stone, cold water coming in, someone you love going up. She wanted me to recognize that trying to go through the mining bay or in the transports isn't safe. She wanted me to see *her* as my way to the Above.

Instead, she has reminded me of another way that I can leave.

I can't leave Atlantia the way my sister did.

But I can try to leave the way my mother did.

Of course, there will be one significant difference.

When I go through the floodgates, I'll be alive.

CH*A*PTER 8

I wonder how much a tank of air will cost. What if it's five hundred and seven coin, exactly the amount of the money that Maire says Bay left for me? If so, would that be a message from Bay, a signal that she wanted me to find a way to follow her to the surface?

The day after Maire takes me to the floodgates, I go straight to the deepmarket when I've finished work and make my way through the stalls, listening to the air vendors, the ones who sell shots of pure, heady air flavored with scents and spices.

I make several passes up and down the rows of sellers, paying attention to how each vendor sounds and to what they're saying, wondering who to choose. I find myself slowing down, stopping, in front of the stall bearing a placard that says: ENNIO, AIR MERCHANT. Ennio is a slight young man, full of movement. When he sees me, he holds up a small canister. "Our most popular scent," he says. "Lavender. It's restful, if you're having trouble sleeping."

I shake my head at him. "I need more air than that," I say. "Plain air."

I don't know if I'm using the right words—will Ennio know what I'm really asking? He does. His eyes shutter, and his voice becomes tight and low. He wants me gone and that lets me know that I might be on the right track.

"No," he says. "*No.* I don't sell that kind. My air is for people who want to stay comfortable right here in Atlantia."

I think he's lying to me. Why? Because I'm young? A girl? Because he doesn't like the sound of my voice? I'm tired of that getting in my way. "How much *would* plain air cost, if someone were to sell that kind?" I press. "A tank of it, pressurized? Can you tell me that, at least?"

I think he won't answer, but he does. "A thousand at best," he says, "and there's no guarantee that you're even getting what you pay for. You might have an empty canister or one that won't do you a bit of good because it hasn't been pressurized correctly. And you won't live long enough to take more than one or two breaths of that. Some want to try to go up on their own, and there are those who don't mind profiting from the stupidity of others. But no one's ever made it Above unless the Council's taken them up."

A thousand coin. Almost twice the amount Bay left me.

"I should turn you in," Ennio says, watching me. "The Council likes to know who asks these kinds of questions."

"There's no need," I say. "I wouldn't try it. I wanted to know what was possible."

"Going Above isn't possible," Ennio says. "You're young. Don't throw everything away." I nod and do my best to appear chagrined.

He's no siren. He told me what I need to know, but he doesn't have the power to change my mind.

Aldo has pinned up the brackets in the usual place on the wall of the market stalls nearest the racing lanes. I'm surprised to find that I feel a stirring of excitement. It will be nice to have a distraction, something to do with my body. I've been restless since Bay left and I stopped swimming, and of course there are reasons for what I'm going to do— I have to get strong enough to swim to the Above and fast enough to get around the mines, and I have to win enough coin to buy an air tank to take with me. I don't think Ennio will refuse to sell to me if I show up with a thousand coin in hand. And the way he spoke about the air and the sellers tells me that he, at least, attempts to sell air that will work.

But I don't see my last name—Conwy—on any of the brackets. I read them over again and turn around to see Aldo walking in my direction. He shakes his head.

"They said no," he tells me, when he gets close. "Neither the bettors nor the other racers were willing for you to take her place."

"Why not?" I ask. "Didn't you tell them that I could keep up with her in training?"

"Yes," Aldo says, "and they know it anyway from seeing the two of you swim together. But you didn't earn her place. Bay did, and she's gone."

I suppose I can understand this. Although I've seen Bay and myself as two halves of the same whole for years, everyone else might not feel that way. "All right," I say. "I'll start at the bottom. In the low brackets."

Aldo shakes his head. "You can't race. At all."

"Why not?" I clench my hands into fists. "They raced Bay. Why am I any different?"

"You just are," Aldo says. "There's something wrong about you."

If they only knew. *Everything* is wrong about me.

How am I supposed to get faster—and stronger—without anyone to race?

There's nothing I can do about it.

Except, there is.

I could speak to Aldo, putting barely any sound behind the word; it could be made mostly of air, my breath against his neck as I leaned in. I would hardly have to use any of my real voice. But he'd hear a hint of it, close to him and only for him. *"Please,"* I'd whisper, and in spite of himself he'd close his eyes. He'd do whatever I said. I know he would.

But I don't do it.

In that moment I remember the money I brought with me.

"Then I'll rent a lane," I say. "Right now."

"For what?" he asks. "You'll waste your coin. No one's going to race you."

A few of the bettors and other racers have gathered around to listen, to see what I'll do. I don't look at any of them. I keep my eyes on Aldo.

"I'll swim against myself," I say.

Aldo laughs. "No one will watch that," he says. "No one will bet on it."

"That's fine," I say. "I'm not doing it for them." My mind buzzes with ways to make swimming harder, to push myself. Should I use some of my money to buy one of the fancier training suits, the kind with resistance to make you stronger? And then I realize I'm already wearing the perfect suit. My machinist's gear from work will weigh me down. It will be hard to swim in this, and I can let it dry overnight so I can wear it again tomorrow.

I step down into the lane. The water drags on me and it's hard to walk. I hear people laughing, someone saying that I'd do better to take everything off, someone else saying that there's always been something odd about the other Conwy girl. I duck my head under the water and I no longer hear anything they say.

I can barely swim the first few strokes after I push away from the wall. The weight of my clothing pulls me down. But then I remind myself. *It's going to be harder than this to get to the surface. And you don't know how far you'll have to swim once you get up there. This is nothing. This is the very beginning of what you'll have to do.*

I look down at the black line along the center of the lane, the one that keeps you away from the sides if you follow it. I keep to that line, with all the drag and pull from my suit weighing on me, and I don't stop until I've made it all the way down and back, over and over again, until I'm afraid that I will actually drown.

I climb back out. My clothes are soaked, and my muscles tremble from the effort.

People are watching. Some of them laugh. Some of them cheer. But they're all paying attention, and I fight down a smile. They have reminded me of something I have always known, something that my mother knew how to play upon. People love a spectacle, an event. Give them something to watch and you will make them happy. "So much of life is in the smallness of moments," my mother said. "But they are harder to mark. So we need the grander celebrations and occasions. People like to feel significant."

Maybe if I give them something good enough to watch when I swim alone, they'll pay me for it. What if I made it so interesting that I could draw a crowd? The thought terrifies me, but then my time in the lanes would serve two purposes: I could train for the swim to the Above, *and* I could make money to buy the air tank I need.

"I'll rent a lane again, same time tomorrow," I tell Aldo. "Tell anyone who's interested. And I'll do something new next time."

"You think they're going to care?" he asks.

"They already do," I say, pointing at the crowd. They think I'm odd. No one wants to swim against me. But they don't mind watching me take risks myself.

I don't have extra clothes with me, so I have to drip my way home. I pass one of the stalls that sells pastries cut into wedges, with flaky crusts and nuts and raisins and brown sugar inside. My stomach rolls with hunger. But I need to save my coin. Every bit of it. I worry already about how much I've spent. I need to make all the money back, and much more besides.

I pause for a moment near a stall where a vendor sells tiny bottles of dirt (marked as REAL AND FROM ABOVE). In spite of the labels, I feel certain that the dirt must be counterfeit, and I want to say something to the woman who counts out coin with shaking hands to buy a bottle from the smarmy-looking vendor. *I've seen the real thing up close,* I want to tell her, *and this isn't it.*

I know what dirt looks like because my mother let us look at the large jar of earth that sits on top of the altar. She even let us open the jar. We couldn't touch the dirt, but we could certainly see how dark and rich it was, and sometimes I felt that the smell of it was the smell of home.

But not everyone is as lucky as I was, and if this woman wants to think she has a tiny jar of real soil, perhaps it's worth it. After all, I liked believing that my sister and I told each other everything, and that turned out not to be true.

Was it ever true?

I know it was.

When did it change?

I have no idea.

I don't realize that I've stopped walking until someone bumps into me and *tsk*s at my waterlogged clothes. A few children point and laugh at me.

Everything is heavy.

I want this pain off my back. I want to stop thinking about why Bay left and whether or not I can believe Maire. The swimming has worn me out, which is good, because I didn't have to think of Bay while I was doing it, but it's also when I'm exhausted that the dark loneliness breaks in.

And I realize that in order to go up through the floodgates, I have to trade places with someone else. I have to slip into the morgue and arrange myself like a body. I have to hide the real corpse, whoever it is they mean to send up. And, of course, in hoping for the floodgates to open, I am hoping for someone to die. I am hoping for someone to die so that I can leave.

I pass the vendors who sell jewelry—ornate silver; round, carved beads; puddles of stone and glass held together with wire and metal—and then I see something that stops me in my tracks.

It's a ring, arranged on black velvet in a glass-lidded case, and even though I don't care anything about jewelry, I know that ring.

It's the one that belonged to my mother. The one Bay forgot to bring to the morgue that day.

The ring is made of platinum and inlaid with brown and blue. My father gave it to my mother on their wedding day. It is extremely precious, because the blue is a gem called turquoise and the brown is wood, both rare materials from Above. My father had my mother's name engraved inside the band, and then, when Bay and I were born, he had our names engraved there, too.

After my mother went up through the floodgates, Bay wore this ring every day.

Was she wearing it the day she went Above?

I can't remember.

You're not allowed to take anything valuable with you when you choose the Above. Only the clothes on your back. So did someone take this from Bay after she chose the Divide? And bring it to the deepmarket to sell?

Or was it gone before then?

Could Bay have sold it?

I shiver and stare, trying to make sense of what I see. Could this ring be a counterfeit, like the dirt sold in bottles? If so, it's a perfect replica, and the closer I look, the more I recognize that silver band inlaid with wood and blue stone, smooth, circling.

"It's not for sale," says the older woman tending the stall, and the large, burly man next to her—her son?—folds his arms and glares at me.

"That ring is mine," I say. "It was my mother's."

"What makes you think that?" she asks.

"It has the name Oceana carved inside the band," I say. "And my name. Rio. And my sister's name. Bay. No one else would know that. You couldn't see the engravings while she was wearing it."

"This ring did indeed belong to Oceana the Minister," the woman says. She speaks my mother's name with a touch of reverence, the way Elinor did earlier. "You're right about that."

"And it should be mine," I say. "You could come with me right now to the temple, and every priest there would vouch for me. They'd tell you that I'm her daughter."

"I'm sorry," the woman says. "But I paid for it. If the boy who sold it to me stole it from you, then you need to take it up with him."

"Boy?" I ask.

"Yes," she says. "A young man brought me this ring. If he was a thief, that's not my fault, but I will sell it back to you if you can come up with the money. I won't even raise the price." She seems pleased with herself for being so fair.

"But who was the boy?" I ask.

"He didn't give a name," she says. "But he had blond hair. He was young. Handsome. He looked well-off."

The description could be any of dozens of people in Atlantia, but it also matches Fen Cardiff.

"When did he bring it to you?"

"Two days before the anniversary of the Divide," she says. "I remember it well. I've been glad to have it. It's a beautiful piece and serves its purpose nicely."

I'm about to ask the woman what she means—what purpose can a ring have, except to be worn?—when a man comes up holding a tiny jar of water, much like the ones in the other stall that contain the fake dirt. "It's five coin," the woman says, and the man nods. He gives her the money and holds out the jar, and the woman takes it from him. She picks up my mother's ring and drops it into the jar of water.

It's a struggle to keep my voice level. "What are you doing?"

"You're not the only one who recognizes this ring," the woman says, holding up the jar to the faint deepmarket light. The ring clinks against the glass. "Everyone knows Oceana the Minister wore it on her blessing hand."

The man watching is rapt. "Thank you," he says.

"You're pretending the ring has power to bless the water," I say.

"No pretense about it," the woman says, carefully fishing out the ring with a long, thin metal skewer. "You said yourself this was your mother's ring."

The man gapes at me. "Oceana's daughter?" he asks.

"Never mind that," the woman says. "It's Oceana's ring, and now your water is blessed. Off you go."

After he takes the jar and leaves, the woman sighs. "I shouldn't have said that about Oceana being your mother," she says. "I'm sorry. You can't have everyone following you around the deepmarket hoping that some of your mother's magic has rubbed off on you."

"My mother wasn't magic."

"I meant that figuratively," the woman says. "But you do sound like a girl who takes things literally." She polishes the ring and then puts it back in its case. "Of course, I suppose everyone knows who you are anyway, but it's better not to draw attention to that fact. Although you're doing your best to get noticed, standing there in those dripping clothes."

"Why would everyone know who I am?" I ask. Atlantia is a large city. And my mother may have been a public figure, but Bay and I kept to ourselves. We always did a good job of blending in, or so I thought.

"There are thousands of us, but one Minister," the woman says. "Anyone who ever bothered to enter the doors of the temple for a service probably had you pointed out to them at some point."

This is not what I want to hear. I knew people paid attention to my mother, of course, but I always imagined myself slipping unnoticed through the streets and the deepmarket. It is true that Josiah and Elinor and Bien all knew who I was, though I assumed that was because they'd been told before I came down from the temple. "*You* didn't recognize me right away," I point out.

"My eyesight isn't what it used to be," the woman says. "And I didn't expect the Minister's daughter to be wandering around the deepmarket soaked to the bone." Then she holds out her hand. "My name is Cara."

I don't care what her name is, and I don't shake her hand. "You're ruining the ring," I say. "It's not meant to be put into water—you're going to make it rust, or damage the wood, or wear off the inscriptions."

"Not everyone wants blessed water," Cara says. "Some people only want to touch the ring. We're careful about that, of course. Can't have them stealing it. Some people want the ring to bless a scrap of fabric or an object from their home. And don't worry. I've got a special oil to restore the moisture to the wood."

"Why are you doing this?" I ask. "Why are people paying good money for it?"

"Some people down here worship Oceana, you know," Cara says quietly. "I've seen them lighting candles to her the way they do to the other gods. And I've heard people whispering that she died early because she was actually one of the gods and it was time for her to go back home."

"Blasphemy," I say. Again. I never knew there was so much of it. But it's everywhere. At the workplace, here in the deepmarket.

"Or piety," Cara says. She takes out a vial of oil and drops some onto the wood of the ring, rubbing it carefully with a soft cloth.

It hurts me physically to see my mother's ring in someone else's hands. Would Bay give the ring to a boy to pawn instead of giving it to me? Perhaps there's another explanation. Maybe Fen stole it from her, and she didn't want to tell me.

I could tell Cara, "Give me the ring," and she would have to do it.

It's getting harder to hold back.

"I know you want this," Cara says, "but I'm sorry. I paid too much for it to let it go. I will give the ring back to you if you can bring me five hundred and seven coin. That's how much I paid for it."

The words I was about to say catch in my throat. I stare at Cara.

Five hundred and seven coin.

The money *is* from Bay. She *did* sell the ring.

And I used some of the coin to purchase time in the swimming lanes. If I hadn't done that, I could go right home and come back with the rest of the money to buy the ring today.

But Bay wouldn't sell the ring just so I could buy it back. She must have wanted me to use the money for something else, something so important that she was willing to sell our mother's most prized possession. What could it be?

Did Bay want to help me buy an air tank so I could try to swim for the surface? Or did she intend me to use the money to get there in another way? Should I be trying to bribe some

Council member to get me on a transport? Or did Bay give the money to Maire to indicate that I *could* trust my aunt, that I should follow her Above?

I wonder if True knows anything about the ring. Did Fen talk to him about it?

"Do you know anyone named True?" I ask Cara. "A boy, about my age? Brown hair, brown eyes? He says he comes to the deepmarket most evenings."

"Yes," she says. "He's often around, pushing that cart of his, selling those fish he makes."

Fish?

I don't think I've heard her right.

Someone else brushes past me to buy a blessing from my mother's ring, and I take a step back. So True works as a vendor in the evenings. Unlike the stalls, the carts are always on the move. How am I supposed to find him?

As I start scanning the crowd, he comes into view, pushing a cart very carefully. He's not calling out for customers; he's looking down to make sure he doesn't lose any of his wares.

Seeing him right now feels like I offered up a prayer and the gods answered it immediately. Like I threw a coin in the wishing pools and what I wanted appeared before my eyes. I'm not sure I like it. It seems suspicious. Things like that don't happen, and they especially don't happen to me.

I leave behind Cara and my mother's ring and walk toward True. As I come closer, he glances up and his eyes meet mine. He looks surprised as he takes in my wild, wet hair, my still-dripping clothes, but he doesn't say anything. He seems to think I should be the one to speak.

"There's a question I need to ask you," I say. "About Bay and Fen."

True glances around at the busy deepmarket. "Can you ask it here?"

"Maybe not," I say.

True nods and starts pushing his cart again. "Come with me," he says. I follow him around the corner of a row of stalls. The plastic-and-wire slats keep out much of the light and it's a bit dim and deserted. "There," he says. "It's quieter here."

I mean to ask him about Fen and the ring, but I'm distracted by the wares in True's cart. They're *moving*.

Small metal fish swim in glass bowls filled with turquoise-colored water.

The fish are simple and beautiful, a few pieces of scrap metal put together, and even though there is very little detail on them, somehow you know exactly what they are.

"How do you do it?" I bend down to examine them more closely. "What kind of join did you use so they can move like that?"

True's face lights up and he takes a fish out of the bowl to show me. "I call it a fishtail solder," he says. "You attach it at the front and the back with a smaller rod. It's actually three pieces instead of two."

"How do you know to do this?"

"I work on the gondolas," he says. "I repair them, at night. So I'm used to working with metal and machinery."

"When do you sleep?" I can't imagine when he has time, between night work on the gondolas and making and selling his creations in the deepmarket.

"For a few hours in the mornings," True says. When he smiles, it goes all the way to his eyes, making them crinkle. Everything about him seems warm—his smile, the open way he looks at me, his hand when it brushes against mine as he gives me the fish so I can take a closer look. "I don't mind missing out on some rest. I like working on the gondolas, and I like making machines of my own. But how do you know about joins and solders?"

"I used to put the leaves back on the trees," I tell him. "At the temple. They had to be flexible, too. But we should have done something like this. It would have given the leaves greater range of motion."

The fish are so fast and fluid. If I had some to practice with, I could use them to simulate the mines. I've chosen the floodgates because they're nearer to the surface than the mining bays—I'll have a better chance of survival with a shorter swim and less of a change in pressure—but there will still be plenty of mines to get around. I could try to avoid the fish while I swam in the tanks. It would give the people in the stands something different to watch. They could make bets on how many times I come up against the fish, how fast I can make it to the end of the lane.

True's fish are exactly what I need.

"How long can they go like this?" I ask.

"Almost ten minutes," he says. "Then you have to take them out and rewind the machinery."

"Do you sell many?"

He shakes his head. "People buy them now and then for their children's birthdays. I wish I could afford a stall so I could have a chance at selling more, but to pay for a stall, I'd have to sell more fish." He laughs.

"But they're beautiful," I say. "People should be saving their coin to buy them." I wish I could tell him this in my real voice.

But I think that somehow he understands, because he sounds very sincere when he says, "Thank you."

A bucket of metal parts set behind the bowls catches my eye. "What's this?"

True tries to grab it away from me, but I've seen some claws, a gargoyle mouth, a stretch of silver, meshy metal wing. "It's something I'm working on," True says.

"You're trying to make the bats," I say.

"It's hard to get them to fly," True admits. "They keep crashing and breaking."

It would be interesting to ask him more, to try to help him figure out how to make the bats work. But I don't have time. I have to get Above. And I can't tell True about my plans to get there. He can't help me, and he might try to stop me. Or worse, tell someone what I'm trying to do.

"So what was it you wanted to ask me?" True says. "About Bay and Fen?"

"It's about a ring," I say. "It used to be my mother's, but after she died, Bay wore it every day. I guess I thought it had gone to the surface with her, if I thought about it at all. But I saw it today. The vendor said that a boy who looks like Fen brought the ring to her two days before the anniversary of the Divide. So Bay must have asked him to sell it. Unless he stole it from her."

"No," True says immediately. "He wasn't that kind of a person. He *isn't* that kind of a person." He frowns. "What did they get in exchange?"

"Five hundred and seven coin," I say.

"That's a lot of money," True says. "What do you think they used it for?"

I don't want to tell him that I have the money. I don't know him well enough. But I also don't want to lie to him. "I'm cold," I say. "I've got to get home. I just wanted to see if you knew anything about this."

"No," True says. "But I can try to find out more." He smiles at me. "Does this mean you changed your mind? About working together to find out why they left?"

"Yes," I say, and I feel a twinge of guilt that it will have to be an uneven partnership. I want to know what he knows. I want his help in discovering what we can. But my main focus is to get to the Above, and I can't tell him anything about that.

"How much do you charge for each of these fish?" I ask True.

"Ten coin," he says, sounding surprised at the sudden change of subject.

I try not to smile. A pittance, when you consider all the use they will be to me. "I want to buy ten," I say, reaching into my bag and counting out twenty coin. "I have enough money to buy two right now. Will you save eight more for me? I'll pay you the rest tomorrow. I don't need the bowls or the water."

True's face is astonished and happy. "Of course," he says. And then he reaches into the bowls and stills the fish. "You can have them all now," he says. "I trust you." He counts out ten and puts them into a sack. It's heavy when I take it from him.

"Thank you," I say.

"I'll see you tomorrow," he says.

I'm sure that I make a fine sight on the gondola, shivering in my sodden machinist's clothing. I find myself wishing that Bay could see me right now, sailing toward the temple with a bag full of metal fish. Would she laugh? Would she cry? Is this anything like what she planned for me?

All I know is that it's the best I can do.

CHAPTER 9

When I swim in the lanes, I keep my eyes open wide and turn to the side, slither, slip. My body feels like it is not my own and like it is exactly, only me. I evade the fish, glide away from them. The ocean sings to me. My sister sings to me.

And then I lose the rhythm, and the fish brush against my body. One. Two. Three. Four. I'm dead four times before I get to the end of the lane.

It's not good enough. I'm not good enough.

But I will learn. Nothing can be as hard as holding in my voice all these years. I will do this. I'll learn to swim around the mines, and I'll earn enough money to buy the air I need.

I stand up in the swimming lane.

Today more people are watching.

One of them is True.

I wave to him. He lifts his hand in response and comes over to the side of the lane to talk to me. I pull off the cap I wear to keep my hair out of the way. The metal fish swim around me—I'll have to catch them in a moment. I meant to find True in the deepmarket after I finished racing, but he's found me first.

True's not smiling, but he seems—I can't think of a better word for it—enchanted. It's the way people sometimes look when sirens speak. But I don't know why, because I haven't said anything at all, and certainly I haven't spoken to him with my real voice.

"You're very beautiful," he says.

He looks as stunned to have said it as I am to hear it.

"I mean," he says, "the way you swim. It's beautiful."

"Thank you," I say, and I feel like he has dropped a piece of light into the dark sorrow of my heart, like a coin into a wishing pool. The warm gold feeling doesn't last, but it flickers as it goes down. "How did you know I was racing?"

"I didn't," he says. "I was here for something else. This was luck."

"I have your money," I say. "Let me get out and I'll give it to you." I rented one of Aldo's temporary lockers for today so I could keep the coin secure until I finished swimming.

True shakes his head. "They're a gift," he says. "I want you to have them."

But he needs to take the money. He's got to earn enough to rent a stall in the deepmarket. I'm about to argue, but Aldo has come over to join us. He ignores True and leans over the lane, addressing me. "They liked it," he says. "I had people asking when you'd swim again. They thought it was interesting, the way you tried to get past the flickers in the water."

"Could they see everything all right from the stands?" I ask.

Aldo nods. "And if we get a bigger crowd, we can use some of the broadcast screens like we do for the larger races."

Bigger crowds mean more money. More money means that I can get to the surface faster. I've spent my life avoiding attention, but I'm going to have to court it if I want to get Above.

"Now that you've given them a taste for free," Aldo says, "we can charge a fee to watch you, set times for your swims so that spectators know when to come. And the bettors liked it, too. They can take bets on how many hits you get during a swim. It's nice to have something new to watch for a change. The races have been going on the same way forever." He looks at True. "Was it you? Were you holding mirrors to reflect on the water?"

"They're not lights or mirrors," I say. "They're fish. Made out of metal." I scoop one up and hold out my hand to show Aldo.

"Whatever it is," Aldo says, "we've got enough interest to give it a try. You can have free practice times in the lane if you'll split the winnings with me."

This is excellent. Even better than I'd hoped. Of course, people will be watching me but it's not as though I'll have to talk. I can have Aldo announce me. "Not down the middle," I say. "Seventy-thirty, the same as any racer."

Aldo shakes his head. "It's a risk," he says. "I know people will bet on and watch the races. I'm not sure that this will take off."

"Seventy-thirty," I say. "All I need you to do is provide the water and the lanes and announce for me. I'll supply the rest, at no cost to you. I have more ideas in mind."

And I do. Aldo thinking that the fish were light and mirrors—a trick—has made my mind swim with possibilities.

"Like what?" Aldo asks.

"We'll show people the fish," I say, "and tell the crowd that we're going to up the ante every time I swim. We'll put more fish in the water. True can make them faster. We could rig them so that they give off an electrical charge when they touch me." That would be even better practice for getting around the mines—if I could train my mind to equate brushing up against the fish with pain, I'd work even harder to avoid them.

"That sounds too risky," True says.

"I'm sure there's a way we could do it without it hurting too much," I say. "And the more dangerous we make it seem, the more people will come to watch. We'll keep changing things up, make them interesting." What if I lock my hands or feet together to make swimming more difficult? What if I go under, deep, and see how fast I can come to the surface with weights tied on?

Aldo nods. "All right," he says. "We can split it seventy-thirty."

True looks upset. "Why do you want to take so many risks?" he asks, but no sooner has he finished the question than an expression of understanding crosses his face and he falls silent. I find it much more disconcerting than Aldo's complete disregard for my safety. Does True really understand me?

If so, then he is dangerous to me, more dangerous than anything I do in the swimming lanes.

Aldo and I set a time for my next event. "We can't call them races," Aldo says, "so we'll call them performances." I nod in agreement. Though I'm thinking of them as training sessions, I don't suggest we use that term instead. I don't want anyone to guess my other purpose in doing this. Especially not True.

After Aldo leaves, True leans farther over the lane to talk to me.

"I know why you're doing this," he says. "Why you're taking so many risks."

My heart sinks. How did he figure it out? How did I give myself away?

"The ring," he says.

The ring? Of course. My mother's ring. He thinks I'm trying to earn enough coin to buy it back.

"I'll help you," he says. "I won't charge you anything for any of the fish you use. I'll help you make them."

"Why?" I ask. "Why would you do all of this for free?"

"Because I know how much you want that ring," he says. "And because I need your help to find out why Fen and Bay went Above."

Of course. There's always a price to be paid. True doesn't know that I'm going to get Above and *then* ask my sister why she went.

"We know that there has to be a reason why Bay and Fen went Above," True says. "We know it can't just be that they were in love, because they could have stayed down here and been together."

"We don't even know that they *were* in love," I say.

True hesitates.

"So you think you *do* know that?" I ask.

"Well," True says, "I used to see them sometimes. Kissing."

"Kissing," I say, even more flatly than usual.

"Right," True says.

Could Bay have been in love with Fen? Is *that* why she left? I don't understand.

"When they were kissing . . . did it *seem* like they were in love?" It's truly funny to hear me speaking about love and passion in my false, emotionless voice, but to True's credit, he doesn't laugh.

"I wasn't doing the kissing," True says. "I don't want to speak for them. But yes, it did seem like there was something between them. Something real."

"But even if there was, you're right that they could have stayed Below," I say. "They could have been married here someday. They didn't have to go Above for that."

"I know," True says. "So there must be more to it."

He's right. They must have had other reasons. Deeper than love, perhaps darker.

"Last night I went over and talked to Fen's brother, Caleb," True says. "He's young—ten years old—and he's devastated about Fen leaving. The family can't understand why he'd go. But Caleb said that Fen left him a note. He showed it to me." True holds out a paper. "It's not the real thing," he says, "but Caleb let me copy it down."

The note is short.

> *It might seem like me choosing the Above means that I don't care about you, but that's not true. I do care and I always will.*

Fen wrote those words for his brother, but I want to pretend that Bay wrote them for me.

"Caleb also told me," True says, "that Fen went out at night and came home with his hair wet. Caleb used to see Fen come in but Caleb would pretend to go back to sleep."

"The night races," I say. Those contests, which take place after the deepmarket closes, are the most dangerous. You risk hypothermia if you swim at night, and also time in the holding cells if the peacekeepers catch you. But the stakes are high, and you can make money fast if you don't get sick and don't get caught. It's a completely different kind of racing than what Bay used to do. It's for the truly reckless.

"I've never been to the night races," True says. "I had no idea Fen was in them. But I should have realized. He always liked a risk. That's why I came down to the lanes today. I was asking around to see if anyone here knew Fen. They did, but none of them had any idea he was planning to go Above."

"Do you think that's how they met?" I ask. "Bay must have gone to watch the night races. Or to swim in them." It makes sense now—how I'd find her next to me when I woke up, her body burrowed close for warmth. Did all of this begin because my sister couldn't sleep and I was greedy for my dreams?

"I think so," True says. "And I think they started looking for something together. Maybe something that had to do with your mother, and with how she died." He stops. He's finding it hard to say the words, so I do it for him.

"You think," I say, "that my mother was killed. Murdered."

"Yes," True says. "I'm sorry."

This is all conjecture, but in spite of myself, I feel truth in it. Bay and I both thought there was something wrong about our mother's death. I never thought Bay would leave me, but I know she loved our mother. Did Bay learn something that meant she had to go Above? What about our mother's death could possibly lead Bay there?

"You're not the first one who's suggested it," I say.

"But *why* would someone do it?" True asks. "How could anyone want to hurt Oceana the Minister?"

It's too much. I can't think about it anymore, not now.

I start trying to grab the fish left swimming in the lanes, but my fingers have gotten cold and I miss.

"I'll help you," True says, folding up the note and putting it away.

"You'll get wet," I say.

"That doesn't matter," True says.

The fish are fast and True and I are clumsy, which makes him laugh, and that sets me free for a moment because I like the way he sounds. *I* can't laugh, because a little of my real voice always comes through when I do, but I let myself smile. We are like children, splashing as we catch at the fish, children who used to do this in pools and streams Above. That word is what sobers me.

Above. I have to go Above.

"How can you be so happy when they're gone?" I ask. "Don't you miss him?"

True stops smiling. I feel sorry. "Of course I do," he says. "He was my best friend. I miss him all the time." He bends down, catches another fish, and I watch the muscles in his back move smooth as water underneath his shirt. Then he straightens up and says, "But I can't help being happy. I'm alive."

I have nothing to say to that.

I'm alive, he said, and he is.

I don't know that I am.

But if I make it Above, I think I could be.

CHAPTER 10

$\mathcal{I}$ 've just changed out of my racing suit when I hear the bells chiming, the ones that signify closing time for the deep-market. "It's too early," I say out loud, and someone in the dressing stall next to me says, "Not for the third Wednesday."

Of course. I'd forgotten, lost track of the days. The Minister always gives a broadcast on the third Wednesday of each month. I wonder what the Council wants us to hear tonight.

The broadcast goes out to schools and churches throughout Atlantia, but I've always listened at the temple. So I ride the crowded gondola up there, hoping I can find a seat somewhere now that I no longer have a reserved spot at the front with the other acolytes.

The temple is jam-packed, as is always the case for these sermons, and there is a strange buzz in the air, an excitement that feels heightened. I see a spot at the back, high up in the gallery, and as I make my way toward it I hear Nevio begin talking at the pulpit, his voice magnified by speakers set up throughout the building.

"I speak for both the Ministry and the temple," Nevio says, "for we are in perfect agreement about how to address this situation." His voice sounds fulsome and rich, with something underneath it, some steel sound that I've never liked. I reach the top of the steps, and someone slides over on the highest wooden bench to make room for me. I barely fit. This place is full.

"The situation," Nevio says, "is the sirens."

My heart jumps in my chest. What is he planning to say? Does this have something to do with Maire breaking into the floodgate chamber?

Does Nevio know that I was with her?

"As some of you are aware," Nevio says, "the sirens' time is ending. The last known siren was born twenty years ago."

Can this be true? If it is, then I am the youngest siren. The last one. My mother never told me that.

"The sirens are a miracle," Nevio says, "but they are *our* miracle, to be contained and controlled for our good. They belong to Atlantia. Just as the bats cannot be allowed to fly about unchecked and need a place of their own and people to feed them, the sirens also need keepers and a safe haven for their protection and ours."

He speaks to Atlantia, but I have the strangest feeling that he also speaks to me specifically. That he's telling any sirens out there—*Could there be others like me?*—that they need to come to him to be safe. That we are capable of terrible things. We might hurt the ones we love. We might turn evil and wrong.

Maybe I should listen to him.

But then I look back at the pulpit and picture my mother there instead of Nevio and I know that was the very thing she tried to protect me from—a life under the control of people who didn't love or understand me.

"And as the time of the sirens ends," Nevio says, "we may look for a new miracle. For the third miracle."

The people rustle hopefully, murmur to one another. They're all too ready to give up the strangeness of the sirens for something else, for something new.

"This is what I want to speak about with you today," Nevio says. "We must prepare for the third miracle. We must be ready." He speaks of sacrifice, and love, and duty, and of the relationship between the Above and the Below and the importance of following the rules set forth by the Council. I stop listening, because I have heard the same thing said before, and much better, by my mother.

What if I *am* the last siren?

What does that mean?

As people exit the temple after the sermon, they push past me on my bench, speculating with animation and excitement about the *when* and *where* and *how* of the third miracle. I don't move. This is my mother's place. She should be here. Everything has been wrong since she died.

Why is she gone?

How did she die?

Who made it happen?

Nevio could have done it.

Or *was* it Maire?

It's not a thought I want to have, but it won't leave me.

Could Maire tell me if I really am the last siren?

I don't know who to trust.

I hear footsteps on the stairs, and then someone appears in the gallery. Justus. He comes and sits down next to me. He looks weary and sad. I wonder if he's thinking of my mother, too.

"When you were a candidate for Minister," I ask him, "what was it like in the floodgate chamber? When they brought in all the sirens to test you?"

"I could resist all of them except for one," Justus says.

"Maire," I say.

Justus closes his eyes. "The words she spoke," he whispers. "The way she said them." He opens his eyes. "She made her voice sound like your mother. And the things she said . . ."

"Terrible things?"

"Wonderful things," Justus says, and a flicker of remembered happiness crosses his face. "But none of it was true, and when I realized that, I wept. When the Council saw the effect Maire's words had on me, that was the end of my chance at being Minister."

My heart goes out to Justus. He always loved my mother. Bay and I knew it, and so did my mother, but she didn't love him back, not that way. I wonder what Maire said to him. It was a cruel thing to do.

"Maire kept me from being the Minister," Justus says. "In the end she brought down Oceana, too. Right before she died, your mother tried to reconcile with Maire, and look how she was rewarded."

When Justus looks at me, I know he wants me to realize what he means, but he doesn't actually want to *say* it. Everyone holds things back when they speak, not just me. Everyone expects and needs other people to give part of the meaning, to make inferences, to put the rest into the little they manage to convey.

Justus thinks that Maire killed my mother.

I want to ask him more, but I suddenly realize we are not alone. I glance up and there stands Nevio, wearing the emblem that used to hang around my mother's neck.

"Justus," he says. "It is time for you to go to work in the tower. The dimming time has begun."

Justus inclines his head. As he leaves he puts his hand on my shoulder. It is the first time he has done that since he found out what I am, and I'm grateful for the gesture and for what he's told me. He is a weak man, too weak for my mother, but that doesn't mean he isn't kind. And he's kept my secret. He hasn't told anyone about my being a siren, or I would have been hauled away to work for the Council by now.

I stand up, too, but Nevio motions for me to sit back down. I don't. Nevio is taller than I am by several inches but I don't look up at him. I look past him.

"I know you have been through a great deal," Nevio says. "I know your mother's death and your sister's choice to go Above have made you not quite yourself."

He's right about that.

"And now you're the last one, left to deal with the aftermath of their actions," Nevio says, and a sharp, sudden bitterness floods through me. He's right again. Bay and my mother are away from everything now. I'm the one they left to gather up the fragments, and I'm not even sure of what I'm trying to piece together.

"I suppose Justus has been telling you about our suspicions regarding your mother's death," Nevio says. "He should know better than to make the same mistake twice. He also told Bay that he thought Maire was responsible."

He did?

"It wasn't a surprise," Nevio says, "when Bay decided to run away from it all by choosing the Above."

But Nevio *was* surprised. I saw him, that day in the temple when Bay said *Above* instead of *Below*.

I *saw* him.

He's made a mistake, and I've caught him.

And then I realize.

Nevio the Minister is a siren. A different kind than I've ever encountered before, but still a siren. A strange, subtle one. I can't put my finger on it.

The Minister is not supposed to be a siren. It's against all the rules.

But he is one nonetheless. I *know*. I know the truth from his lie.

He was convincing me, making me bitter and believing— not about everything, but about my mother and Bay leaving me alone to pick up the pieces—and then he made that mistake. He said that he wasn't surprised. He didn't know I'd seen him, in that short moment in the temple when Bay made her decision.

And an unexpected thought flickers into my mind, bright and right as a fish among the coral in the sea gardens.

When Maire manipulates you, she always lets you know that it's happening. She looks right into your eyes. Even if you can't resist, you know what she's doing and you hate her for it. Nevio is not like that. He doesn't want you to know that you're being manipulated.

Could it be that Maire is an honest kind of siren? Could it be that I *can* trust her?

"I've had to lock your aunt away for a time," Nevio says. "She was breaking into parts of Atlantia that are forbidden to sirens. One of the guards who encountered Maire was fairly certain that he saw someone with her, but she was captured alone. Do you know who that other person might be?"

"No," I say. "But it wasn't me. I'm afraid of my aunt."

Nevio studies me for a moment. Does he believe me? Did I give enough truth in addition to my lie? Does he know that I've figured out his secret? Does he know mine?

"I am glad to hear that," Nevio says, and then he walks past me, along the gallery toward the door to the tower where Justus works. I wait until Nevio closes the door behind him before I breathe again.

Why would someone kill my mother? Was it because of something she knew? Something she did?

Who she was?

⟶

Back in my room, I hold the dark shell that Maire gave me. It feels hard and knobby. It was once inhabited by something alive. Is there life inside it again? Will I hear my aunt's voice?

This seems like magic. It seems dangerous.

But I have so many questions.

On that page of notes, the part Nevio didn't mean for me to see, my mother wrote the word *sirens*. And she wrote to *Ask Maire.*

So I do.

"Can you tell me the history of Atlantia and the sirens?" I say into the shell. "From the very beginning?" It is cool against my lips. I hold it up to my ear and wait.

Yes. Maire's voice comes to me as if it has traveled a great distance, which of course it has, all the way from her prison cell in the Council block to my room in the temple. Her voice sounds small and clear, and I do not know how she has managed to hear me from so far and to send her answer such a long way.

And then Maire repeats the history of the sirens to me, and I am surprised to find myself trying not to laugh, because the voice she uses to tell me the history is a quiet but perfect parody and put-on of Nevio's voice when he sermonizes, his speaking mannerisms exaggerated just enough to make it ridiculous. I didn't know Maire could be funny.

In the beginning there was the Divide.

The world began to fall apart, and so the gods helped the engineers and the Minister create Atlantia. But not everyone could go down. To ensure that the system would work, they made sure that every person who had to stay Above had a loved one Below. Many agreed to remain Above because they wanted their loved ones to be safe. They selected numerous adults for life in Atlantia, of course, because they could keep Atlantia running and fix any problems that occurred. But there were also plenty of children chosen. Children were particularly effective selections for the Below, because you could convince multiple adults—parents, grandparents, uncles, aunts, teachers—to stay for a single child. This is how it was in the beginning.

"I know all of this," I say. "Can you tell me more?" I stop and try to think of what I really want to know, what I want her to make clear. "Is there another history?"

Yes, Maire says again. *To tell it to you means that I must tell you a secret. One that could ruin me if you share it with anyone else.*

I hold my breath. Maire has another secret? I already know that she is extremely powerful, that she can save voices in the shells.

She says nothing, and I realize that I have to ask.

"What is your secret?"

I can hear voices from people who are gone, Maire says. *Who died hundreds of years ago.*

I hear voices in the walls of Atlantia, especially siren voices. They've been saved up, embedded in the walls. The dead are always speaking, but not everyone hears them. I can, and I think that gift must be connected in some way to my ability to save the voices in the shells.

I'm silent for a moment. Then I say, "I don't know if I believe you."

Maire laughs.

"Can you tell me what they said?" I ask. "Those voices in the walls? What did *they* tell you about the history of the Below? About the sirens?"

Yes, Maire says. And her voice changes, becomes the voice of someone else.

In the end there was the Divide.

It's very different from when she mimics, the way she did with Nevio moments ago. It seems that a real and other person is speaking. The voice belongs to a woman who sounds very old, and it is not the voice of a siren.

Those of us chosen to live Below knew we were lucky, but our hearts were also broken. We wept for those left Above. We wandered the streets of our beautiful city and we felt so cold. Though we knew it meant death, we began to want to get back to the Above. We didn't believe that we belonged so far underwater. We felt that if our world was dying, we might as well die with it. Our leaders told us to remember how fortunate we were. To live so that we made the sacrifice of the others worthwhile. Tears streamed down their cheeks as they said these things, so we knew they understood how we felt.

We all tried. But nothing tasted the same. Nothing looked right or sounded the way it had in the Above. There were so many walls, so many echoes. And even with all of the lights, you could feel the dark outside. Some people attempted to get Above. They stowed away in the food transports and suffocated within minutes. They went out through the mining bays and drowned.

Even some of the children tried.

There were so many children sent down without parents. We all did our best to take care of them. They had it the hardest of everyone who came Below. They tried to be happy, because that's what we all said their parents wanted. They cried to themselves, silent tears all day long, as they learned and worked and grew. They became strong, because children are resilient, but I could swear that even after they stopped weeping outwardly, their hearts wept inside. But—and I will always believe this was what made the first miracle possible, that in fact it may have been the first miracle—the children became strong without becoming hard. They steadied their hearts but didn't let them turn to stone.

And then, as they grew up and began having children of their own, a miracle happened.

The sirens.

They were born as I was getting very old, but I lived long enough to hear their voices. I am glad for that.

They sang peace to us. They reminded us what laughter sounded like.

They were beautiful and joyful. Their parents loved them. We all loved them. We loved them so much that we could at last bear the pain of missing those we'd left Above.

When they told us to live, somehow we could. They looked into our eyes and asked us to be happy, and we found we wanted to obey.

The bats came soon after the sirens. Looking back, I think that the bats must have been here all along but didn't show themselves until the siren children sang in the temples and skipped through the courtyards. The bats loved the siren children. They flew about and landed on the children's shoulders and stretched out their wings, as if they wanted to protect the beauty of the sirens' songs.

The sirens were so beautiful and so terrible. Beautiful because of their voices. Terrible because little children should not have such a great responsibility.

But there is no doubt that the sirens saved us.

The voice stops.

What if the children who didn't harden their hearts *were* the first miracle?

Then we have already had all three, and the people are waiting for something that will never come.

"How do you know this?" I ask Maire. "Where did you find that voice?"

I heard it in the walls one day, Maire says. *I think a siren saved it there long ago, asked the walls to hold someone's voice when they were speaking so we could know the truth later. I think that in the past there were many sirens with that ability. But I don't know anyone else who can do it now.*

"How did you hear it?"

I was listening.

"Why?"

Because that is another important part of a siren's power, Maire says. *Most of the sirens now do not understand that part at all. But you do.*

"Am I the last siren?"

You are the last one that I know of, Maire says. *But I do not know everything.*

"Do you think there are more?"

I hope so.

It's frustrating that I have to ask for every piece of information, that she can't volunteer more than I request. Maire did this so that I would trust her and it's helping, but I also wonder what she would say if she hadn't made these rules.

And there's something else. Maire set the rules and spoke them. So does this mean she can control herself? If I make a promise, in my real voice, will I be unable to break it, no matter what?

Stop thinking too far ahead, I tell myself. *You can do this. You can earn money for the air tank and get Above.*

"Where can I get pressurized air?" I ask.

Silence. I can imagine what she wants to say:

You can't get out on your own, Rio. The mines will kill you. Don't try to go through those doors in the ocean room.

But that's not how I plan to leave.

I ask again. "Where can I get a tank full of pressurized air?"

And it must be that she can't break the rules she set, because the words sound almost torn from her. *Ennio in the deepmarket,* she says.

"Is he a crook?" I ask.

When he sells air, it is good. It's not his fault everyone dies.

Ennio. I knew it.

"How could someone convince him to sell her a tank of air," I ask, "without having to use her real voice?"

And again she has to answer.

I think.

I'm almost sure.

But I'm never *completely* sure, when it comes to Maire.

Tell Ennio, Maire says, *that he owes me a favor, and that I'm calling it in on your behalf.*

"Will he believe me?" I ask.

If you tell him a name, Maire says, *he will.*

"What's the name?"

Asha, Maire says.

I almost ask who Asha is, but then I decide I don't want to know. I have too much to hold in and keep back as it is.

"Thank you," I say to Maire. "Do you know why I want the air?"

Yes, she says. Of course she knows. She isn't stupid. She knows what I want to do. But she doesn't know *how* I'll do it.

"Is there a better way to the surface?" I ask. "If my voice is strong enough, can I just tell the Council to put me on a transport and send me Above?"

The Council doesn't tell the public this, Maire says, *but the transports are controlled by the people Above. They are kept at the surface except when in use.*

"Then what *is* the best way to go Above?"

The best way to go Above is with me.

Her voice sounds small and strained. I can barely hear it. Even Maire's power has its limits, and she is growing tired.

In a strange way, I trust the mines in the water. They are made to do something and they do it. They're not alive. They're not complicated, like my mother and Maire and Bay.

There are more questions I want to ask Maire. *Do you know who killed my mother?* and *Was it you?*

But I don't. Something stops me. Maybe I don't want to hear the truth. Maybe I'm afraid she'll find a way to lie to me. Or I'm afraid that if I ask her those questions, she won't answer any others, and there is so much I need to know.

"That's all," I say, after a few moments.

It's not a question, so Maire doesn't answer. The shell is

silent, except for the sound that's always there, the ocean or the wind.

I put down Maire's shell and pick up Bay's instead. I know Maire told me the sounds were captured earlier, but it's easy to imagine that Bay really is singing to me, missing me, right this moment. I whisper a question for Bay. *"Why did you leave?"*

She doesn't answer. She keeps on singing.

I lean back and close my eyes, thinking of all that Maire can do. Like all sirens, she has the ability to persuade, but she can also mimic voices perfectly, ask questions that people from the past have been waiting to answer, and save what someone has said inside the small world of a shell.

The woman speaking from the past was right.

It *is* beautiful and terrible to be a siren.

CHAPTER 11

"I thought of something," True says. "They're not quite ready for you to use yet, but I'm pleased with them."

He's brought his cart all the way over to the racing lanes again, and he takes a bucket from one of the shelves at the back. "Thanks to your last swim, I've had some more interest in my fish," he says. "I thought I'd bring the cart right down here to take advantage of that. I've sold seven already. We'll have that ring back for you soon."

He hoists the bucket up onto the top of the cart. "I wish I were having better luck talking to Fen's family, though. I've been trying, but they're still distraught and they don't seem to know anything. And Caleb's told me everything he can."

"Bay spoke with my aunt before she left," I say, "but so far I haven't been able to find out much about what they said."

"We'll keep trying," True says. "We'll get there." Then he reaches into the bucket and pulls out something silver and sinuous.

"You made an eel," I say.

He nods. "I thought of it after I saw you swim."

"You're comparing me to an *eel?*"

"Yes," True says, grinning. "It's a compliment."

He winds the mechanism on the eel and drops it into the water, and it swims, beautiful and smooth, undulating the length of the lane. True was right. If I swim anything like this, it's a compliment.

The eel bumps into the wall, turns, and swims back.

"Touch it," True says as it gets closer. I do, and a little jolt of electricity fires through me.

"You did it," I say. "Already."

"I couldn't sleep this morning," True says. "So I got up and worked on them. I made five. But I need more time. The charge on this one seems fine, but I haven't been able to test the others enough to be sure they're safe."

But what we don't have is time. The crowd gathering near us expects more than what I did before. We have momentum and we need to build on it if we can.

"So it was fish last time," someone calls out. "What today?"

"More fish," True calls back, and someone boos.

"We've already seen that!" someone else shouts.

I need this to work. I'm not ready to trust Maire to get Above. "This one works fine," I say. "I'm sure the others are safe, too."

"I *think* they are," True says, "but I need to make sure. It won't take long. You can use them tomorrow."

I turn my back on him and climb on the starting block near the lanes, holding up the dripping eel in my hand. "These," I say to the crowd as loud as I can without losing control. "I'll be using these today."

"What do they do?" one of the bettors asks me, coming closer. I drop the eel in the water and it swims.

"Like the fish," the bettor says, sounding unimpressed. Which makes me angry. Because even without the electrical charge, even without me trying to swim around them, these inventions are beautiful. True's workmanship should be worth something all on its own. People should be lining up to buy things from his cart.

So I tell the bettor, "Touch it," and when he does and steps back, surprised at the shock, I smile.

"See," I say. "There's more to it than you think."

"I'll tell the others," he says grudgingly. "But can you feel it through your wetsuit?"

I dip into the water and touch the eel with my elbow, which is covered by the suit. I feel a slight push of pressure, but most of the shock is absorbed by the material.

"Not much," I admit. It would be better if I could. I think fast. I need a full wetsuit to get to the surface. But I have an extra—I have Bay's. "Do you have a knife?"

"We're in the deepmarket," he says. "I'm sure there's someone who does." He goes out into the crowd and a few moments later he's back, before True can even finish the speech he's giving me about how dangerous this might be.

I take the knife into one of the dressing stalls, remove my suit, and cut the fabric so that my arms and legs will be mostly exposed. I put the suit back on and walk out, and the bettor smiles as he takes the knife. "Yes," he says. "That's better. And you're the Minister's daughter?"

"Oceana's," I say. "Not Nevio's."

This makes him laugh. "Right," he says. "People will like that." He walks over to the others and starts talking and gesturing with them, and I wonder what he means. Does he think that they'll like seeing Oceana's daughter risk injury because they didn't love her, or that they'll find me interesting because they cared about her?

True looks unhappy and angry. "This isn't a good idea," he tells me in a low tone. "What I have is a prototype, not a finished product."

"They're going to leave if I don't do something new," I say. "I need to impress them *today*."

"Give me another day," True says.

"It has to be now," I say. "Or they'll forget. You wouldn't believe how fast people can forget about someone."

People are climbing into the stands. It's time.

I reach down and pick up the bucket of eels and fish. True grabs the bucket, too, his hand over mine. His grip is strong and he's not smiling. "I'm sorry," he says. "But they're not ready."

"True," I say. "Please."

I can't put anything I really feel into the word, but True draws in a deep breath, almost as if I have. His fingers tighten on mine for a moment, and I see small burns on the backs of his hands, which must have come from working on the eels and the fish. Did he get any sleep at all?

And then True lets go of the bucket. Neither of us speaks but I wish I could thank him the right way, with my real voice. I start winding up the fish and eels and dropping them back into the water.

They're lovely. He has done perfect work. It's a pleasure to see.

True folds his arms. He doesn't climb up into the stands—he stays right down by the lane to watch. When I glance back at him, his eyes lock on mine. He's trying to understand me, but he never can, because I'm holding back too much of what he needs to know.

I climb up onto the platform and realize that Aldo is still among the bettors, preoccupied with making money. He's forgotten that he's supposed to announce my race. I feel a rush of panic. I'll have to do it myself. I should have told the bettor to stay here and call out for me. I'm going to take all the excitement away from my performance if I announce it in my flat, false voice.

Then True steps up onto the platform next to me. I think he's changed his mind, that he's going to try to stop me, but instead he raises his arms, and the crowd goes quiet. And then True calls out, "Rio Conwy, racer and risk-taker."

That sounds all right. This might work.

True's face is very animated, and his voice carries well as he tells the audience about the eels. I like watching him speak from this perspective, from the side, when I see his mouth move and his eyes smile from a different angle.

True makes what I'm about to do sound more dangerous than it really is. He talks about the eels and how they'll burn my skin if they touch it. He tells the spectators that the fish aren't charged, but they still represent a hit. He says the bettors are taking bets on how many hits I take in one pass down the lane, and on how fast I can go. I see a flurry of activity in the stands as people make their wagers.

"Rio Conwy," True says again, to finish. He shouts my name. Cheers it. Invites everyone to look at me.

I raise my arms into the air, a gesture foreign to me, but it feels right. I hear a smattering of applause and a few whistles from the stands and I almost smile. It's easy to perform in front of people when you don't have to say anything.

And then, into this moment of buoyancy, I feel that sudden, deep despair creep in.

This is never going to work, a voice says to me. *You think metal fish can replace mines? You think that an air tank will be as good as a pressurized transport? You're going to die, Rio Conwy. You're pretending to be a showman, and you're pretending you can get to the Above on your own, and the only one you've tricked is yourself.*

You're never going to get Above.

People keep cheering. The official timer in the stands holds up his arm, raising the red flag that means I'm about to begin.

"Be careful," True says.

I'm the last, I think. The last siren.

The timer lowers his arm.

I jump in and swim.

I'm the last, so there's no reason I shouldn't also be the first. The first to get Above.

That argument makes no sense. It doesn't have to. I've seen the black line, and I swim. I'll see the black water, and I'll go up.

Only three fish hit me, but the eels are faster, and I have several burns on my arms and legs. I pull myself out of the water and stand dripping next to True.

"It could have been worse," True says. He's shaking his head and looks worried, but there's also a trace of that expression I've seen once before, when he said I was beautiful.

The spectators loved it. They cheer loudly and come down from the stands to surround me. I can hear them calling out questions, especially the bettors, who have a new race on their hands: Rio Conwy vs. Rio Conwy.

I'm about to say thank you when I remember that my voice will ruin the spell.

"Tell them I don't speak before or after the performances," I whisper to True. *"Tell them it's part of my routine. It's better that way. You know. You've heard me. But tell them this is just the beginning. We'll get more eels. I'll be faster next time. There will be more at stake."*

True gets a strange look on his face; he seems almost sorrowful. But he nods and turns to intercept the crowd while I hold my head high and walk away to the changing rooms. Once I'm inside I stay quiet and listen to the crowd outside. All of that noise is for me.

～

"This won't interest them forever," I say to True, after everyone else has gone. I keep thinking about my mother and what she said about people liking a spectacle. "I need to do something big before they get tired of me. Build up to some kind of final event, take their money, and be done."

"Like what?" True asks.

"I'm not sure yet."

We dry off the fish and the eels, cleaning and oiling them and wrapping them in soft cloths so they'll stay in good shape between swims. We bundle them up like babies, and that makes me smile. And then True touches my hand to get my attention.

"How much more dangerous do you plan to make this?" he asks. He turns my hand over, carefully, so that we're both looking at a small, red burn on my palm. It happened when one of the eels swam too close to my face and I had to push it away. I know exactly when I got that injury, though I can't pinpoint the moments when I came by all the others.

"I don't know," I say.

CHAPTER 12

J've been promoted. Josiah meets me at the door at work the next morning and tells me that it's time. "We're moving you to the ocean room today," he says.

"Congratulations," Elinor says as I stop near our table to say good-bye. She works quick and capable, and I wonder why they didn't move her to the ocean room long ago.

"I like it here," she says. My face must reveal what I'm thinking, or else it's a question others have asked before. "I've requested to stay. The ocean room is—too much."

I think I can see what she means. Through the window that separates us, I've watched the people in the other room and I've noticed a tension there that isn't in the sky room, a striving among the workers. You can see it in the way they work and interact. I wonder if it's the proximity to the sea, and the fact that real water can be glimpsed through the window in the portal door. I think the ocean can make people anxious. It's like seeing a real sky. It's seeing the world as it is, not as we made it to be.

When I sit down at my new workstation, I hear Atlantia breathe deep and even around me.

Somewhere, far away, I think I hear a voice screaming. But

when I try to listen more closely, to narrow my hearing down to that sound alone, it disappears.

It's your imagination, I tell myself. *You're remembering what Maire thinks she can hear.*

Bien watches me from her table, her gaze clear and unkind, and I drop my eyes. I still can't control people, not without revealing myself. I need to be careful.

The morning passes quickly. Josiah shows me the screens that demonstrate and diagnose the more complicated drone injuries that we fix in the ocean room, and it's easy to see how to repair them from the graphics. My hands are capable and I feel confident as I clamp my visor down and get back to work.

Everyone except Bien is friendly enough, which is to say they ignore me and concentrate on their own work. The damage on the drones is fascinating—ashy scars of injury, torn wires jutting out of their metal bellies—and it turns my stomach when I think of what the mines could do to a person.

That won't happen to me, I tell myself. *I won't let it.*

I wish I could show True the drones. He'd love them.

After work everyone walks to the nearest wishing pool and throws in their coins for me. Elinor comes; Bien, too. People are polite, but they don't know me well and I never have much to say, and after Elinor leaves, I sit alone at the well looking down at all the glittering coin. It's a great deal of money, and I find myself touched that they'd do this on my behalf. Of course they might have used the wish for themselves, the way I did with Bien, but I don't mind that.

I count fifty-three coin, and the amount makes me wonder. Is there a way to gather all of this up? It's illegal, of course. The money is supposed to go to the people Above. I glance around. The plaza is almost empty, except for an occasional worker or peacekeeper walking across.

And someone else.

Maire sits down next to me on the rim of the pool. She reaches into her pocket and takes something out. I can't see what it is.

"I thought you were in prison," I say.

"The Council had something they needed me to do," Maire says, her voice dry. "They let me out." She's unescorted—no peacekeepers, no Council members in sight. So they trust her enough—or need her badly enough—to let her free, even after the incident at the floodgates.

"What was it they wanted from you?" I ask.

She smiles. "Don't you want to save these questions for the shell?"

"No," I say.

"That's good," she says. "Some things are better discussed face-to-face." She opens her hand and there's a coin sitting in the middle of her palm. "Take it," she says. "Make a wish for yourself."

"No," I say. "Thank you."

Maire shrugs and tosses the coin into the water. *Fifty-four.* She gives no outward sign that she wishes for anything.

"I want to know more about the sirens," I say. "Is it safe to ask you about them here?"

Maire doesn't even look around to see how many people are near us. But she tilts her head, and I realize she is listening. "Yes," she says. "For now."

I keep my voice low. "How did the sirens go from being loved to hated?"

"There was a step in between," Maire says. "They were worshipped."

"What do you mean? Like the gods?"

Maire smiles. "No," she says. "I mean they *were* the gods."

"I don't understand," I say. "The gods have existed since long before the Divide."

"People worshipped gods for thousands of years," Maire says. "So yes, gods have existed long before the Divide. But *our* gods—the ones you see in the temple—were only sculptures in the beginning, brought down from the Above. They were salvaged from the ancient cathedrals on the surface and used as decorations. Embellishments. People didn't believe in gods at the time of the Divide. It had been years since anyone believed in anything." Maire puts her hand in the water, trails her fingers through it. "Then the sirens came and changed all of that.

"There was no scientific or logical explanation for them. So the people began to turn elsewhere for an answer. And when they looked up, they saw those statues in the temple looking down, and they began to wonder. They wondered if there were gods after all, and if they had sent the sirens. Some people even believed that the sirens *were* gods. That's when the miracles and our religion all came about. Did you know that the first Minister was a siren?"

"No," I say. "They don't teach us any of this."

"The Council changed the history long ago," Maire says. "Even most of our own Council now doesn't know what happened. They believe as you did, as most people do, the version that you've been taught."

Could this be true? I think back to that voice Maire saved, that long-ago woman who came Below and who witnessed the siren children. The only even remotely religious word she used was *miracle*. That might have been the beginning of their belief.

Who else knows this? Did my mother know? Did Bay? I can't bring myself to ask. I don't want to know how many more things they kept from me.

"Did that first siren Minister invent our religion?" I ask. "And then force everyone to believe it?" That could be a reason for people to come to hate the sirens—if they felt manipulated in their belief.

Maire shakes her head. "The religion was agreed upon by the sirens and the people together. They studied old histories. They learned about the gods. And then they shaped it all to fit the way their lives were. The Council took our religion to the Above, and the Above began to believe as well."

"Did the Above hate the sirens and the people Below for that?" I ask. "Because we told them what to believe?"

"No," Maire says. "At first both the Above and the Below believed the religion was right, that it made the most sense. In fact, they came to believe that they had *not* created their faith and belief system. Rather, they felt that they had been led to the truth by the miracle of the sirens. But the religion became warped and twisted as both the Councils Above and Below used it for their purposes. As I said, a very few people in Atlantia know the truth. Now you are one of them."

"What evidence do you have of all this?"

"The siren voices," Maire says. "This is what they told me. And I believe them."

"Do you have any of them that I can hear?" I ask. "Like the voice of that other woman in the shell?" If I could hear the sirens say all of this, I would know that it's true.

"No," Maire says. "The siren voices were too strong to save. I heard them once, and then they were gone. They had been waiting a long time."

So I can't hear them myself. *That's convenient,* I think. Do I believe Maire?

"The siren voices are gone," Maire says, "but you can still hear some of the others. Like the one I caught in the shell. I was listening, and when I found one that I knew would be good for you to hear, I saved as much of it as I could before it was gone. They can all only speak once, you know. But they have things worth saying, too. Haven't you heard any of the voices before?"

"Not speaking," I say. "I've heard breathing. Screaming. I thought it was Atlantia."

"It is," Maire says.

I'm not sure I understand what she means, but there is something else I want desperately to know.

"How do you do it?" I ask her. "With the shells?"

"I tell them what I want," Maire says. "I tell them to hold the voices, and they do."

She makes it sound so simple.

"Could I do it?" I ask. "Control things that aren't living?" I wait for Maire to laugh at me. I wait for her to tell me that I can't. That I'm not powerful enough. Or that I shouldn't try. Or that it's not safe. That's what my mother would say. She cared so much about keeping me safe.

But Maire doesn't say any of those things.

"You can't be afraid," she says. "I failed in my first attempts at saving the voices because I was afraid."

"You were afraid of the shells?"

"I was afraid of what I was asking them to do," she says.

"Are there any other rules?"

"The sirens of the past told me that we can only control physical things that have been made," Maire says. "We cannot control things that are more elemental. Air, wind, water—you cannot control the things that have almost always been."

"And we can control people," I say.

"Their bodies," Maire says. "But we cannot control their souls."

"Is there anything else?"

"You have to be near the object when you command it," Maire says, her tone practical, instructive. "At least that is how it is for me. And eventually your command will wear off. You and I won't be able to communicate through the shell forever."

She stands up. "I need to get back."

"Wait," I say. I've realized that this information isn't just interesting in abstract—it's useful for me *now*. I could use this in the tanks. "You're saying you can command other things," I say. "Not just people. Not just shells."

"That's right," Maire says.

"And the trick is to not be afraid," I say.

"It's not a trick," Maire says. "It's the way it is. And you have to listen." She pulls her black robes tightly around herself. "It's time for me to go."

She doesn't look back. I don't follow after her.

When I glance down at the pool, I see that all the coins have come up to the surface. They're floating there. All I have to do is pluck them from the water and put them in my bag, if I want them. But coins sink. They don't float. Unless—

My aunt must have told them to do it.

Maire has done something very dangerous, I realize, by teaching me so many things when she knows sirens are to be taught only under Council supervision. But what Maire's done isn't public. I'm the only one who knows. She's put herself in my hands. I could go to the priests, I could tell Nevio the Minister, I could warn the Council about what she can do and what she's said to me.

I have the power to make things very difficult for my aunt, and she is the one who gave that power to me.

Does that mean *Maire* trusts *me*?

I don't know. But I do know that she's told me something that could help me make it Above, alive.

As I walk to the gondola stop, I think about my new idea and try not to jangle the coin I've taken from the pool. It's heavy in my pocket. When I pick up my pace to pass a group of people, I think I hear a voice, a person crying out, and I turn too fast. I slip unexpectedly and fall hard to the ground, hitting my knees and hands and sending an aching, sharp song through my bones.

A woman near me exclaims and reaches down to take my arm and help me up.

"Thank you," I say, after a brief pause, to make sure the pain won't come out in my voice. I'm still stunned by the suddenness of the fall. I should have been more careful.

"Are you all right?" someone else asks.

"Yes," I say. "I don't know why I slipped—"

And then we see it.

A small puddle of water, right there on the ground. In unison we all look up to try to find a source.

"Is it a leak?" someone asks.

A drop of water sails down from somewhere up high.

"Where did it come from?" I ask.

"I think it's coming from one of the rivets near that fifth seam," someone else says. "Can you see?"

I try to focus on the ribs of metal sky arching above.

A peacekeeper pushes through the crowd. "What's the problem?" he asks.

"It looks like a leak," says the woman who caught me. "This poor girl slipped in the water from it."

"Don't worry," the peacekeeper says. "We'll get it fixed straightaway."

I've heard of tiny leaks before, but I've never seen one. I'm fascinated by the growing pool of water on the ground, and I have this strange desire to kneel down and touch it, maybe even taste it. Real seawater, sneaking in from the outside.

⌒

When I change into my racing suit, all I feel is focus. I have to see if this will work. If what Maire says is true. And if I am strong enough, powerful enough.

Once I'm in the water for my practice swim, I open my mouth, and I speak. Unafraid.

I use my real voice, but it sounds different under here. And of course my mouth fills with water even though I try to let in as little as possible. There is only so much you can say like this, but all I need is a word or two.

"*Come,*" I say.

And the fish and the eels come to me, without hesitation.

"*Go,*" I say, and they swim away.

I am exhilarated.

I might survive this after all.

The fish and eels are small. But if I can control them, is there also a chance that I could control the mines out there in the water? And could I tell the doors of the morgue to unlock and let me in when it's time for me to shroud myself and go up through the floodgates?

For once in my life, something is easy. I used my voice, and it worked exactly the way I wanted. Does the water magnify my voice? Make me more powerful? There's so much I don't know, and it feels wonderful for the first time, instead of miserable.

I swim up and down and up and down the lane, wearing myself out, practicing telling the fish what to do.

Maire and I are not like the other sirens.

Even things that aren't alive have to obey us.

For once I'm glad to be like my aunt.

When I get home, I look at my pile of coin and my pile of fish and I feel a deep satisfaction. I'm not there yet. But it's coming together.

Except for one thing.

When I lift up Bay's shell, it has gone silent.

No singing, no breathing. Not even the sound of the ocean. Nothing at all.

Is it because I am getting closer to the Above? Because I am going to hear Bay's real voice again soon, in person? Or has the magic worn out? Maire said it wouldn't last forever.

My sister is gone again.

CHAPTER 13

*I*t feels like I might be the last person alive in Atlantia. The deepmarket stalls are shuttered and locked against thieves, and it's dark and quiet. But then I hear sounds, hiding sounds, hurrying sounds, and I move fast and keep my eyes straight ahead and make sure I stand tall and walk with my shoulders squared.

Without Bay singing, it was too hard to sleep, and I decided to do what she did when she couldn't rest.

I decided to go to the night races.

When I get to the racing lanes, I climb up into the stands. The water doesn't look blue in the dim lighting. It's no color at all. People talk in murmurs as they make high-stakes bets. They don't laugh and joke the way they do during the day. When a bettor comes up and asks what I want to wager, I shake my head. I don't have money for this.

"Then why are you here?" he asks.

"I came to watch," I say. In the dark my flat voice sounds different—inarguable and unapproachable instead of stupid. It matches the gray light. He mutters but leaves me alone.

How often did Bay come here? I wonder. I have her shell in my pocket, for comfort, but I won't get it out. In the dark, crowded stands, it would take one bump or jostle and I could lose hold of the shell, and then it would clatter and shatter on the hard ground below.

Even thinking about it makes me feel sick.

Maybe her voice will come back. Maybe I need to give it time.

I brought Maire's shell with me, too. I couldn't bring myself to leave it behind. And then there's the air mask, slung over my back, as if I'm trying to pretend like tonight is just a normal outing to the deepmarket, no different from any other. As if by obeying the rule about carrying the mask, I won't get in trouble for breaking curfew.

The announcer doesn't shout out the names of the racers. Instead he holds up a sign and someone shines a spotlight on it so we can see who's up next. Everything is more discreet, more serious. If the peacekeepers decide to make a raid, everyone caught out after curfew could go to prison. But I've heard that some Council members like to come betting, too, and so the races aren't ever shut down permanently.

I feel sad that Bay came here without me. And I wonder how she felt all those years before my mother died, knowing that I planned to leave. I didn't mean to be unkind. I just knew I couldn't stay. I always felt close to Bay, because she was the one who knew my secret about the Above. But I wonder if knowing that secret made her feel far away from me. She always knew I had to leave her.

And I didn't know that being apart would feel like this. If I'd known, would I still have gone?

Did Bay ever race at night? She always came home cold but dry, but she could have worn a cap, covered her hair.

The thought of her being in that water makes me shiver. But watching the swimmers, who are constantly, quietly moving to keep themselves from getting too cold, who have gray faces in the grainy light, I realize that I should probably try this, too.

Swimming in the cold and the dark is what it will be like when I try to go up. Even if the sun shines Above, it won't reach me for a long, long time.

But I don't want to race here. I've heard what people say about the racers, and I watch how they swim. These are the races for people who no longer hope. These people want something singular and unattainable, something no one else can understand.

These are the people who are not happy in Atlantia, who have things they cannot forget or who feel wrong in some way, as though they do not belong.

I understand them, and it frightens me.

I wish I knew a siren who would soothe me, tell me it was all right, that I can be happy, that I belong here Below.

But the siren I know does not soothe.

I lift the other shell to my ear.

"Where do you live?" I ask.

It's late. It's dark. She could be sleeping.

But she answers.

Maire lives in an apartment in a neighborhood not far from the deepmarket. It looks completely unremarkable from the outside, one door among many all lined up in a row. The sky is low here, so the narrow building is only two stories high. It appears that there are only two small rooms per apartment, one room set on top of another. I have to squint in the dim light of the streetlamps to make sure I have the right number.

Even though I knew my mother died on Maire's doorstep, I've never known where Maire lived. I assumed she would live up in the Council blocks with the other sirens. I pictured my mother dying there, in one of their clean-swept, candy-colored entryways. The steps at Maire's apartment are gray, like everything else in this kind of light.

I've seen everything now. My mother's dead body in the morgue, her insignia worn around another Minister's neck, her office cluttered with someone else's books, and now this, the place where she died.

I've seen everything and I still feel like I know nothing.

Before I can knock on the door, Maire opens it. Compared to the dimness outside, the hallway behind her is a flood of light, like she's cracked open the sun. "Come in," she says.

"I thought you would live up near the Council," I say.

"I prefer to live down here," she says. "Up there they're always listening. Down here Atlantia is too loud for them to hear much."

"I'm surprised they allow it."

The lower room is a kitchen area with a bathroom at the back. Maire leads me through it and up the stairs to the apartment's other room, a sitting room with a couch, where I assume she must sleep. The shades on the windows are dark and thick—blackout shades, to keep in the light. I couldn't even see a sliver of it from outside. Though the neighborhood is not one of the nicer ones in Atlantia and the apartment is small, it appears that Maire lives here alone—a very grand luxury in a city where space is at a premium.

"I told you I was selfish," Maire says, as if she knows what I'm thinking. "This is part of what I've bargained for, all these years. There are times when they need a siren who is not an empty, vacant puppet. Sometimes they require someone who has actual power. I do what they say, and they let me live where I want." She gestures for me to sit down on a red chair, upholstered in thick, fine velvet.

The room looks nothing like I expected. I thought there would be shelves crowded with jars full of mysterious things, shadows everywhere, not this place of order and light. I expected more of a deepmarket jumble, but the few things here are well-made, cared for—two chairs and a couch; a table; a delicate, green glass vase; a shelf of books; a jar of dirt. I wonder if it's real.

On the table between us sits a large, golden bowl full of different-colored shells. It's odd to see so many in one place. "How did you get all of these?"

Maire shrugs. "How does one get a collection of anything?" she asks. "I kept an eye out in the deepmarket. When I saw one I liked, I bought it. I've been gathering them for years."

"Is that how you hear me?" I ask Maire, gesturing to the shells. "Do you pick up one and listen?"

"No," Maire says. "Those shells are all empty."

"That's what you said about the sirens," I say. "You said they were empty. Vacant."

"Yes," Maire says. "That's how the Council wants them to be. And over the years, the Council has become very good at breaking sirens down."

"What happened?" I ask. "You told me about the time when the sirens were worshipped. When did they come to be hated?"

"It's a terrible story," Maire says. "Are you sure you want to hear it?"

I am, but I'm not sure I want to hear *her* tell it. It's one thing to hear of the past from a distance, in the shell, removed from the power of Maire's voice. It's another to sit in her home, to look her in the eye as she speaks.

"Did my mother ever come inside this room?" I ask.

"Not on the day she died," Maire says.

She doesn't have to answer me directly, because we're speaking with each other in person. For a moment I want to ask her questions in the shell, see her dance. But that feels wrong. She is not a puppet. Neither am I. She gave me the shell as a gift for when we are apart, so I can keep learning.

But right now we are together.

What does Maire know? I still feel that she hasn't told me everything about my mother's death. And is Maire aware that Nevio is a siren? Even though the thought of Nevio fills me with revulsion, I have a strange feeling that the three of us— Nevio, Maire, and me—are connected in some way. We are all sirens who have secrets.

In the full light, Maire looks old and young, as if she has always been and as if she is very new. The light dances on her hair and in her eyes. She waits for me to decide whether or not I will listen as if she has all the time in the world. At the same time, her very stillness lets me know that we do not, because in that stillness I hear Atlantia breathe. And then I hear something more. Voices.

I draw in my breath.

"Yes," Maire says. "It's like I told you at the wishing pool. The voices are all there. Waiting for someone to hear. I've listened to many of them over the years, but I'm finished with that now. I've heard enough. Now it's my time to tell."

"And it's still my time to listen." I keep the bitterness from my voice, but my heart is full of it.

"Yes," Maire says. "But not for much longer, Rio. Not for much longer at all."

She's going to tell me the story, and I'm going to listen. And I am afraid. I wonder if this is how my mother felt, when she went into the floodgate chamber for her trial to be Minister and the doors opened and her sister came inside.

"After several generations," Maire begins, "some of the sirens began to use their power to control the people. And to control one another."

Her words are simple, no embellishments. Her voice is soft, no force or threat behind it. No anger. No judgment. Only: This is what was, and I am telling it to you.

"When this happened, the majority of the sirens agreed that they should no longer be able to serve as Ministers. They didn't want the leader of Atlantia to have too much opportunity for unfair persuasion.

"Then, several years later, there was an awful day in the temple when two of the sirens stood up and argued right before the Minister's sermon.

"One siren stood up and screamed; the other sang.

The one singing said she had to tell the people the truth about our world. The one screaming said the people weren't ready to hear it, that the truth could ruin them.

"After that no one could make out any of their words, only the sounds, and the sounds were terrible.

"So terrible that some of the worshippers in the temple that day died.

"They fell with blood streaming from their ears and terror in their eyes.

"They died under the statues of the gods and in full view of the congregation, and after they fell, the two sirens stopped screaming and singing. One knelt by the bodies and begged them to come back to life, but of course that didn't work. Even a siren can't command such a thing. The other began to weep and could not stop. The peacekeepers broke through at last and took away the sirens and, later, the bodies. No one could believe such a terrible thing had happened in the temple, where everyone is supposed to be safe.

"After that disastrous day, the Council decreed that the sirens should be under their protection and governance. The sirens were so distraught over what had happened that they agreed. They thought it was better for everyone."

When Maire finishes, Atlantia is quiet. "And so," Maire says, "began the long domestication and decline of the sirens."

"Those two sirens," I ask, "what became of them?"

"One of them agreed to abide by the new rules," Maire says. "The other committed suicide."

"How?"

"She drowned herself in the wishing pool," Maire says. "The one where I met you the other day. She used locks to chain her hands and feet together, and then she threw herself into the water, at night, when she knew no one would come along to save her. Hers was the first voice I was able to hear clearly, years ago. It's gone now. She's gone now."

I don't know about that. I can picture her in my mind, seaweed-haired, blue-limbed after all these years, lurking at the bottom of the pool, two flat coins settled in the sockets where her eyes used to be. The thought makes me shiver.

"Your mother did love you," Maire says. "But it made her afraid. You can't let love make you afraid."

How can she say that? And how could she leave my mother out on the doorstep that day? If Bay died like that, I would bring her inside, away from prying eyes. I would use my real voice and pray to have her back. Even though it wouldn't work, I'd have to try.

I stand up to leave. Maire follows me downstairs, turning off the lights as she goes, darkening down the house for the last of the night.

"You know what they were, don't you?" Maire says as I open the door. "The two sirens in the temple."

She's right. I do. Though I don't know their names, and though Maire didn't tell me this straight-out, I heard it in her voice. I knew it from the story. "They were sisters," I say.

"Yes," Maire says. "No one else knows this anymore but you and I. There had never been two sirens in a family before. There have never been two since."

Until the two of us.

Until now.

CHAPTER 14

By the time I walk all the way from Maire's apartment back up to the main part of Atlantia, it's almost morning. The lights will come up soon. I have to hurry. I crouch under the temple trees, and carefully gather the metal leaves into the bag that holds my air mask. I hear the rustling of something, and at first I feel afraid, but then I realize how high the sound is.

It must be one of the temple bats.

It settles in a tree above me and I smile to myself. "Knock down all you want this time," I say, and as if to oblige, the bat moves and a silver leaf comes shaking to the ground. I gather that leaf, too.

The light begins to rise in our false sky.

I hear the bat lift off out of the tree above me, and I look up hoping for a glimpse of it, but all I catch is a slip shadow flitting in the faint light. This is the time when Bay would be climbing back into bed, when she would have stolen an hour or two of sleep before we put on our robes and began another day of work in the temple.

I stand up and pull the bag over my shoulder. It's heavy, full of leaves. I hope no one looks at it too closely.

The story of the two sirens in the temple has given me an idea, and I need to talk to True. There are several gondola stations large enough to have sheds where the gondolas can be taken for repair, but I've seen True's work and I think he must be one of the best machinists. So I hazard a guess and go to the biggest station in Atlantia, the one near the Council blocks. I hope I'm right about where he works. I hope his shift hasn't ended yet.

Workers spill out of the station, laughing, talking. I listen for True's voice among them and, to my relief, I hear it.

I'll have to follow him until he separates from the others. They'll wonder what I'm doing out so early. The only people allowed out now are those leaving work.

It doesn't take long, thankfully. True calls a good-bye to the group and then starts off down a road on his own. It's lighter every moment. I follow him for a few steps, gathering my thoughts, preparing to flatten out my voice.

I haven't yet called to him, but his back stiffens. He knows someone's following. Is this what it feels like to be Maire? Spying, waiting, hiding?

"True," I say, and he turns.

"*Rio,*" he says, relief and concern in his voice. "Is everything all right?"

"I've had an idea," I say. "Can I talk to you?"

"Of course," he says. "In here." He guides me the short distance back to the gondola shed, keying in a number on the door and then pulling it closed behind us.

The shed is well-lit, and I blink, taking in True. His fingernails are black with dirt and he smells like oil, and yet there's that cleanness about him, and I think, *He is exactly the kind of person that Atlantia was designed to save.*

"What is it?" he asks. "What can I do?"

"I'm wondering if you could make me some locks."

"Locks?" he asks. "Like for a door?"

"For me," I say. "To wear on my hands and feet when I swim."

"I don't understand," True says.

"Remember how I said that the best way to get the coin fast is to do one big event? So that I can get the money and be finished?" I wait for him to nod. "Imagine that I'm at one end of the lane, hands and feet locked together, and that there are dozens of eels and fish coming for me from the other end of the lane, and the crowd knows that the eels and fish are electrically charged. And they know that I have to break free of the locks before I can even move."

Can True picture it? I can.

I've had a long walk up to think about everything that I learned in my aunt's house, in the place where my mother died. And I've decided I want to follow my mother to the surface—not take my chances with Maire.

From now on, my focus is on the floodgates. On getting through them alive. Not on listening to voices from the past or to Maire. I don't trust her.

I've decided that when I create this moment, I will be Oceana, alive against all odds. I will find a robe to wear that looks like hers. I will fetter myself with locks and chains, symbols of death. The fish with their sharp currents and winding ways will represent Nevio and others like him, and then, as Oceana, I will break away and swim past it all. I will come to the surface and breathe again.

"This will draw a crowd," I say. "I think people will want to bet on it. We can advertise. Aldo will tell everyone. If you can get the locks made fast enough, we could do it soon. Like next week."

But True shakes his head. "Too dangerous," he says. "If you didn't get out of the locks in time, and if enough of the fish and the eels got to you, you could go into shock and drown. You could actually *die*, even though I've tried to make them as safe as I can. They're still charged."

"That's the point," I say. "People *want* to see something dangerous."

"Then let them go to the night races," True says. "Take it more slowly. The crowd hasn't lost interest in you. They like what we've done so far."

He's right, of course. And, if I take more time to earn the money, that gives me more time to train.

But I don't know how much longer I can last here. How much longer I can go without saying something in my real voice. It's getting worse than it's ever been—as I miss my sister more each day, as I learn more about my power and about the sirens who came before. Listening to Bay's shell each night helped me have enough strength to keep myself in control, but now her voice is gone.

"I don't think I can wait," I say. That's all I tell him. But as always, True seems to know that there is more I can't say. He seems to understand.

I don't know how or why.

"So how will you get out of the locks?" True asks.

"That's the hard part," I say. "We want the audience to feel like they've seen a miracle, but not like they've been tricked, once we tell them how it was done. Which we'll have to do, at the end. And we'll probably have to let someone else put the locks on me so that they know that part is fair. Aldo, maybe. Someone the bettors trust."

True nods. He looks interested. In the problem, or in me?

It doesn't matter. But it does.

"And look what I have," I say, opening my bag. "All these leaves. All this metal. It has to be good for something. If not for this, you can use it for your fish." I reach for one of the buckets among the work gear on the shelves and dump the leaves inside. "There," I say. "For you."

True looks shocked. "Where did you get those?"

I flush. Does he think I'm a thief? I suppose I am. "From the trees by the temple," I say.

For some reason that answer seems to satisfy True. "I'll help you," he says, "but you have to promise me that you won't try this before it's safe. You can't do what you did with the eels and jump right in."

"I promise. I'll wait until it's safe."

"I can't tell if you're lying." He sounds as if this surprises him.

"I'm not lying," I say. I'm not, but I don't know how to get him to believe me. And I *have* lied to him before.

True smiles. "Good," he says. "Now, how can we get you a key for the locks without it looking like a trick?" His face lights up. "Maybe we could rig one of the fish to bring it to you in the water."

I like this idea. "Yes," I say. "I'll have to hold my breath and get myself unlocked, and then I'll swim."

"The unlocking is just the beginning," True says. "You still have to make it through all of the metal creatures to the other end of the lane."

"I'm getting better at avoiding them," I say. True doesn't know that I can move the fish and eels. That, if I have to, I can tell the fish with the key to glide right into my palm. "I can do it."

"I know you can," True says.

"So you'll help me?"

"Of course."

"Thank you, True." Relief and exhaustion settle over me. "We'll earn enough money to get what I need and to buy a stall for you, too. This is the beginning, for both of us."

True nods. "I'll get to work on it," he says. "Right now."

"Thank you," I say again. I wish I could stay and help him, but I have to get to the mining bays to report for work.

I'm almost at the door when True says my name.

"Rio."

I look back. "You could buy the locks, and we could alter them," True says. "That would save time."

I shake my head. "No," I say. "It has to be you who makes them."

"Why?"

"Because I trust you," I say. "If you make the locks, I know they'll work." I've been afraid of many things, but I feel no fear about this. I know that both True and his creations are good, and I'm not afraid of what I'm asking the locks to do—to come undone so that I can live. I trust my voice.

It takes True a few days to come up with locks and keys. We schedule an extra practice session in the lane, and we pay Aldo more than the usual rate to make sure that no one will be in the stands or practicing near us.

Bay's shell stays silent. I don't ask Maire any more questions, and she doesn't try to contact me. I'm sure Maire has her own plans, her own work to do, and I'm focused on swimming, getting stronger, using my voice to make things come to me. All small things, so far.

But I feel my voice growing.

True helps me snap the locks into place around my wrists and ankles. On the day of the real event, Aldo will check to make sure that they're secure. For now it's enough that *I* know they are.

"If I think it's been too long," True says, "I'm going to come in and get you out."

"I might drown you," I say. "Pull you under. Can you even swim?"

He laughs. "Of course I can."

"I've never seen you."

"I learned when I was young," he says. "But you don't forget."

He's right. And as I watch True walk down to the other lane, pushing the cart full of eels and fish, I know I won't forget this—what he's done for me, and how he did it.

When True raises his arm a few minutes later, I know he's ready, and I duck under the water. That's his sign to begin. He'll put in the fish with the key first and then everything else.

Here they come. I see the swirl of bubbles around each of them as they make their way for me. They are fast, beautiful, precise, and one of them reaches me just as my lungs start to burn from holding my breath. An eel stings me.

"Unlock," I say, and I feel the locks loosen around my ankles and wrists.

It works.

I let the fish with the key come to me, so that True won't know that I don't even need it at all, that I unlocked everything with a word underwater. Once the fish brushes against me, I catch it in my hand, slip the key from under its belly, and tell the locks to *fall*. They do, and I swim.

An eel shocks me.

Another.

Move away from me, I think, but of course nothing happens. My power is in my voice.

I almost open my mouth to say something to them, let water in and words out, but instead I keep swimming. I go around and through their darting, small bodies with my long, strong one. We are dancing, almost, the whole turquoise length of the lane.

My mind is sometimes a hard place to be, but I have always liked having a body. I like the feeling of having fingers to flex and use, a back to stretch, hair to swing in a braid, eyes to see. Does my mother have a body somewhere or is she only soul now? I can't imagine such a thing.

My body is strong, and my voice is, too. As I get closer to the end of the lane, I can't resist any more.

I've never tried to control so many things at once.

The words come out of my mouth and the water comes in as I tell the metal sea creatures to move away from me, and they do like a pulse, a compulsion.

My power is growing, changing. I can feel it. Was it speaking in the temple that began it? Letting out that single word when Bay left? Or has it been from learning from Maire or wanting even more desperately to go Above?

When I surface at the end of the lane, True studies me. He knows something's different. He knows that all is not quite as it should be.

"What happened?" he asks. "In there? In the water?"

I shake my head as if I don't know what he means. "It's working exactly the way we wanted."

I am beginning to know what I can do, and this makes me smile.

"You did it," True says, reaching to help me out of the lane. There is a brief, charged moment when we touch. My happiness makes him glad, but his eyes still look worried. Does he know? Was he close enough to see me speaking underwater? But why would that tell him anything? He doesn't know I'm a siren, and even if he did, most sirens can only control other humans.

"Anyone who sees you swim," True says, "will remember it forever."

What he says echoes what I thought earlier, that I will not forget what True has done for me. And he speaks with sincerity, with that warmth that radiates all through him, and I wish it were all around me. I wish he would put his hands on my face and warm me all the way through.

It's a wild thought, but I'm cold and crazy with relief and exhaustion. It's hard to wait for a moment to let it all settle before I speak again.

"Anyone who sees what you can make will do the same," I say. "This is going to work. Perfectly. I'll tell Aldo to set the date. Three days from now." It will be a spectacle. No. It will be more than that.

It will be a celebration.

True starts laughing. It's the kind of laughing people do when they're children, the kind I've always been envious of, where you can't seem to stop, something is *that* bright and funny. The sound is beautiful and his eyes crinkle almost shut.

"What is it?" I ask. "What did I say?"

"In that bucket of leaves that you gave me," True says, "there was a tiger head. From one of the gods. Did you put it in there on purpose?"

"No," I say, shocked. I'm surprised I didn't notice such a thing, even in the dark. But it makes sense, the way the gods were always coming apart. "Where is it? What did you do with it?"

"I melted it down with the rest," True says. "It's one of the fish now. The one with the key."

And now I cover my mouth with both hands, whether in horror or mirth, I'm not certain. The word I manage to say is *"Blasphemy,"* in a whisper, and True puts his arm around me like we're old friends, which in some ways we are. In some ways, he is the oldest friend I have. I feel his body, still shaking with laughter, against mine.

"Don't you believe in the gods?" I ask.

"Of course," he says. "I believe in them so much that I don't think they need statues everywhere to be powerful. None of that makes any difference."

～

He waits for me outside the changing room, and as I put on my other clothes I find myself laughing, too, without a sound. I feel almost happy. And I feel terrible, because I have learned many things—about sirens, and the nature of them, and the ancient past of Atlantia, and about myself—and I can't tell True any of it. He has been a good friend the past few weeks, and I have kept so much from him.

155

There is one discovery, however, that I *have* to share with True. I can't go to the Above without letting him know the truth about Nevio. "I have a secret," I say, when I come back outside.

"What is it?" True asks. He doesn't seem surprised but interested and eager. His expression almost seems to say *I know* and *At last!* which gives me pause for a second. What does he think I'm about to tell him?

I'm about to tell True that our Minister is a siren. This is not something that's easy to say without any emotion or accusation in your voice. I've got to hold back.

This also isn't something anyone else should hear.

So I lean in closer to True.

He moves in, too, and ducks his head a bit so I can whisper in his ear. To an outsider we might look normal, a girl and a boy sharing secrets in the deepmarket.

"Nevio the Minister," I whisper, *"is a siren."*

True doesn't pull away, but when he whispers back, he sounds stunned. Whatever he thought I was going to say, it wasn't this. *"How do you know?"*

Does he believe me? "Nevio lied," I say. "And I knew it because I'd seen the truth. Otherwise I might have gone on believing him. But once he lied, I knew, and then I could feel it when he was speaking. He is a siren. I'm sure."

"This means he's been hiding his ability," True says. "He must be extremely powerful to manage that."

"I know," I say. This is the most frightening part of all. Nevio knows how to sound like everyone else, and he can put just the right amount of power into his voice to give effective sermons and exhortations without the people suspecting anything more. It must take an uncanny amount of self-control.

Nevio is very, *very* strong.

"Do you think your mother knew that Nevio is a siren?" True asks.

I've wondered the same thing. I don't think she did. My mother didn't tell me everything—she kept her own counsel. I'm painfully aware of this. But so much of what she did was to protect me. I can't imagine her bringing me to live at the temple school or urging me to take up a temple vocation if she thought Nevio was dangerous or knew that he was a siren. And if she'd discovered such a thing, she would have removed Bay and me immediately.

Was *that* what she was coming to tell Maire the night she died? Had my mother found out Nevio's secret?

If she knew his secret, it would be a very good reason for him to kill her.

The expression on True's face makes me think that his thoughts are similar to mine.

"I don't know if she found out," I say. "I can't be certain. If she did, she didn't have time to tell me."

"Do you think any of the priests know what he is?"

"I don't think so," I say, "at least, not if they believe as my mother did, that the church and temple can best help if the people come to them without being persuaded. A siren changes that dynamic automatically." But there could be priests who don't believe as my mother did, or ones who feel loyal to Nevio. "Do you think the Council knows?" I ask True. "Should we tell them?"

"I'm not sure," True says. "Maybe they do know. Maybe that's *why* they wanted Nevio to be the Minister." He shakes his head. "The more we find out, the more confusing it all becomes."

"But you believe me?"

"Yes," True says. "I do." His eyes narrow; his lips press together. For the first time since I've known him, I have to look hard to see the kindness in his face. For a moment his expression is different—closed-down, cool, and still.

We're both quiet as we walk out into the deepmarket. I listen to the people laugh and talk, and I try to catch the sound of Atlantia breathing in the gaps.

The two of us pass Cara's stall. A new cluster of people has gathered around my mother's ring.

"We'll get it back," True says. "Don't worry."

I feel another needle of guilt. He doesn't even know that I'm not trying to buy the ring, that I'm saving for an air tank instead.

He doesn't even know that I'm going to leave him.

A woman has bought the chance for her child to touch my mother's ring. This makes me nervous. What if the child drops it? What if the mother is a crook and has another ring like it to palm and trade back?

But then I see the girl touch the ring, reverence in her expression.

"Maybe it's not so bad that the ring is here for now," I say to True. "It's a way for the people to remember her."

As I say this to True, I realize that this might have been exactly what Bay intended.

Maybe she had Fen sell the ring to keep my mother's memory alive in a way that our having the ring could never do.

Or *was* she trying to help me by leaving me the money?

Or both?

Tears of relief rush to my eyes. I still know Bay. Not perfectly, but in some ways.

"While we're telling secrets," True says, "I have one, too."

"You do?"

"I'm immune to sirens," he says. "And not many people know it. My father and Fen. And now, you."

I should have realized. There is something unmovable about True, in spite of all the laughter on his face and the gentleness in his eyes. Something at his core that can't be taken away or changed.

I have a very strange and interesting thought—could True resist *me*, if I used my real voice?

"So you could be the Minister someday," I say. My attempts at humor usually fall as flat as my voice, but True smiles.

"There's more to being the Minister than that," he says. "Isn't there?"

"Of course," I say. "But that's an important step."

"If you're immune, you're supposed to declare it to the Council, but I never have."

"Why not?" I ask.

"My mother thought we should keep it to ourselves," he said. "My father went along with her wishes because he loved her. And after she died, it was too late to tell anyone. They'd wonder why we'd been keeping it secret for so long."

There are so many secrets in Atlantia. And maybe this is part of why I'm drawn to True. He's been keeping a secret, too. Not one as dangerous as mine. But he knows what it's like to hide at least some of what you are.

"My father doesn't care anyway," True says. "I don't live with him anymore—not since I started working full-time on the gondolas."

"I'm sorry," I say. I wish I could say it better.

"It's hard," True says. "He hasn't taken much interest in anything except his work since my mother died." Before I can ask how—though I don't know if I would have dared—True tells me.

"Water-lung," he says. "I know not many people get it, but she did."

"My father died of it, too," I say.

"The Council would never let you and I marry," True says thoughtfully. "Because the illness was so recent in both of our families."

I must look surprised, because he hurries to clarify. "I was thinking out loud," he says. "I was thinking *that* might be a reason for Bay and Fen to go up, if they both had the illness in their lines. But there's no water-lung in Fen's recent family history. I'm sure of it. His parents and grandparents are all still alive, and his brother is fine."

"Do *you* have any brothers or sisters?" I ask True.

"No."

"I see," I say, and I feel sorry for him, not only because he doesn't have a sibling, although it's always seemed to me like a terrible thing to grow up alone. He can never go Above. He would never have had the choice.

"So you've always known you couldn't go," I say.

He nods. "And you always dreamed you would."

I look at him in surprise. How did he know?

"I can just tell," he says simply.

There are many things I could like about him if I weren't so ruined.

"Well," I say. "We don't always get what we want."

"No," True says. "We don't."

CHAPTER 15

There's one more thing I need for my Oceana costume, and I don't see why I shouldn't have it.

I need the insignia. The waves that turn into trees.

Nevio never takes it off, but I also know that the Minister has two insignia. One to wear and one kept in a safe in the Minister's office as a backup. The Minister is the only one who has a key to both office and safe.

But that is no longer a problem for me.

I take a piece of soap from the temple and hurry down the hallways while the Minister and the priests are at dinner. I should have plenty of time. All I have to do is press the insignia into the soap, to make an imprint that I can use as a template. I'll make my own insignia, with melted-down silver from the trees and a stolen torch from the temple workroom.

"Unlock," I whisper to the door.

It doesn't open.

Could it be that I have to be underwater?

You are *underwater,* I imagine Maire saying. *Everything in this city is underwater.*

I envision all the weight of the ocean above Atlantia pressing down. I can't control the water, but something about it seems to be a conduit for the sirens, a channel for our power. "Unlock," I say again.

This time it works.

I close the office door silently behind me.

For a moment I have a childish desire to vandalize everything that is Nevio's—his books, his trinkets, the painting he's hung on the wall to replace the one my mother had. I'd tear out pages, rip up the canvas, smash things, write all over his notes, read his journals, and leave everything that belonged to my mother untouched.

But I can't. I have to stay focused.

The safe is behind the painting he's hung, one that shows a man kneeling in prayer. When I get closer, I realize something about the image that I hadn't seen before.

The man is Nevio. He's in shadow, turned away so that it won't be obvious to the casual viewer, but when you come close there's no mistaking it.

He's hung his own image on the wall.

I wish True were here to see this.

I take down the painting and wonder what became of the one my mother used to display there. It was a simple painting: water and light.

Water.

"Unlock," I say to the safe, and I hear a *click* and pull it open.

There's the box. I open it up and take out the second insignia. I press the soap against it and take the print, deep. It's perfect.

A sound in the hall. At the door?

They can't be finished eating yet.

I rub the insignia with my sleeve to make sure that I leave no trace of soap, and then I close the box quickly and put it back inside the safe. As I do my fingers brush something else, and in spite of the sound in the hall, I pull out the item to take a look.

My skin knows exactly what it is even before my eyes register the sight.

A shell.

The kind Maire gave to me, but this one is pure white.

Another sound in the hall. I put the shell back, close the safe, hang the painting on the wall, and wait.

I hear speaking. Two people, neither of them Nevio.

They move on, and I slip back out the door and up to my room in the temple. I sit down on the bed, the soap melting in my hand, almost forgotten.

There was no time to ask a question into the shell, but I know who would answer.

Maire.

My aunt is in contact with Nevio.

"We haven't spoken in some time," I say, careful to keep my voice even. I hold the black, spiny shell with shaking fingers. "Where are you?"

Back in prison, Maire says. *And seems that this is where I'll stay, at least for the time being.*

"But you can make things move," I say. "Why don't you unlock the doors and walk free?"

I've chosen not to reveal that particular talent to the Council, Maire says, *because it's helpful for them to believe they can control me. And I discovered long ago that some of the best voices can be heard in the prison walls. More recently, it was a way for me to keep myself away from you, to put another barrier between us. You have no idea how difficult it has been not to try to mold you, to experiment with your voice. That's why I gave you the shell—so you could control your own learning.*

"Do you," I ask into the shell, "communicate with Nevio the Minister?"

Of course. There's no hesitation. She doesn't sound ashamed. She doesn't explain. And that makes me sick. Nevio took my mother's place. He stole and read her personal papers. And Maire still speaks with him. Does she know he's a siren? Does she care?

I'm not going to get caught up or bogged down in all of this. I don't want to let her keep me from getting to the surface, don't want to allow her voice in my head when everything is about to come together. But I can't help myself. There are two final things I *want* to know.

"Did you kill my mother?"

No.

"Do you know who did?"

Yes.

She knows. But she doesn't want to tell me anything more. She's going to make me ask again, each specific question.

"Who was it?"

There is a moment of nothing, and I press the shell closer to my ear.

The Council.

"Which one?"

All of them.

"How?"

They called her in for a meeting. When she arrived, they gave her something to drink, as was the custom, and they had each put some of the poison in her cup. They all did it.

"Why?"

She knew too much.

I don't want to believe Maire.

But I do.

The Council killed my mother.

A cold fury, as implacable and full as water through the floodgates, comes over me. Maire didn't kill my mother. But she knows who did. And she hasn't told anyone. She hasn't cried out to Atlantia as I know she could, telling them of the evil the Council has done, calling the people to help bring about justice. She has done *nothing*.

"How do you know this?"

Nevio told me, after it happened. He helped them arrange it.

And Maire's still in communication with him. She gave him a shell. I can't speak because my voice will be full of hate.

And she told me. Your mother told me, too. She realized what had happened.

"Why would the Council let her go?" I ask. "Why would they risk her telling someone?"

Because they knew exactly who she would tell. Her sister. And they wanted her death to serve as a warning to me. When I found her, I made sure she was dead and then I stood over her body waiting for the Council to come take her away. I had received the warning. There was nothing more I could do.

I'm sick, hearing this. "How could you let them take her away? When you knew what they'd done?"

It was what I had to do.

All I have to throw in Maire's face right now is my perfect, practiced control. So I do it. I hold everything in. "You know her killers, but you've done nothing to make them accountable. And you still work with the Council and with Nevio. Oceana's murderers. *Why?*"

Love.

Of course.

Maire told me who she loves, who she protects at all costs. Herself.

That's why Maire sometimes sits in her cell instead of unlocking her doors. Sometimes you can't speak, not because others won't let you, but because you are afraid of what you'll say. You can't trust your voice. You can't trust yourself. You stay silent and contained for your own protection.

And I understand, because even though part of me wants to go scream in the streets, telling everyone what the Council has done, I won't. Because that will put my plan to escape at risk.

I'm looking out for myself, just like Maire.

But at least I won't go up with her. I'll go up my own way. My mother's way.

I never thought Maire could replace my mother or my sister. But somewhere, deep down, I must have hoped that I could love her. Was I stupid enough to think that she might come to love me, too?

You always have more to lose, until you die.

I find myself asking Maire one final question.

"Does being a siren mean that you are always lonely?"

Yes, Maire says.

She's right.

I have *always* been lonely.

Even when Bay was here, I often felt alone.

This is what I need to face. Even when I care about other people, there's a part of me that can't seem to stop being alone. Maybe it means those people are right, the ones who say that sirens don't have souls.

If I had one, would I be less lonely? If you have a soul, are you always companioned?

But then I realize that even if I did have a soul, it's not as though someone else would be there. It would only be more of me.

CHAPTER 16

"So," Aldo asks, "are you ready for tonight?"

I nod. In the days since I last spoke with Maire, I've focused completely on preparing for this evening. For the spectacle. The celebration. When I talk to True, that's what I call it because that makes me feel stronger, more like Oceana. I'm as ready as I'm going to be. I've practiced in the lanes and worked with True on the fish and eels. I've made an insignia from the print I took in the bar of soap, and it's cruder than I would have liked, but I did the best I could.

Aldo looks at the pile of turquoise fabric in my arms. "Is that your costume?"

"Yes," I say. I used some of the coin to buy the cloth and had a seamstress sew it to my cut-down wetsuit. It's more like streamers than a robe, but the fabric is supposed to hold together in water, and the effect when I swim is that I'm part of the water and also separate, something different to watch. I think of the costume as my Oceana robes, because this was the color she always wore at the pulpit. And the color she wore when we sent her body through the floodgates.

Aldo unlocks the stall where I plan to store my costume. I've come here before work to leave some of my things for the event tonight. True should be along any minute with the fish and eels in their buckets. I think Aldo will do his best to keep things secure, but I can't risk anyone tampering with the locks, and the single fish that will bring me the key. They'll stay safe in my room until it's time for the swim.

"We should have a big crowd," Aldo says. "The bettors are in a frenzy. They're wondering what you'll do after this."

"Who knows," I say.

Posters hang in the deepmarket, advertising the event tonight. People have started to recognize me as I walk through the stalls. Notoriety will bring me more money, but it also makes it more necessary for me to leave. Attention is a dangerous thing.

But it's all coming together. This evening I'll be back to swim. And *then*, with the money I earn, I'll be able to buy the air from Ennio and take it with me when I leave the deepmarket.

If this goes as planned, then I'll have everything I need to leave Atlantia very soon.

All I'll need after tonight is for someone to die.

True walks toward us, pushing the cart. He nods to Aldo and hands everything off to him except for a bucket with the fish and the key and the locks, which he hands to me, and another bucket, which he keeps for himself.

The entire time his mouth is set in that firm line I've seen once before.

"Are you ready, then?" Aldo asks, when we've finished.

"Yes," I say. "We'll see you tonight."

We start back up into the deepmarket. I'm not sure what True is thinking. Neither of us says anything, and then True takes my arm and pulls me into an empty stall with him.

"This is for you," he says, holding out the bucket. Not smiling.

"Did you think of something new?" I ask.

"No," he says. "It's not for tonight. It's five hundred coin. Now you don't have to swim."

I draw in my breath. Is he serious? I kneel down and pull back the cover on the bucket slightly. True wasn't joking.

"Where did you get this?" I ask.

"All of the publicity from your swims has made people interested in buying the fish," he says. "I can't keep up with the demand. But I've been saving it for you. It means you can buy the ring back. Right now. And you won't have to swim tonight."

With this much money, and what Bay left me and what I've earned in the lanes so far, I have enough to buy the air tank. True's right. As far as the money is concerned, I don't have to swim tonight.

But I still need the practice. I need the added pressure of performance, the time in the water.

And True doesn't even know that it's not the ring I'm trying to buy.

"You should use this money to buy a stall in the deep-market," I say. "Or more supplies."

"I want you to have it," True says. "Please."

"Why are you doing this?" I ask. "We had everything planned."

"What if it doesn't work? What if too many eels shock you? Or the locks don't work right, and I can't get into the lane in time?"

"It *is* going to work," I say.

Light flickers through the slats, and I wish it were the light of the Above.

I wish I could tell True the full truth, that I have to leave. And I wish I could tell him this in my real voice. But I remember the expression on Justus's face in the temple on the day Bay left. I can't tell True. I don't want to change how he sees me.

"You don't know that," he says.

"I do," I say.

"So you're going to swim anyway?" he asks. "Even though you have enough money?"

"Yes," I say.

"Rio," he says. I see anger and anguish on his face, all the happiness and laughter gone. There is something he wants to say and he's fighting against saying it. Whatever it is, he knows it will change something, perhaps ruin everything.

"Tell me," I say. I whisper it. Because if I speak now, I'll reveal myself.

He shakes his head. He kneels down and I kneel down next to him and he runs his fingers over the money in the bucket. I trust his hands. And his heart. I want him to touch me. He is dangerous to me.

He knows too much. No one can know me this well, because then they will leave me. That's what happened with my mother. That's what happened with Bay.

"I have to do it," I say. I make myself sound the way I always do, flat and false.

It hurts both of us.

I knew it would.

"I can't be a part of this," he says. "I can't announce you tonight. But you can keep everything. The locks and the keys. The fish. The coin."

"Thank you," I say again. "Will you be watching in the stands?" I want to see him one more time. It is the most I have wanted anything besides finding my sister and going Above. It is hard to say the words.

"I can't be a part of this," he says again.

"You *are* a part of this," I say.

"I know," he says. And then he leaves, walking fast, because he has nothing left to carry. He's given it all to me.

Standing in the dappled light of the stall, I fight back the tears. Crying is dangerous. Crying reveals too much. I have everything I need. I have the fish and the locks and the costume and the key. I have the insignia. And I have money.

I will spend it all now. I have the coin True gave me and the other money, too, worn in the bag with my air mask on my back. I will buy the air I need and hide it in my room at the temple. Then I'll be ready to go at any time, as soon as someone dies.

I know it's wrong, but I hope it happens quickly.

There is no longer any reason for me to stay.

When I tell Ennio what Maire said, and when I say the name Asha to him, he turns pale. Without speaking he takes the money and gives me an air tank, heavy and made of ancient-looking metal. He rolls it up neatly in a cloth so that it appears to be a bulky but uninteresting, unspecific bundle.

"It works exactly like the air masks for the drills," he says. "You're familiar with those. Attach the mask and breathe the same way. But this one will last longer. And it's pressurized for an ascent."

"How do you know that?" I ask. "If no one's ever made it to the surface?"

"I found an old cache of air," he says. "From when they were building Atlantia. Sometimes they had to work out in the water. Sometimes they had to go up."

This sounds far from safe. And it's going to be hard to speak while I'm wearing the mask attached to the air tank. How will I let the words out without letting the water in?

Am I trying to do something impossible? Am I crazy?

I've never known if what they say is true, if I'm broken and strange, or if I just belong somewhere else and, if I can get there, I will finally feel right.

That's what I've hoped for all my life.

"Go," Ennio says. "And don't come back." He says that in a nice way, like he means for me to escape instead of die, and so I leave without another word. On my way out of the deepmarket, the bundle heavy on my back, I walk past my mother's ring. People have gathered around it.

In spite of everything, she can still draw a crowd.

Hopefully, tonight, so will I.

———

I hide the air tank in my room with the fish and the locks and the last of the money. I'll win more tonight, but I plan to give all of that to True to pay him back. Then he can buy more supplies and a stall in the deepmarket. Perhaps someday, without me asking for help with other things, he will find a way to make the mechanical bats stay aloft. I wish I could see that.

I glance over at Bay's and Maire's shells, but I resist the temptation to try to listen to one or to ask questions of the other. I've decided to trust myself and True, and I don't want any doubt to creep in.

As I ride the gondola down to work, the sounds of Atlantia breathing press in on me, becoming louder and louder. No one else seems to notice.

And when I come into the workplace, the breathing becomes screaming.

I resist the urge to press my hands against the sides of my head to block out the sound. Again, no one else seems to notice it. I look around the room and see Bien watching me. Does she hear it?

Why is Atlantia screaming? Or is it the sirens? Has Maire driven me mad? She said she was trying to help me. Was she trying to break me instead?

And then everyone else looks up, and some of them reach to cover their ears. But it's not the screaming they've noticed—it's a new sound. The shrill whistle signifying a breach drill sounds down the halls and into our workroom.

Everyone reaches for their air masks, and I reach for mine, but it isn't there.

In the excitement of everything—True giving me the money, buying the air tank, preparing for tonight—I forgot to bring it with me. I took it off at home and left it with my other things.

I've neglected to bring my mask before—we all have—but never during a drill. This will result in a reprimand, certainly, and perhaps more. I swear under my breath. I don't want anything to mess up tonight.

Bien pulls on her mask and so do the other workers. I hear them breathing as they start their oxygen. A girl near me shudders as she gets ready to seal the mask shut. "I hate this," she mutters to her friend.

And then she notices me. "No mask?" she asks.

"I forgot it," I say, and her eyes widen.

"Uh-oh," she says. "You could have gotten away with it if it weren't for the drill."

I know. My timing is terrible. At least the sound of the whistle drowns out the screaming in the walls for now.

I seem to be the only one in the ocean room who didn't remember to bring a mask today. I suppose the water outside the portal is a constant reminder of how close we are to being unable to breathe.

Emergency procedure apparently dictates that the workers should file into the sky room, because that's what everyone does. I'm glad. I look for Elinor, walk toward her.

Josiah rushes into the room, mask already in place, and surveys us. His eyes stop on me.

"I need a spare mask," I say.

He nods. There are always a few on hand in every building, even though we're supposed to carry our own. He leaves the room to find one for me.

It's strange not to have mine on, but mostly I'm glad. I don't have to pretend to breathe the air. And it's funny to hear the other workers talking to one another through the masks in monotone, depersonalized voices. I've always wondered if this is what I sound like to everyone else.

After a few more minutes, the door flies open and Josiah comes back inside. "I haven't found one yet," he says. "The closet was empty."

"It's all right," I say. "It's my own fault."

Josiah stares at me for a second and his eyes are wide with fear and concern. Why is he so worried about this?

I realize the answer a moment before the whistle stops and a siren's voice—not Maire's—comes over the loudspeaker.

"This," the siren says, her voice pleasant and urgent, "is not a drill. Please follow instructions exactly. If you haven't done so already, go to your designated gathering location and then remain where you are, with your mask on, breathing regularly and normally. The situation will be remedied as soon as possible."

And now everyone in the room stares at me.

"Perhaps she could share one. . . ." Elinor begins, making a move to take off her mask.

"No," Josiah says. "That compromises the survival of both. It's against the rules."

His voice sounds flat, but his eyes look sorry.

Everyone is still watching.

What do they think I'll do? Run? Cry? Scream? The first option doesn't make any sense, because I don't know where Atlantia is leaking. For all I know, I could run right into the breach. And crying and screaming are going to use up what air I do have. If it's a breach in the air system, the oxygen in the room will be gone soon enough.

My heart pounds so hard that I swear I can feel it in my palms as well as in my chest. It strikes me that I'm providing a good diversion for the others—the smaller drama of *Will Rio die?* is, for now, overshadowing the larger issue of *Are we all going to die?*

Should I risk everything and command them to let me leave? Then I can go hunt for a mask.

But the voices in the walls of Atlantia start up again, and this time they are screaming at *me.* Telling me to *stay. Stay.*

Who are they? The sirens? Maire heard them speak to her from the walls of the city. Am I hearing them, too? But that can't be right. Maire said they were gone.

Elinor moves to put her hand on my arm, but I'm crawling inside and outside with all these voices and I edge away.

It's growing dark in our workroom, though it isn't the dimming time, and that feels ominous. Why lower the lights? Has the breach affected the power in some way?

I have no memory of this ever happening before.

And what about True? Where is he? Is he safe?

It's cold.

I do *not* want to die like this—drowned or suffocated in the Below without ever having seen the Above. For a moment I'm tempted to ask doors to open and mines to move, to get out right now.

But I'll die for certain that way. *Wait a little longer,* I tell myself. *If the water starts coming in, you can do that. You can die out in the ocean instead of trapped in here. And if you survive, then don't wait any longer to leave. Get the air tank. Get out. Don't wait until there's a body you can trade places with in the morgue. Go to the floodgates and go up.*

Eventually the sirens' screams die down. People are no longer talking, and I feel weak. Most of us shiver.

There isn't much air left in the room.

We all wait to see if the water will come rushing in or the air out or both.

Just when you think you don't have anything else to lose.

You die.

⌒

I don't cry at all while we watch the minutes pass on the clock and I breathe in and hope it won't be for the last time.

I don't cry when some of the people start looking at me less and some more. I can tell they think I'm going to die soon, that the air is almost gone. Some would rather not see it happen. Some want to watch. They want to see what it's like.

We hope to observe, not inhabit, the moment of our own deaths.

My mother wrote that. Nevio didn't intend for me to read those words, but I remember every one of them.

I don't cry when the siren comes over the loudspeaker to tell us all that the breach has been sealed off, that we are not in danger anymore, that we can take off our masks now. I feel the air rushing back into the room, and I draw it into my lungs.

I don't cry when the siren tells us that we will soon be able to return to our homes, to be patient for a little longer.

When my mother died, there were times when I wept like Bay did, like I would never stop. But of course I stopped eventually. You have to stop crying if you plan to survive.

"Where was the breach?" someone asks.

"We don't know yet," Josiah says.

"How bad was it?"

"We don't know that, either," Josiah says. "They'll tell us when they can."

"You were so brave," someone says to me. Now everyone smiles at me, seems pleased with how well I handled myself.

"It turned out all right," I say.

"You didn't know that would be the case," Elinor says. "We should have shared with you. Even though it's against the rules." She looks ashen, shocked at herself. "But we didn't."

"It doesn't matter," I say. "I would have done the same." I wouldn't have shared my air with any of these people. Not even with Elinor. Bay and my mother and True—they are the people I'd risk my life to save. "There's no need to apologize."

"I never knew I was so coldhearted," Elinor says.

"Rio's not surprised," Bien says. "She knows what people are capable of."

Right then the siren speaks from the walls. "We regret to say that the breach was in the deepmarket," she says. "We have had to seal it off to preserve the safety of the rest of the city."

What does that mean? I want to ask, but I know and I am so cold.

"They sealed it off," a man says, sounding stunned. "That means there will be no survivors."

The people of the deepmarket, gone. Aldo. The bettors. Cara and the man who worked with her.

I will never swim in the deepmarket again.

And *True*.

Did he go back there today? To sell the fish in his cart?

Maire is safe, locked away in the holding cells up closer to the surface.

But *True*.

Elinor sinks to her knees. Bien has forgotten me. There is a look of terror in her eyes.

Everyone whispers and cries out their questions. What kind of a breach was it? Too much water or not enough air? Did they drown or suffocate? Which would have been worse?

"The gondolas are not working," the siren says, "but you may walk back to your homes. None of the neighborhoods were destroyed. We will give you more information as soon as we can."

And then there is singing over the speaker. Siren singing. They are comforting us, telling us to wait and see, to go home, go home, go home. But these voices are tame, not like the ones screaming from the walls. These sirens are telling us what the Council wants us to hear.

I hurry for the door, but once I'm outside I stop in my tracks. It's foggy.

And we don't have weather here.

Elinor catches up with me. She draws in her breath at the sight.

"Have you ever seen anything like this before?" I whisper.

"Once," she says. "When your mother died. It's one of the reasons some people think she might be a god."

"I didn't go out that night," I say. I was inside, with Bay, promising her over and over again that I wouldn't leave. "I didn't see anything like this."

Elinor and I both start to run. We pass the wishing pool and then we are caught up in masses of people, all hurrying, and I can't see Elinor anymore.

My feet carry me in the direction of the temple, because that is where I first saw True, and no one stops me because I am also going home. Home through the fog, the siren voices singing overhead, loosed at last.

I pray silently, and it's not to Efram or any of the tiger gods, or any of the gods at all. It's not their faces I picture; it's hers. My mother's.

I hear other people around me saying her name. They are remembering that other night when the fog came. They are remembering *her*.

I've joined my blasphemy with those in the deep-market who worshipped her. Did they pray to my mother when the water came in or the air went out? Did she help them? Can she help me? I'm going to the temple, and I need a miracle.

Please let True be there.

Please let True be there.

Please let True be.

CHAPTER 17

I have eyes for him, and so I see.

True walks through the temple, pushing past people, looking around. Looking for me. He's at the other end of the nave, too far ahead, and there are many bodies in between us and I don't trust my voice to call out his name.

But part of me *wants* to call it out, because if he hears me say it now, he will know. I would like for him to know.

And then, as if I've spoken after all, True stops and turns back toward the entrance. Across all the people mourning and seeking, under all the gods watching, unmoving, he sees me.

"Rio," he calls out. He starts toward me so fast that he knocks someone off balance and reaches out to steady them, but his eyes never leave my face. He pushes the wrong way through the crowd, and I push, too, against people and the pews and anything else that gets in my way.

I think he will stop when he reaches me, but he keeps moving, pulling me right into his arms. "You're safe," he says, his lips in my hair.

Then I notice light and stained-glass windows and candles and people, because I'm looking away from True, trying to keep the tears from falling, tears of relief that he is alive. True is alive.

There are too many people in the temple and more coming every minute. The sirens told us to go home, and, for many of the people, that means the temple, in a spiritual sense at least. My mother always said that. *This is the home of their belief.*

I take True's hand and lead him outside and into the fog.

When he sees how thick it has become, his eyes widen and he looks at me as if this might be my doing, as if I am powerful instead of plain.

And I remember how, earlier, seeing him kneel by the bucket of coin in the deepmarket, I knew that there was something he wanted to tell me.

I pull him under one of the trees. In the patchiness of the fog, I can make out glimpses of him—the back of his hand marked with scars from cutting metal; his face closer to me; his body lean and dark in the dim light. *"Tell me,"* I whisper, my voice the only sound besides the leaves moving above us, almost invisible in the fog.

This time he does.

"I heard you," he says. "That day at the temple."

Somewhere near us a leaf falls to the ground, making a small silver sound.

"You thought I meant that I heard you crying," True says. "But that's not what I was trying to say."

And I understand.

He heard me.

Not when I was crying at the temple.

Before.

When Bay left.

He knows I'm a siren.

True's hands come to either side of my face, and his fingers brush my lips. "You're whispering something," he says softly. "What are you saying?"

I didn't know I was whispering, but I realize he's right. When did I start?

I'm saying *please*, and I'm not sure why.

"All I could hear during the breach was your voice," True says. "I could hear you calling out with the same agony that I heard when Bay left. But you weren't calling for her. You were calling for me, and there was nothing I could do to help you."

He shifts his body so he can see me better, but I don't say anything. I look at him. He has the same shadows underneath his eyes that I noticed the first time we met. He's been worried. About me.

"You're all right," he says. "You're here."

"True," I say, giving him a double answer. Saying his name and saying that *yes I am here.*

He kisses me.

Right here under the trees, right here on my lips, and then on my neck, his fingers strong on my back, pulling me hard and close to him. We are nearly the same height, and we fit together right.

He is good at this. I am good at this. We are good at this.

I close my eyes, and I listen. To his breathing, mine.

"Let's go to the deepmarket," True says. "Let's see if there is anything we can do."

The sirens still call out for the people in Atlantia to go home, go home, but True is immune to them, and I find that they are not so hard to resist anymore. I have grown stronger.

Perhaps it's because I don't hear Maire's voice among the others.

True and I walk through the trees toward the nearest gondola stop, where one of the boats sits, still and dry. The fog grows thicker, and the lights dim. But we are close, and I can see his face, his kind eyes, his lips.

"Now," True whispers, and he pulls me, the two of us running blind through the white. He stops suddenly, and we're next to the canal. True lets go of my hand and leaps over the side and into the canal right in front of the boat. I follow.

When I crouch down beside him, True has already found a way to open a panel in the boat. It's strange to see the metal inner workings of the gondola. "I can make it go," he says. "It might not take us all the way down to the deepmarket, but we'll get there faster this way."

"The peacekeepers will see the gondola," I say. "Or hear it."

"Of course," he says. "But if the fog is like this all through Atlantia—like it was after your mother died—they might not catch us."

The engine takes, starts whirring. "Get in," True says. "Get low. I'll be right there."

I climb over the side and sink down between two benches. After a moment True appears beside me, landing lightly, and as he does the gondola moves.

We slip through the fog, whisper-white.

Neither True nor I say anything.

When we kissed under the trees, anyone could have found us and still there we stood, touching each other, clinging on.

Now that we're alone, we don't do anything but look. Even when the wisps of clouds come between us, I feel his gaze on mine, as certain and deep as the way he kissed.

No one stops us on the gondola. It's eerie how empty this part of Atlantia is. But then, as we get closer to the deepmarket, I hear shouting. A few dozen people have gathered near a barricade. They are either immune to the sirens' song or so worried about someone in the deepmarket that they are able to resist, for now. One woman holds her hands over her ears and weeps, shaking her head back and forth against the song, her body trembling.

Peacekeepers call out to us to leave. "There's nothing you can do here," they say. "There are no survivors. Go home or you risk arrest."

"Tell us," a man calls out. "Was it water or air?"

"Did they suffer?"

"It was water," someone says, and everyone turns to see who's spoken.

Maire.

She comes from behind the barricade, and she's wearing dry clothes, but her hair is braided back and wet.

I thought she was in prison. What is she doing down here?

"And it was air," Maire says. "It was water that drowned them, but they may have been unconscious if there was a loss of air pressure first, which we believe was the case."

Everyone listens to her, even the peacekeepers, although she's not using her voice in the way she usually does. She's simply speaking and telling us something, matter-of-fact. Not manipulating.

At least that's what I think.

"They are recovering what they can," she says, "and they hope to have bodies to be identified soon."

Someone shouts out in anger and agony.

Maire closes her eyes. She's about to use her voice. She always gives some kind of signal, I realize. She always lets you know.

"More peacekeepers are coming," she says, the tones of her speaking rich with warning, "and some of the Council and Nevio the Minister. If you are still here, they will take you to the holding cells in the prison to preserve the peace. I can promise you that prison is not a pleasant place to grieve."

A few people turn away, still weeping. But others stand their ground.

Maire begins to sing, joining with the other sirens whose voices come over the speakers around us, telling us to go home.

How long has she been out of holding? The Council let her out before to help them. Did they free her this time so that she could help in the deepmarket? Or was she released before that?

Did the Council ask her to do something else?

A terrible, dark thought crosses my mind.

The Council killed my mother. They are capable of killing when it suits their purposes.

Is Maire?

Her eyes light on me, and an expression of surprise crosses her face. She didn't see me until now. Still singing, she moves in our direction. She pushes past True and leans to hiss something into my ear.

"Save your voice," Maire whispers. *"Whatever you do now, do not speak."*

Then she turns her back on me and walks toward the woman who is still trying to resist, who shivers with the effort. Maire leans down and sings right near her, and though it's terrible what she's doing—trying to make someone do something against their will—there is a gentleness in my aunt's eyes, an anguish in her expression that hurts me to see.

She couldn't have caused the breach in the deepmarket. She's strange, but she isn't evil. She can't be. I can't be.

True touches my arm. "We should go," he says. "I don't think either of us would do well in prison."

He's right. We're both hiding too much.

We find the gondola where we left it sitting silent in the fog. True brings the boat to life, and we slide back toward the temple. The fog hides us, and so do the screams of the people as the Council members and Nevio reach them.

"The last time the fog came," True says, "some people called it the breath of Oceana. They wondered if it was the third miracle."

"I don't think that it is," I say.

"Neither do I," True says. And then, "I'm sorry about the ring."

"The ring?" Then I remember. My mother's ring, the one True thought that I was trying to buy.

"It's all right," I say. "Much more than that was lost today." All those people—Aldo, Cara, the bettors.

And I truly am a terrible person, because tears come to my eyes, and they're for the people who died, but they are also because I will never perform for them again, I will never see how fast and good I could have been in the lanes today. I will never stand up in my Oceana robe and show them that even though they didn't want me to race, I found a way to get what I needed, and I never even had to use my voice.

My mother was right when she said that thinking of the greater good doesn't come naturally to me. So this is why I really wanted to swim in the lanes. It wasn't to prepare. It *was* to perform.

"I'm sorry," True says, "that I won't get to see you swim again."

"You said you weren't coming," I remind him.

"I wouldn't have been able to keep away." I feel True's hand on mine. "You're not planning to stay Below," he says.

"I want to find my sister," I say. "I want to be with her."

"Finding out why she left won't be good enough?"

"No," I say, and I'm sorry to have to tell him this, but it's true and it's time. "It will never be good enough. I have to see her again."

"Why?" True asks. He heard my meaning the day Bay left, when I said that single word in the temple, and I hear his now. He cares about me. He might even love me. So why can't I stay?

I have to tell him so that he understands when he finds me gone.

"I miss her," I say, "so much that it feels like I'm alone in an ocean that covers all the world. I miss her so much that I think I'm not really a person anymore, only pain. And then sometimes I think it's the opposite. I *do* have a body. It's a mess of organs and muscle and bones lying on a shore, and the salty seawater comes over me in waves that never end and it hurts. All the time."

"This is how you feel without her," True says.

"Yes," I say.

The moment I spoke in the temple, True knew that I was a siren. And, knowing who my mother was and who my aunt is, he must have realized that I had another siren in my family. That I am not just a siren but a strange one at that. But he didn't say anything to anyone. He's been keeping secrets for me all along.

What would it be like to stay here in the gondola, the fog around us, the sound of the bats winging their way across the skies, Atlantia breathing, lulling us to sleep?

True's lips brush against mine and I kiss him back. We hold each other tight. Earlier, under the trees, we were hungry and relieved to touch each other.

We are still hungry.

The gondola stops. We need to get out and get home before the peacekeepers find us.

"I'll walk with you to the temple," True says.

As we come closer to the temple, the fog lifts. It is lighter here. And so we can see that the trees have lost their leaves, all of them, in silver drifts on the ground. The gods are naked in the branches, their broken arms and shining teeth there for all to see, and as I watch a temple bat drifts down to land on Efram's shoulder.

I have never seen Atlantia like this, unleaved, unloosed. The breach, the fog, the trees undone.

The city is decaying before our eyes, and I realize that it has always been this way. It is such work to keep Atlantia alive, to keep any of us alive. But the work is what draws us in, what gives us purpose. This city is our ship, sealed tight to keep us safe, and it is breaking.

"How could this happen so fast?" True asks. "We haven't been gone for long. The trees were fine an hour ago."

"Maire was right," I say. "We need to go home."

"We will," True says, and I wonder how his voice is so deep and so clear. How his hands can be both strong and gentle. How he can know what I am and still be unafraid to kiss me like this.

I can't see True again after tonight.

My mother was right. She told me that one word could undo the work of years; could be overheard by many.

First Justus, then Maire, now True. Who is the most dangerous of the three?

I know the answer to that. I've known for some time.

CHAPTER 18

*D*uring a special broadcast the next day, Nevio tells us that the breach was a terrible accident. That the water that came in was too powerful, too fast, that there was nothing to be done but seal off the deepmarket to prevent the water from reaching the neighborhoods.

Hundreds of people died. There's no way to give everyone an individual burial with a death toll so high, no time for family members to prepare the bodies. The priests are working all day and late into the night to bless and shroud the dead, and the bodies will have to go up through the floodgates in groups. There is not enough time to bury them one by one. Nevio tells us that the first group will be released tomorrow morning.

We lost more people in the deepmarket breach than we have ever lost in a single day in Atlantia. This is a terrible tragedy.

And I am a terrible person, because in the tragedy I see an opportunity.

This is my chance to go through the floodgates.

And it's even better than I could have hoped.

The mass burials are the perfect cover for my attempt to get Above.

Instead of just one body, there will be dozens going up at the same time. I'll wear Bay's wetsuit, the one I didn't cut up for a costume, and find a robe to shroud myself in and conceal my air tank.

This time *I* will be the one who leaves.

⌐

I wait until it's late at night, until the hours when even the priests have to steal a little sleep, and I slip into the morgue, find a shroud in a pile, and put it on over my wetsuit and air tank. The dead rest in their rows, and I lie down and pull the shroud over my face, making sure that the air tank is adjusted and strapped on tight.

I lie on the cold floor and wait. Wondering whether I've timed everything right, wondering if this will work.

And then people come inside. They move body after body. When it's my turn, I hold very still. I pretend not to breathe.

The workers bring me from the morgue out to the floodgate chamber. They carry me on a stretcher, so they don't touch the air tank, which is a mercy, and they settle me on the chamber floor. I know where I am by the echoes in the room and the smell of cold stone and salt water. I hear the workers placing other bodies around me. The floor feels very hard through my shroud.

A chill of foreboding shivers down the back of my neck. *What if it all ends here? What if I drown before I even get out of the chamber?*

Think about something else. Think about True.

I wonder if he is watching the burial. He won't know that I'm here with the other bodies, but soon enough he'll know that I'm gone, that I left Atlantia somehow. I wanted to leave a message for True, but I realized it was complicated—who could I trust to give it to him?—and, in the end, unnecessary.

I told him everything last night in the gondola. I didn't tell him when I was going, but he knows I've always wanted to go Above, and he knows how much I miss my sister.

In the end True will think that I loved Bay more than I love him, which is true in some ways.

I have loved her longer.

⌒

The priests begin to say the prayers over us. They speak as one, and I can't make out Justus's voice.

I hold so very, very still. The priests are everywhere, walking among the rows. I wonder if any of them think they see a flutter of breath when they come past my body. My mask is in place, the tank still undiscovered, the control to the airflow in my hand. It will take a tiny movement to switch it on, one that I hope no one sees. And then I'll have to hope that the air is good and the ascent slow enough that my lungs don't burst.

The priests stop chanting. I hear the door to the chamber close as they leave us alone.

Somewhere in the viewing area, Nevio and the Council are watching. Is Maire with them?

The water coming from the gods' open mouths hits the floor. I wonder if True will understand when he finds out what

I have done. I hope he knows how I feel about him, that I didn't want it to have to be like this. But how else could I go?

My shroud is soon sodden.

The last time I was in this chamber was with Maire. That's when I had the idea to go up through the floodgates.

This is the perfect way to escape. But it's also the perfect way to get rid of the last remaining daughter of a Minister you wanted dead, a Minister who knew too much. The Council killed my mother. Did they ask Maire to kill me?

What if going up through the floodgates wasn't my idea after all? What if it was hers?

All it takes is a little fear to creep in. It's like the water in the deepmarket. Once it breaks, you will soon have a flood. And then there's no telling what could happen.

Don't panic. Don't be afraid. You're meant for the Above. Your inner voice has always told you this. Trust it.

It is a good thing that I practiced in the lanes, because as the water lifts me I am buffeted and spun around, and I have to adjust and move without seeming to do so. I have to work to keep my head upright, hoping that with so many bodies they won't notice. I switch on the air, and it flows into my mask.

Up, up, up, I go. They accelerate the water once the bodies have lifted off the ground. Artificial currents keep us away from the walls and toward the center, but we bump into one another.

Bile rises into my throat, though I've eaten nothing.

Don't think. Just breathe.

I feel the cold of the water, even through the wetsuit. I know that the exposure might send me into shock. I know the suit might not be enough to protect me.

Up. Up.

The shroud comes loose over my face. I must not have tightened it enough. I can't help it. I open my eyes.

The petals above me spin, and it is all I can do to keep staring up and not swim straight for the exit. It's bright. So bright. Is that real light or artificial light? I don't think the sun can reach this far down, but other things I've thought were certain have been proven wrong.

Some of the bodies reach the opening of the chamber before I do.

They become blazing, brilliant, bright; they disappear.

Is this the third miracle? Do I believe in the miracles?

I do. I believe in the sirens, because they exist and I am one of them. I believe in the bats, because I've seen them. I've scrubbed up their leavings and marveled at their wings. So a third miracle could be true, too.

But something is happening. A darkening. A pulling down on the inside, the very heart of me, on my body.

Am I dying?

The petals spin inward instead of outward, closing instead of opening.

"Open," I say. *"Open back up. Let me out."*

But it doesn't work. Because of the mask? Because I am too far away?

The water is lowering.

They are bringing me back down.

They know.

CHAPTER 19

How do they know?

Did Nevio figure it out somehow?

Or did I give myself away? Did someone notice that the shroud came open or see me move?

I want to pull the shroud closed, but I can't risk it. Perhaps they shut the gates for another reason. Maybe it's not me at all.

On the way down, I get caught in a current as the water swirls toward the floor. My head bobs under, and water floods into my mask. The seal must not have been tight enough, and I choke, my body convulsing. I can't breathe, and I'm moving far too much. I reach up inside the shroud and fix the mask, hoping that in the whirl of bodies going down, no one will notice the movement.

The water settles me roughly on the bottom of the flood-gate chamber. I lie perfectly still, on my side, flung there as haphazardly as the rest of the bodies.

I didn't even make it out of the chamber.

For several long minutes, I rest there on the floor, surrounded by corpse-filled shrouds, trying to keep my chest from heaving up and down, willing myself not to shake with the cold, listening to the last of the water drain away.

Peacekeepers take me straight to holding and put me in a room by myself. It's small, with a dark-glassed window and a table and two chairs inside, nothing more. But the chairs are beautifully carved and made of wood, true treasures from the ancient Above. Why would they put such things in a holding cell?

They don't give me anything else to wear, even though the air coming through the vents feels icy. I stand in the middle of the room in my wetsuit and drip and shiver. *I'm alive,* I think. *I'm caught.*

Maire comes inside, a rush of warm air from the hall following her.

She looks neat and tidy, her hair braided in a way that reminds me of how Bay and I wore ours on that day in the temple. There's even a ribbon, brown velvet, winding through Maire's hair, and her clothes are neatly pressed. "Raise the temperature in here," she says to a guard in her gorgeous, dangerous voice. "Bring her dry clothes. Now."

Then she turns to me. "They've sent me in to talk with you," she says. "Sit down."

I stay standing. I don't want to obey her. And I don't want to ruin the chair. Salt water on that old wood—I can't bring myself to do it.

"The Council wanted to interrogate you," Maire says, "to find out why you tried to go up through the floodgates. I told them that it wasn't necessary to question you. That you simply wanted to go Above because you missed your sister."

I don't say anything.

"You're very quiet, Rio," Maire says. "Is there anything you'd like to tell us?" She gestures to the mirrored window at the back of the room.

I wonder how many people are listening.

I know what Maire wants me to say.

I'm not sure if I hear it in her voice or see it in her eyes, but I know. She's not commanding, but she is asking.

She wants me to say that I'm a siren.

In front of her. In front of whoever watches from behind that window. She wants me to give myself away, even though all this time she's told me to save my voice.

A guard appears at the door with the clothes Maire requested—shirt and pants, underclothes, socks, and they're all *dry*. I want to wear them so badly that my teeth chatter. There's a blanket, too. Maire holds it up to screen me from the window.

"Go ahead and change," Maire says.

I want to resist her, the way I refused to sit down on the chair, but I'm too cold. As fast as I can, I slip on the dry underclothes, the pants and shirt. My chilled fingers fumble with the buttons.

"Finished?" Maire asks, and when I don't answer, she lowers the blanket. "There," she says. "That's better."

And then she takes my chin in her hands and looks right into my eyes.

"Rio," Maire says, "it's time." She leans in and whispers into my ear, *"You need to tell us who you are."*

She pulls away. "The people from Above are tired of helping us," Maire says, her voice brutal and clear. "Our mines are depleted and useless to them now, and they have stopped sending us food. We're a drain on their resources. And you know what happened in the deep-market."

Is she saying that the people Above caused the breach somehow?

The door opens, and Nevio comes into the room. So *he* was behind the dark glass. "You've said too much," he says. "As always."

"I'm right, *as always*," Maire says. "By telling Rio what's happening, I'm giving Atlantia a chance." She nods to me. Her lips form the word *speak*. But she doesn't command me to say it. Why? Even now, she still wants me to have the choice?

I don't understand any of this. They're working together, that much is clear, but I see nothing warm, no sign of collaboration between the two of them. In fact, when Maire addresses Nevio, I hear a simmering, long-brewed hatred that she doesn't bother to hide.

Maire meets my gaze. "This is the last chance, Rio," she says. "We're out of time. If you want to go to the surface, this is the way."

My mother trusted Maire. So did Bay. And Maire gave me the shell and told me many things I'd never known. And I have no other way to the surface. I have to trust her, too.

And I *want* to speak. I *want* to go to the surface.

I tried to get there myself, and I failed.

So I do it. I use my real voice. I say what I've wanted to say all my life.

"I am a siren."

Maire closes her eyes.

I've spoken the truth. I've said what I am as loud as I can.

It sounds so powerful that I feel my heart will break, or break free from me.

I am.

A siren.

CHAPTER 20

*N*evio stares at me.

"But that's not possible," he says. "You're related to Maire by blood."

"Nevertheless," Maire says. "She is a siren. You heard her."

Nevio keeps looking at me. Then he smiles. "Bring her to my office," he says, and he walks out of the room, leaving my aunt and me alone.

"Why now?" I ask Maire as soon as Nevio leaves. I use my false voice. It's hard to do after speaking in my real one.

She takes me by the arm, and I try to twist away, but her grip is strong.

"Good," she says. "Keep using your old voice. Save the true one. You will need it Above." And then the peacekeepers catch up to us, and Maire lets go.

I expect them to take us to Nevio's office in the temple, but instead we walk down a long corridor and to another door. So he also has an office in the Council buildings. They offered one to my mother, but she never used it. She liked to do all her work in the temple.

A peacekeeper opens the door for us, and I stand there and gape. I can't help it.

Nevio's office here is like nothing I've ever seen. The walls are paneled entirely in wood. I feel like I'm standing inside a tree, where its heart should be, and I don't like it.

"We need to take her with us to the surface," Nevio says.

"Yes," Maire says.

"I should have known." Nevio paces around me. "That dull voice. It stood to reason that you were hiding something." He laughs, a truly ugly sound because it's full of anger and condescension, no mirth at all. He turns on Maire. "How long have you known?"

"Not long," Maire says. "I heard her that day in the temple when her sister went Above."

"And you didn't tell me?"

"I didn't," Maire agrees.

"Did anyone else hear you?" Nevio asks me.

"Justus did," Maire says.

"Justus," Nevio says dismissively, as if Justus is nothing at all. "Anyone else?"

The Minister pacing, Maire betraying, neither one of them treating me as if I'm a person at all. I told them what I was, but nothing has changed—

"That boy she's been running around with," Maire says, and my head snaps up. "His name is—"

"Stop," I say, and I don't hold anything back.

For one long, long second, they do stop. Nevio quits pacing. Maire doesn't speak.

Then Maire says, "True Beck."

No. Not True. How did she know?

"Impressive," Nevio says, his eyes running over me like I'm a fascinating piece of sculpture to admire; a line of scripture to decipher; a thing, not a person. "She told us to stop, and we did. How long did it last?" he asks Maire.

"Just for a moment," Maire says. "And you?"

"The same," he says.

For a few seconds, I made them do what I wanted.

Nevio watches me, calculating. Is he changing his mind about what should be done with me? Why does he get to decide?

He doesn't.

"I am going Above," I say, in my true voice.

I've known it all along. I've known it since I could first think or feel. Hearing myself say it now takes away all uncertainty. Maire shakes her head at me. She told me that she wants me to save my voice. For what? Why does it matter now?

I'm going Above.

"You are," Nevio says. "Take care of everything," he tells Maire. "We leave as soon as they send down the transports."

❧

"I know you hate me," Maire says as we hurry down the hall together. The peacekeepers have vanished, and Maire and I follow the winding pathways of the Council buildings, a place I know only from the artfully constructed exteriors, the sand- and candy-colored stuccos of the buildings.

I don't deny it. "You said that you'd let me choose."

"You were the one who made the final choice, who said the words just now," Maire says. "Which is good. Because this won't work if it isn't what *you* want. And we are running out of time. If you don't come up with us now, you'll be stuck Below forever."

"What won't work?" I ask. "What am I supposed to do Above? And why did you tell him about True?"

Maire doesn't answer. She pulls me to a window in the long hallway. "It's all falling apart," she says. "Look."

The plaza is flooded. Not by much, but the entire surface is sheeted in several inches' worth of water. It's so beautiful that I can't keep from staring—a pool, shining like a lake in pictures of the world before the Divide. The bare silver trees reflect on the water, making two of each of them—one in the water, one above.

"Another problem," Maire says. "It began last night. A small, slow leak, but we haven't been able to stop it or drain it yet."

"How can you work with Nevio?" I ask. "He's part of the Council that killed my mother."

"You know what he is," Maire says.

So she does know that he's a siren. Of course she would.

"I know what he is," I agree. "And I know what you are." I can't hide the hatred in my voice. "You gave Nevio a shell. I saw it in the safe in his office. You're his collaborator."

"I have never spoken with Nevio that way," Maire says. "There's only one other person I've spoken back and forth with through a shell the way I have with you. And that was your mother."

Out in the plaza, peacekeepers direct people away from the water. Maire touches the wall next to the window, and I wonder if there are voices in here, too.

"The shell you found in his office," she says. "Was it white?"

"Yes."

"That was the shell Oceana and I used to communicate, near the end, when they were watching her," Maire says. "She had it with her when the Council poisoned her. I'll never forget that, hearing her whisper what they'd done, and then the silence after." Maire's eyes stay dry, but her voice sounds rough and sad. "Nevio took it from her just after that, before she ran away to find me. He knew the shell was important, but he didn't understand why or what it did. He must not have seen her speaking into it. I'm not surprised he's kept the shell. He doesn't like mysteries."

"She tried to keep you safe," I say, "but you didn't do the same thing for her. What kind of sister are you?"

Maire turns away from the water, and I take a step back. For the first time, I think that she looks like Oceana. I see the same weariness in her eyes that I used to notice in my mother's, but in Maire's it is even more profound.

"I need you to do what you do best for a moment," Maire says. *"Listen."*

"To *you*?"

"To the city," she says.

And I do. I can't help myself. Atlantia no longer screams, but breathes the way a child does after he has cried all he can and is tired and broken and empty. I listen to Atlantia's sounds and I look out at all her sights: the colorful houses, the iron rivets, the metal trees, the sky, the people who are so sure they are blessed.

"When I first heard you, that day in the temple," Maire says, "I knew we needed you. I knew how powerful you might be. You've had to keep your voice hidden, which means that when you *do* speak with your full voice, you have a raw power that the rest of us no longer possess."

"Did my mother know that?" I ask. Was she trying not to hide me, but to make me strong?

Maire smiles. "Yes," she says. "Of course, making a siren hide her voice can also have the opposite effect. It can destroy a child who isn't strong enough."

This is what I hate about Maire. Right as she tells me something I desperately want to know, she gives me terrible answers to questions I never thought to ask.

"I have been waiting for you," Maire says. "But I can't wait any longer. We might succeed, if you join us. We've found you just in time." She shakes her head and smiles, a sad smile. "How could Oceana hide you so long from me? Especially when we were friends again, near the end, and she told me *everything* else?"

I hear tenderness when she speaks of my mother, and I can't bear it. "Don't talk about her," I say.

"So you won't allow me to speak of my own sister," Maire says. Her eyes flash and she looks dangerous, but she keeps her voice on an even keel. "Then let's continue to speak about you and your extremely useful voice. Pure and untrained. The most powerful voice I've ever heard."

That can't be right. "The Minister—" I begin.

Maire shakes her head. "Nevio isn't as powerful as you. But his talent *is* unusual, and I don't know that any siren in history has been able to mask their voice as well as he has masked his. The sirens have changed. The Minister can hide *and* use his voice. You and I are in the same family, and we can control things in addition to people. It seems that even miracles evolve."

Even miracles evolve. The bats did. They made their wings blue like glass and water. They changed to suit their environment.

And now they are dying.

"The Minister is speaking to the other sirens right now," Maire says. "He is telling them that we are the Below's last chance for survival. He will let them know that we are going to the Above to remind the people there of their place in the world, and of ours. He will say that the people of the Above are tired of providing for us Below, and they do not plan to continue to do so. The Minister will say that this mission is essential to the survival of Atlantia. He is right."

"Atlantia will die without us?"

"Yes," Maire says. "It will. Two weeks ago the Above stopped sending food, and our stores are almost depleted. The city is breaking, and we are running out of materials to repair it."

She doesn't use her voice to convince me. She doesn't have to. This all makes sense to me, so much so that I wonder why it's taken the people Above this long. Why *wouldn't* they hate us? Why *wouldn't* they want our better lives? But I also have the distinct feeling that there is something Maire isn't telling me.

"Do they want us dead so that they can take over Atlantia?" I ask. Is that it? Then they could have our city and our longer, easier lives.

"They want us dead," Maire says to me very quietly, her voice sounding the way it did in the shell. "*They're* the ones who put the mines in the water to keep us from coming up. And they don't care about Atlantia."

So Josiah was wrong, or he lied to me. The people *Above* are the ones who put the mines in the water to prevent us from trying to escape.

They don't care about us, and they don't care about our city.

I have always wanted to leave Atlantia, but I never wanted it to die.

The temple, with its aquamarine-painted wooden door and rusty hinges. The plaza, shimmering now with water. The gods in the trees and the leaves we take such care to put back on, the apartments painted pink and blue and white and orange.

The mining bays, the beautiful broken drones, the dark ocean room and the metal scraps glinting in the sky room. The prows and bellies of the gondolas, their sleek way of moving through the canals. The priests, who wear robes and minister to others, and the workers who throw gold coins into the wishing pools and the children who sing as they run across the plazas, their feet fast and their arms open wide.

And True. Most of all, True.

"We may lose everything," Maire says. "We need you to join us. Will you?"

When she says it like that, there is only one answer I can give.

CHAPTER 21

$\mathscr{P}$eacekeepers lead Maire and me through a tunnel at the back of the Council buildings and to a waiting transport. It's full of people—the other sirens are already here. I count heads quickly. Including Maire, there are twenty-seven of them, far fewer than I would have expected. One of the sirens asks who I am, and when she does, I recognize her voice. She's the siren who spoke to Atlantia during the breach in the deepmarket.

"Rio is another siren," Maire says, gesturing to me. "One who's managed to stay hidden until now."

"Can we hear her speak?" asks another siren, a man.

"No," Maire says. "Nevio wants her to save her voice. It will be more powerful that way."

Something about the way Maire tells them this forestalls further questions, though I can see that the others are intrigued.

I am the youngest siren on the transport. "So I *am* the last," I say to Maire under my breath.

"As far as we know," Maire says. "But I believe there may be many more to come, if Atlantia survives."

Someone hands us blue robes to wear over our clothes. For a moment I am speechless at the beautiful cloth in my hands—it is a lovely, iridescent turquoise, shot through with golden threads and silver and green and white and even black. I am wearing the ocean. The cloth feels ancient, a remnant of a finer time.

"Sirens used to wear these when they went to the surface," Maire says. "The cloth was made with a technique unique to the Below that we have since lost."

I slip my arms into the robes. The sirens also wear make-up—including the men. The cheekbones and contours of their faces are brought out with shading. They—we—bring to mind those sharp-faced animals from the Above, the ones called birds. I've seen them in pictures. One of the sirens comes toward Maire and begins marking up her face.

It's not hard to see that, to the people Above, we are supposed to appear otherworldly, powerful and strange. We are meant to impress and convince them.

"Don't we need to wear masks?" I ask. "Isn't the air dangerous up there?"

"We won't wear masks today," Maire says. "It's more powerful that way."

The other sirens have decided to be civil to me. Some of them look guarded, but most seem to regard me with something bordering on reverence. "Oceana's daughter, a siren," one says.

So they've figured out who I am. I wonder if they'll also make the connection between Maire and me, if they'll realize that she's my aunt.

"See?" Maire says, her voice dry. "You're not alone in worshipping her."

Everyone speaks of my mother, but I can't stop thinking of Bay. This could be the very transport she used to go to the surface. *I'm going to the surface.* I wish there were windows. I want to see what it's like, all the way up.

"You'll love it," one of the sirens says, leaning close to me as she brushes my face with iridescent powder. "Do you know what they think about us Above?" She smiles. "They think we *are* the gods." She reaches for a dark pencil, smudges lines above my eyes. "It's intoxicating."

"It's magic," one of the other sirens says.

"How do you know this?" I ask. "Have any of you been Above?" And how much do they know of the real history of the Below, the one I heard from the shell and from Maire?

They all fall silent.

"No," Maire says. "None of us have ever seen the Above."

"But Nevio and the Council told us how it would be," another siren says, "and we're ready. The people of Atlantia will love us again after this. We're about to perform the third miracle."

Maire smiles and there is no mirth in it. She doesn't believe that the people Above think we are gods anymore. She doesn't believe that the people Below are going to worship and love us again.

Maire's eyes meet mine, and I think, *The people Below will never know what the sirens do today.* Nevio will never tell them. If this doesn't work, Atlantia will die, and if it *does* work, Atlantia will go on as it always has. Nevio won't give the sirens credit for this.

"Where do we go when we get Above?" I ask Maire. I've always pictured myself walking alone on a shore, where there are trees and sun and sand. But I know it won't be like that.

"The Above is a large island," Maire says, "with many smaller surrounding islands. The dock for the transports that bring people up is on one of those smaller islands. We are to wait on a platform there for the citizens of the Above to come meet us."

"Is it the same spot where they brought Bay?" I ask.

"Yes," Maire says. "It's been the meeting place since the Divide."

"How is this going to work?" I ask.

"They say that our voices are even more powerful up here," the deepmarket siren tells me. She has a clear, calming inflection. "That when we speak, our voices go much farther and last much longer. There is no way to avoid us or disobey us once we have given a command. If they try, they hear our voices in their minds speaking to them again, even though we have long since gone back Below. Our voices haunt them. It's why they stopped us from coming Above long ago. But the Council agrees that it is time for us to go back."

"Who told you all this?" I ask.

"The knowledge has been passed down among generations," Maire says. "From siren to siren."

I wish I knew if she were speaking the truth. I wish I trusted her.

I wanted to love her.

"If we can really do all of this, why would the Above let us come up again?" I ask.

"Nevio arranged it," Maire says.

The door to the transport opens, and the Minister himself appears. Everyone hushes instantly.

Nevio paces in front of the sirens as if we are a row of acolytes awaiting instruction in the temple. "It is our duty as sirens," he says, "to remind the people Above of their place in the order of things."

So the sirens know what he is. He has identified himself as one of them in words, and he does it with his voice as well, speaking without holding back. "We must remind those Above of their obligation to honor the gods. Their Council understands this. They believe that their people have become too wicked, too dismissive of their religion. They have agreed to let us come Above to remind and convince the people there of the rightness of the Divide."

Now he looks at Maire. She smiles at him. It is the coldest thing I have ever seen.

"We have been trying to decide if we should command or persuade," one of the sirens says. "And if we should speak in unison or cacophony."

"Ah," Nevio says. "I think it must be a command. How else can we make sure that they listen to us? But as for the other matter—well. Let me hear you."

The sirens nod eagerly. How long have they known that he is one of them? How long have they let themselves be under his spell?

"What are the gifts given to we who live Below?" he asks. In his full, real voice, his siren voice.

It is honey and blood, dark and warm, golden and full of shadow. It is a beautiful voice, a decayed voice. I catch my breath. Nevio notices. He smiles.

"Long life, health, strength, and happiness," the other sirens answer, and I am afraid to move. I've never heard anything like this, and my heart fills with joy at the beauty of their voices, at the power behind them. They are angels singing to their god, their voices hopeful and full of belief.

But their faith has been misdirected.

He has taken their power and turned it all toward himself. Do they understand that?

"What is the curse of those who live Above?" Nevio asks.

"Short life, illness, weakness, and misery."

"Is this fair?"

"It is fair. It is as the gods decreed at the time of the Divide. Some have to stay Above so that humanity might survive Below."

They go on through all the rest of it. Neither Maire nor I join in.

"Maire and the new siren didn't say anything," someone says, when they have finished.

"It's all right," Nevio says. "They've been instructed to save their voices. Some sirens who don't train as you do aren't prepared to use their voices more than once in the space of a few hours." He smiles. "But they may still be of use."

He's insulting us, I realize. But he's also lying. He knows that Maire and I are powerful. Why is he pretending that we're not?

"Now," Nevio says, "let's try the other way."

This time, the sirens speak in cacophony. All saying the same things but not at the same time, each using their voice's own particular, potent power—screaming, shrieking, singing, whispering, calling.

It's unsettling, ugly, and powerful in a completely different way. I feel like my bones are rearranging, scraping against one another inside my body, that my brain is itchy and agitated and my blood hot.

"Unison," Nevio decides. "We will have you speak in unison. You have trained, and you know all the words."

I knew the words from listening to them in the temple, but now, after hearing the sirens, it's as if the litany has been seared into my brain.

"We are ready," Nevio says. "I will see you at the surface."

"Aren't you coming with us?" one of the other sirens asks in dismay.

"I am coming up right behind you, in another transport," Nevio says, his voice soothing. "As the Minister, there are matters of prayer I need to attend to, alone, in order to help ensure our success. But I will see you soon in the Above. And I leave my blessing upon you."

He nods to all of us and disappears through the door of the transport. As soon as he's gone through, the door slides shut and I hear the lock engaging. Now that the door is closed, it's hard to see where it was before—it fits into the wall so smoothly. There's no handle or opening mechanism on the inside. "No going back now," one of the sirens says. "Once the door's locked, it won't open again until we're at the surface."

Another siren, one about my mother's age, sits down in front of me. "You've ruined your makeup," she says. She takes out a cloth and wipes my cheeks. She doesn't seem surprised, and I suppose she understands. How could I *not* weep at the siren sounds, both ugly and beautiful?

"I think we're doing this wrong," I say. "All of this. The makeup, the commands. We should try to be *more* human, not less. We should try to talk to them. To the people Above. We should plead with them, convince them that this is what they *want* to do. Use our voices, but then let them make the choice. They won't hate us that way."

The sirens stare at me as if I'm not even speaking their language.

"Is this your idea, Maire?" one of them asks. "It sounds like you."

"I don't know why the Minister and the Council decided to let you come." One of the male sirens sneers at my aunt. I stare in disbelief. How can he treat Maire so casually? Does he have no idea of what she can do?

"Because I'm powerful," Maire says, and there is no anger in her voice. Only sorrow. "And the Minister and the Council know that. Until today they have always wanted me alive."

Until today? What does Maire mean?

Why does she never tell me the whole truth?

I think about what she said earlier:

"The Minister is speaking to the other sirens right now. He is telling them that we are the Below's last chance for survival. He will let them know that we are going to the Above to remind the people there of their place in the world, and of ours. He will say that the people of the Above are tired of providing for us Below, and they do not plan to continue to do so. The Minister will say that this mission is essential to the survival of Atlantia. He is right."

But I also think about what Maire didn't say. She didn't say Nevio was telling the sirens the truth about everything. She only said that this mission is essential to the survival of Atlantia.

Something is very, very wrong here, and I don't know what it is. I think Maire does. And she hasn't told me.

I can't bear it. I stand up and walk to the other end of the transport.

Maire follows me. "Save your tears and your anger," she says. "You're going to need them when we reach the Above."

"Why should I believe anything you say?"

"Because I do tell the truth about some things. Your mother needed me. Your sister did, too. When I said that to you, it wasn't a lie."

She slides a corner of paper out from her sleeve. I know the writing on it.

It's a letter from Bay.

"She told me that I was only to give it to you if you tried to go Above," Maire says.

I snatch the letter from Maire before she can say anything more.

> *Rio,*
>
> *If you read this, it means I've gone Above and that I managed to keep my decision to leave a secret from you.*
>
> *And it means that* you *are trying to go Above. I know you. I know you won't give up until you find a way. But you have to remain Below.*
>
> *I don't know where I should begin, but I know that I have to tell you everything so that you can understand why you have to stay.*
>
> *Our mother didn't tell me until a few weeks before she died that you could never go Above. I wonder if she was starting to suspect what you've always wanted to do. She told me about the history of the sirens. They used to go Above, but they've been banned from doing so for generations. They hate the sirens Above, Rio, and they will kill you as soon as they know what you are. You won't be able to speak Above, not any more than you can speak Below.*
>
> *I asked her why she didn't tell* you *this, and she said it was because she didn't want to break your heart.*
>
> *A few weeks later, she died. And all I could think about, besides who killed her, was keeping you safe.*
>
> *So I made you promise that you would stay. And I decided that I'd have to go Above when the time came. I didn't want to leave Atlantia, but this was the best way to*

*protect you—to guarantee that you couldn't ever go. I had
to hide my plan from you. It felt impossible. You know we
didn't hide things from each other.*

But I'm not leaving you alone.

*I'm giving Maire this letter to give to you, and some
money, too, so you can use it for whatever you might need.*

*Maire will watch over you and make sure you survive.
You need to be where she is, now that our mother is gone.*

I'm so sorry, Rio.

But I have to go to keep you safe.

I love you.

Bay

I swallow. An angry, hard ache in my throat makes it difficult.

This is just like my mother and Bay. Always protecting me.

"Always underestimating you," Maire says out loud next to
me.

I don't want to listen to her. I'm still angry with her. She was
supposed to give me this *before* I was actually on my way to the
surface. Now I'm locked in the transport with no way out.

"You didn't play fair," I say.

"I only cheat when I have to," Maire tells me. "But what I
said now is true. Your mother and your sister loved you, but
they never understood your potential. I do."

I hear the sound of the door unlocking. All the sirens look
dumbfounded. "I thought that, once it was locked, no one else
could enter," someone says.

"That's what they said," another agrees.

"Interesting," Maire says. "Are they letting one of us out?"

They are not.

When the door opens, peacekeepers stand at the ready to keep us from attempting to exit. They escort someone in, and then they close the door behind him.

It's True.

The transport begins to move.

CHAPTER 22

*M*y entire world is in motion, the transport slipping toward the surface, the pieces and people I thought I knew moving into new places.

My mother knew I wanted to come Above.

My sister left to try to save me.

I'm going to the surface with my last family member from Below, one I'm not at all sure I can trust.

And True is here. Why? He is not a siren.

I haven't seen him since that night after the breach in the deepmarket—less than two days ago, but it feels like much longer. Does he know what I tried to do at the floodgates?

True's eyes lock on mine. The lights of the transport flicker briefly off and then back on, and I remember how the light filtered through the slats of the stall in the deepmarket and how it felt to kiss him under the naked silver trees, in the gondola in the fog.

"Who is this?" the deepmarket siren asks.

"Another siren," Maire says. "Nevio found him at the last minute."

True nods, going along with her.

"I hope you're telling the truth," the siren says. "We need you with us, Maire. This mission has to go *perfectly*." She appeals to True and me. "Do you know what the Minister has promised in return for our success?"

I shake my head.

"If we succeed," the siren says, "Nevio is going to make us part of the Council. Can you imagine?"

I can't. Nevio would never let such a thing happen. He's lied to the sirens, and for some reason they've chosen to believe him. I glance over at Maire, and she smiles very slightly. So she knew what the Minister promised. Once again she hasn't been completely honest with me.

One of the sirens hands True a blue robe, and he pulls it on over his clothes. He and Maire and I sit down together at the far end of the transport so that the others can't hear us talk. It feels strange and wrong not to touch him, but there are too many people watching.

"Why are you here?" I ask True. It comes out flat and cold and nothing like my real voice, or my real feelings.

"The Minister found me," True says. When he speaks, I love the sound. But it's my fault he's here. And Maire's, for giving out his name.

"Nevio told me you were going Above," True says. "He wanted to know if I'm a hidden siren, too. I'm not. But I told him what I can do, and he let me come."

I feel us ascending, the slow pull of the transport through the water. I hear the air changing, feel the pressure inside the transport adjusting. Even though I'm worried about everything—Maire, Bay, True—I can't stop the pulse of excitement, the thrill that I am at last going to see the Above. This is what I've wanted for so long. What will it be like?

And True is with me.

It would be safer if he stayed behind, but I don't know if I would wish him away.

"What do you mean?" I ask True. "Did you tell him about all the things you can make?" I'm thinking of the metal fish, the eels, the locks. And then I realize that of course that's not what True means—he means that he told the Minister about being immune. But why would Nevio send True up with us? There are many other people in Atlantia who are immune to the sirens' songs, and they're not here.

"No," True says. He takes a deep breath. "Rio, I haven't told you everything."

What else can there be? He's immune, he heard me speak— isn't that everything? Isn't that enough secrets? "What is it?" I ask.

"I can tell when a siren is lying," he says. His voice sounds shaky. "Once I knew what Nevio was, I listened carefully. And I could tell that he lied in the broadcast when he said the breach was an accident. Someone caused it."

"Who?" I ask.

"I don't know," True says.

I glance at Maire. I remember how I saw her down in the deepmarket, how I wondered if she had had something to do with the break.

"I didn't help them," she says. "It was Nevio, and the Council. They altered the controls and compromised the pressurization system. They wanted the deepmarket dead."

"I believe her," True says.

Maire smiles. She does not seem surprised at True's secret. But I am.

"I've never heard of someone being able to do this," I say.

"I know," True says. "I hadn't, either."

"So you're immune to sirens," I say, trying to get it straight, "*and* you know when they're lying?"

"Yes," True says.

"How can you be sure?" I ask, because how could anyone know that?

True shrugs. "Things have happened," he says. "I know." The laugh lines, the sun on his skin, the brown and gold of his eyes—it is all still the same. He's still the same. But I should have known there was even more to him, that all the empathy he has shown me also indicated an understanding of mystery, of keeping back part of yourself. He knows what it's like to have depths that others don't, that are dangerous to share.

"So I'll have to take your word for it."

True nods.

"Even though you've lied to me," I say, trying to put up one last wall.

"I didn't lie," True says. "I had secrets I wasn't sure I could tell you. You felt the same way." He's right, of course. I never did let him know what I planned to do to get to the Above.

"Does it work with people who aren't sirens?"

"No," True says. "Only with sirens. If I listen closely, I can hear something in their voices when they're not telling the truth. It sounds like the wrong note in a song. I don't know how to explain it better than that."

"But you were affected by *me*," I say, trying to understand everything. "You said that you heard me calling to you in my real voice when the breach happened." Even though that was imaginary, the thought of my real voice was enough to impact him, which shouldn't be the case if he's truly immune.

"Yes," he says. "I'm affected by *you*. Not your voice." I hear him swallow. "Do you believe me?"

"I *want* to believe you," I say.

"Nevio tested me to make sure I was telling the truth," True says. "He told me some things, said for me to tell him if he was lying or not. I guess I passed his test, because he decided to send me with you. He said that I'll be useful, because I can tell if any of the sirens are trying to sabotage the mission. He said it was my responsibility to stop them."

"And you believe that's why he sent you?" Maire asks.

True looks right in her eyes. "No," he says. "I acted like I did. But he knew I was lying. We all know why I'm really here."

"Why *are* you here?" I ask.

I want to hear him say it. I want it almost as much as I want the Above.

"Because of you," he says. "I wanted to come with you."

True's arm and shoulder are warm next to mine, and I want to turn right into him, to have his arms around me and mine around him, as we come to the Above. But I don't want the sirens to see, to think there's any reason for him being there other than the one Maire's given. I want to protect him as much as I can, though it may be too late.

Nevio sent True up so he wouldn't have to worry about True's talent and the problems it could cause for a lying, siren Minister. And Nevio made promises to the sirens because he doesn't think he's going to have to keep those promises.

The Minister doesn't plan on any of us coming back from the Above.

And even though I realize this, I still want to go. Something in my heart feels like it is opening. I imagine the water outside lightening, too, the deep ocean blue of it turning the color of the sky and the sun. If I could get off the transport this moment and go back home, I wouldn't do it. Is it because of Bay? Or because True is here? Or because the Above is where I've always wanted to be?

"We can't stay on the transport when we arrive," Maire tells the two of us, her voice quiet. "They're not going to send it back down with anyone aboard, and we're trapped in here. Our best chance of escape is to get out and do what we can."

"The sirens aren't what I expected," I say. "They're so— tame. So controlled."

"There used to be more of us," Maire says. "There used to be more like me."

"What happened?"

"The others were culled and eliminated," Maire says. "They were too dangerous."

"Why not you?"

"I think Oceana did what she could to protect me," Maire says. "And I told you. I am always willing to do what I must to stay alive."

Her voice is hard. I wonder what she has done. I don't want to ask.

"Stay with me when we get Above," Maire says. "Do what I say. I promised my sister I would take care of you, and I will."

In this moment I believe her. I can see from True's face that he does, too.

If this is the moment of my own death, this time I want to inhabit it. I reach out and hold True's hand, and his fingers tighten around mine. And I imagine what our transport looks like moving up through the water, from dark to light, past the uncurious fish and the dying coral, on to things I have never seen but know enough to imagine, like sand on a shore, and birds swimming on the surface of the ocean, dipping their beaks down to eat.

"Remember," the deepmarket siren says to all of us as the transport stops. "Our voices are the Below's best weapons. We are miracles, meant for this moment."

I don't know that I'm a miracle, but I do believe I was meant for this moment Above, however long or short it may be.

CHAPTER 23

The door slides open, and for the first time in my life I see both sky and land, and they are blue and gray and green and brown and so much lighter than the deep of the ocean that I feel dizzy.

I am Above.

Whatever else happens, I am Above.

It is all glinting light and moving air, light coming down from the sky and reflecting on the water, on the metal bridge that leads from the transport to the shore, air touching every inch of my skin, warm. The sun is a hot, orange circle, like a single piece of coin burning as it dips toward the ocean. I grab on to the rail of the bridge that leads to the land, unsteady on my feet. And then I think I'm going to be sick. It is disconcerting in the extreme to be standing over the water, to see the top of the ocean. It might be how people who live Above would feel if they could stand over the sky.

"It's all right," Maire says, and she holds my arm and helps me cross the bridge.

I take my first step ever on real land—on sand, fine and white and brown and mixed through with grass and shells, so much texture, more than even the woodwork in the temple, more than I've seen in all my life.

I suck in deep lungfuls of the air, rich and warm and oxygenated, even though I know it's also thick with pollution and the particulate matter that will eat my lungs away with cancer. My hands still have salt on them from the sea, from my attempt to surface hours ago.

"Rio," True says. "Trees."

He's right. There are silver-gray trees with ash-colored moss hanging from them growing right up out of the sand a few feet in front of us. The color is similar to the trees I know, but they are not the trees I know—these trees are alive, and when their leaves fall off, no one bothers to put them back on because new ones grow. And you could never reattach these fallen leaves—soft, brittle as paper, crumbling in my hands as I bend down to pick them up. I can't help myself.

And then Maire's voice is in my ear, and she's pulling me back up to my feet and away from the leaves. When I turn around, I am stunned to see that the transport has already disappeared Below.

I didn't even hear it go.

Maire speaks to me quickly as we cross the sand to join the other sirens, who ascend a low, wooden platform. It appears as if it were made from trees like the ones growing on the island. "I have a plan," Maire says, "for you and True to escape."

I listen.

"Behind those rocks on your left," Maire says, "there is a little inlet. Climb in and swim and follow the curve of the inlet. You'll find a cave, farther back along this shore. Hide there. Wait until it's nearly dark, if you can. And then swim from this island to the main isle and go to the temple. You'll see it as soon as you come over that rise." She points across the water to the shore of the main island.

"How do you know all this?" I ask.

"One of the voices told me," Maire says. She sounds sad. "This way is best. You would never have survived the floodgates. Your lungs would have burst in the ascent. That's why I told Nevio what you were doing. We were just in time."

So she *was* the one who betrayed me. But how did she know?

"It was another way up," Maire says, "and you hadn't chosen mine. At least you have a chance this way."

"She's telling the truth," True says to me softly. "But I think you know that."

"No," I say. "I don't."

We've reached the other sirens. They stand in a line on the platform, their robes of blue undulating in the wind.

People sit in boats near the shore, waiting. People from the Above. "What are they carrying?" I ask, loud enough that the other sirens can hear. "Are those weapons?"

"It doesn't matter if they are," one of the sirens says, her tone so confident that I almost believe her.

The sirens have no weapons except for their voices. This is a fool's errand, one of Nevio's devising, one that will end in destruction and silence. Why is he doing this? Does he want to be the last siren in the Below? Does he even want to save Atlantia at all?

Nevio himself is nowhere in sight. The other sirens look around for him, too. "It's all right," one of them says. "He must be here somewhere."

The people in the boats wait. The boats are gray, like the trees.

The deepmarket siren raises her arms. The rest look up at her, eager to respond.

"What are the gifts given to we who live Below?" she asks, exactly as my mother used to do on the anniversary of the Divide, as Nevio did this year on the day Bay left and again on the transport.

Where *is* Nevio now?

And why did he cause the breach in the deepmarket? So that the sirens would come up to try to save the city, thinking that the breach had been an attack from the Above? Will he tell the people Below that the sirens offered themselves as sacrifices to save Atlantia, or will he tell the citizens that the Council purged the Below of our dangerous, evil presence?

Either way, he thinks we are all going to die.

Are we?

"Save your voice," Maire whispers to me. "But move your lips. So that you don't draw attention from the others. Don't try to escape until I tell you."

After a beat of silence, the sirens all begin calling in response, their voices as textured as this land Above. And it is true that their voices are even more powerful here. I feel the air shivering with sound.

"Long life, health, strength, and happiness."

"What is the curse of those who live Above?" the deepmarket siren asks.

"Short life, illness, weakness, and misery."

"Is this fair?"

"It is fair. It is as the gods decreed at the time of the Divide. Some have to stay Above so that humanity might survive Below."

"Then give thanks."

I don't join my voices with the sirens.

I do not speak for the gods. All I ever wanted was to speak for me.

The siren begins asking the questions again. And this time Maire joins her voice with the others.

It is the most sorrowful, singing sound I have ever heard. Through the frightening, layered unison of the other voices, there is Maire's, apart though she speaks at the same time and with the same words. Her voice is the sound of blue and brown, of trees with no leaves and flooded marketplaces and candles lit in memory of people now gone and gods who never were, a begging, pleading, asking the people of the Above to let us live in our place Below. She is not telling like the others, she is asking.

But even Maire's voice is not working. I don't know how I know; I just do. I can't see the faces of the people on the boats. The boats move up and down on the waves, each moment closer to us. The people watch the sirens. They wait for something. Their faces are terribly blank. I have an impression of unmoving lips, staring eyes. I realize that they wear masks. To protect them from the air? To hide their faces?

The sirens' voices swell, like a wave of the sea. They rise and fall, the commanding, the cajoling, the sweetness of some voices, the poison of others.

The deepmarket siren has been calling over the water and now she turns back to us to continue the litany.

She opens her mouth and lifts her hands. But she doesn't speak. She falls.

I don't understand at first. Neither do the others. One voice less, they keep speaking.

"And have mercy on us.

"And on those who live Above."

The fallen siren does not move.

The people of Atlantia always thought we had the upper hand over the people of the Above, that we had the power.

But we were wrong.

Somehow, the sirens' miraculous voices have lost their effect on the people of the Above.

The sirens begin calling for the people of the Above to *go back, go back. Leave. Leave.*

"Why aren't our voices working?" one siren asks another in panic.

Another siren starts to run. Before she's taken more than a few steps, the people in the boats shoot her down, too. True cries out and goes to kneel beside her, to see if there is something he can do, but of course there is nothing. She doesn't even breathe, only bleeds.

I stare in horror at her crumpled body, her robe pooled blue around her. I think, *Like the bat.*

The miracles are dying. The sirens no longer have power to dictate what happens Above.

I open my mouth to beg for True. Perhaps I could tell the people in the boats that True's not a siren, convince them to spare his life.

But then Maire is beside me, speaking into my ear low and urgent. "Save your voice," she says. "You will need it later." She smiles at me. "I have enough power to distract them now while you run. I can make them forget there were two more people on the island today."

"But what about you?" I ask.

Another siren falls, but we three are safe.

Maire takes my hand and presses something hard and fragile into it. I don't even have to look to know that she has given me another shell. "She will tell you everything," she says. "You will believe it, if you hear it from her. But I had to save it for a long time. She will speak just once. Be sure you listen."

"Who?" I ask, hardly daring to hope.

"Your mother," Maire says. She closes her eyes. "My *sister*." Her voice is so full of pride and love that it brings tears to my eyes. It is how I want to speak of Bay. It is how I hope Bay speaks of me.

"You loved her," I say.

"Always," Maire says. "I love her still."

With her eyes closed and her voice soft like this, she looks the smallest bit like my mother, her sister.

"She loved you," I say.

"Of course she did," Maire says. "And I care enough about myself to want redemption for the things I've done." Before I can ask what she means, what she's done, whether she believes in the gods after all, she opens her eyes and looks right at me.

"You didn't care about me until you heard my voice," I say.

"Your voice is part of you," Maire says. "So when I say that I love your voice, which I do, I am also saying that I love you."

"But you didn't love me without it."

"No," she says. "I didn't. Not as much. But that is the kind of person I am." She pauses. "Would you love me without my voice?"

I have a strange thought. Perhaps I could love her *more* without her voice.

She sees what I am thinking.

"Yes," she says. "That is how it has always been for me."

My cheeks are wet.

"Maire," I say, "how do you know you can do this? How do you know *I* can do this?"

"My dear," Maire says, "the only chance of success is to trust in your own power."

And then she gestures for us to run, and she moves away from me, calling out to the people in the boats.

"Listen," she says. In a voice full of power but also hope, and kindness, no curses, no fear. It's golden, beautiful, pure. When I hear it, I believe in her as absolutely as I used to believe in my mother. I *know* Maire has the power to save us.

But we have to go now.

I reach out and try to touch the sleeve of her robe in farewell, but she doesn't turn. True grabs my hand, and we run across the sand, our feet sinking in, our breath coming hard. I glance back once but I can't see Maire.

What has happened to her? Has she disappeared? Is she dead?

True and I pull off our robes and leave them on the shore. I slip into the water, the shell Maire gave me clutched tight in my hand, her perfect voice ringing in my ears. And then, for the first time in my life, I swim in the sea Above.

CHAPTER 24

True and I huddle together inside the cave, wet and waiting. There's not much to hear besides the water as it pushes against the walls of the cave. The constant sound of it reminds me of Atlantia breathing.

We made it.

And the sirens are dying.

My exhilaration over the success of our swim vanishes.

What have I done?

I left Maire behind because I wanted to get True away from the people in the boats, but now he's safe in the cave.

"I need to go back," I say.

"They'll kill you, too," True says. "We have to trust Maire and do what she said."

"I don't know if I can."

"You have to," True says. "It's what she wanted. If you go back, you betray her. You need to let Maire save you." He moves a little, readjusting his position, and then he says, his voice almost angry, "*Why* did you try to go up through the floodgates if Maire told you she could take you up a different way? You could have died."

"Some of us don't have the luxury of knowing when Maire is telling the truth."

"But you could have trusted me," True says. "You could have told me what you planned to do."

"You would have tried to talk me out of it," I say. "You might have even turned me in to the Council to try to save my life."

True's silent.

"I need to go back," I say again. It is all I can do to keep my real voice from breaking through. I have to save it. Maire told me so.

Did she use her voice on me to convince me to leave her with the other sirens? Could it be that she's done all of this just to get me to the surface?

She gave me a shell, one that holds my mother's voice.

What if it tells me something that I desperately need to know?

I want to hear my mother speak. It has been more than a year without her, and I am afraid and Above.

I hold up the shell. I clutched it tight in my hand the whole time we swam, and suddenly I worry that time will have taken away her voice, that there will be nothing left but the sound of water and wind.

"I have to listen to this," I tell True. "I can only hear it once."

He looks at me like he did back at the lanes in the deepmarket, as if he doesn't understand but is with me anyway, and nods.

I put the shell to one ear.

And then I hear her voice and my hands start to shake. True puts his hand over mine to help me hold the shell steady, but he turns his face away to let me listen in privacy.

So, she says. *This is everything I have learned about the sirens and the Divide and our gods.*

It's her. It's really her. She must have told this to Maire, and Maire saved it. How did Maire know she would need it?

The Divide did not happen exactly the way we were taught, my mother says. Her voice is not the one she used over the pulpit. It is low, urgent, intimate, the voice she used with someone she loved. Someone she trusted. *Some of it happened the way we've been told: People were chosen for the Above and the Below. Everyone Above had someone Below who they cared about so they would keep the Below alive.*

But the rest of it, the religion, came later.

The temple, the gods, all of it, was a facade, a conceit. It was a way to make things beautiful Below while evoking the old cultures of the Above. No one believed in the gods as gods. They thought they were gargoyles. Decorations.

But then the miracles began to happen.

First the sirens, and then the bats.

And then the people came to believe. They built their religion around the miracles.

You know all this.

Thank you for unlocking the door to the Council's secret library for me. Thank you for making it so that I could read the papers. So that I could hold the evidence in my hands.

I'm sorry that I couldn't believe in your voices in the walls.

You were right.

I should have listened to you.

Because now it may be too late.

I read other things in those papers.

Did you also know that the air Above became clean enough to live in years ago? Though still polluted, it is much more safe to live there now. But by the time this happened, the Above wanted nothing to do with us. They hated us for our sirens but

loved us for the ore we could deliver. So they reached a con-
clusion—they would keep us alive as long as the mines kept
producing.

But the mines are running out of ore.

The Council of the Below decided that the Minister always
had to be a true believer, which is part of the reason they selected
me. How else could I convince the people if I didn't believe myself? And the people Below had to be convinced, had to believe
their lives were wonderful and safe, so they could keep mining
and keep Atlantia running so that we wouldn't be cut off. The
people of the Above have no desire to live or work in Atlantia.
They think it's dirty, broken. They think we as a people are dirty
and broken, too.

We are not the only Above, and not the only Below. We are an
outpost, one among many, strewn across the great islands of the
sea. The cities Below were where the fortunate once lived and
worked, but now the roles have been reversed.

Sirens have appeared in all the Belows. Our mines have
lasted longer than anyone else. And the other Aboves have—and
I cannot bear to say this—

The other Aboves have killed all their sirens. They found that
it was very easy to do, because even if some of the sirens escaped
the drowning of their cities, even if no one catches or kills them,
they can't survive for more than a few days Above. They belong
to the Below.

What? I am so shocked that I pull the shell away from my
ear, forgetting that I will lose her voice. I pull it back fast, to
listen again. My heart pounds hard inside my chest.

I can't live without the Below. I can't live here Above. And
everyone like me has been or will be killed.

I push my hand, hard, into my mouth so that I won't scream.

We have the last sirens, my mother says, *and it is a matter of time before the Above tells our Council to get rid of our sirens, too. And our Council will listen, because if they don't, they will die. Everything they've done to deceive us has been to save themselves when the time comes.*

So we *have to save the sirens. We have to appeal to the people of the Above and the Below, so that they will see that this is wrong.*

We have to save Atlantia, too. They let us send up our children once a year on the anniversary of the Divide, but I don't know how many more people the Above will allow to come up. I don't think they care about saving all of Atlantia. Though survival is possible in the Above, the people there see us as drains on their resources, as parasites. Which we were, for many years. But as things are right now, the sirens cannot live for long outside Atlantia. They can't last without the water above them.

Will you help me? I have to save you, and I have to save—

My mother stops. She doesn't say my name, but I wonder if that is when Maire realized that I could be a siren. If, when I spoke in the temple, it was the confirmation of something she'd already guessed.

Maybe if you spoke to the people Above—

It has to be a pure siren? What does that mean?

A pause. And then it sounds like she's saying something back that has just been said to her.

Someone who has saved her voice for years. Who has never used her voice for the Council. Who loves the Below as much as she loves herself. Do I know anyone like that?

I hear her breathing. She was thinking of me.

I do not.

She lied. She lied to my aunt, for me.

Or maybe she didn't think I loved the Below enough.

Perhaps you could go up and speak. Let them see what a siren really is. You could use your power for a greater good, instead of for all the Council's little evils.

I know you've done what you had to do to survive, and so have I.

But now we have to do something more.

Together.

It will take both of us to save the sirens.

It will take both of us to save Atlantia.

My mother always protected me.

And Maire was right. My mother always underestimated me.

She underestimated Bay, too.

I press the shell tight against my ear. I listen and listen and listen, but my mother is gone.

How can I tell True all of this?

He can see I'm finished. He takes his hand away from mine and wraps his arms around me. Without saying a word, he pulls me close.

His body feels warm against mine, and his breathing is as steady as the ocean. I match my breathing to his, and my body, too.

The world is coming apart around us—water through the rivets in Atlantia, sirens dying on the shore. I should feel numb, should feel nothing in the presence of too much—learning the truth about my world, learning that I can't survive for long here Above. But what I feel right now, in this moment, is True—and alive.

And he's right. I have to do what Maire said. I trust her.

"I think it's time to swim again," I say. "To the shore this time."

True bends his head so that it rests against mine. He will come with me.

I wonder what waits for us there, if we'll ever be together like this again. True's lips skim my cheekbone and then he finds my mouth and I kiss him back, reaching to touch the beautiful planes of his face. And I am filled with melancholy and triumph. We might die here, but we made it here, together.

Everyone dies. They don't all have the chance to see what they wanted most. At least I've seen the Above. At least I've known True.

CHAPTER 25

The swim to the shore is longer than our quick foray into the cove, and the water feels more wild and dark now, the waves buffeting me on all sides, slapping their way into my mouth and stinging my eyes, but I feel like I recognize the swim in some way. Somehow I know how to push through it all.

That time spent in the tanks wasn't wasted.

I come ashore. True isn't far behind me.

I feel a million tiny grains of sand under my bare feet. We left our shoes in the cave because they were too heavy; they might have weighed us down. A crust of shells on the sand marks the place where the water must come highest. Neither of us says anything, but True takes my hand again as we climb the rise. In my other hand I carry the empty shell that held my mother's voice. I can't let go of it.

Grasses grow sharp in the sand, and so do small, scrubby bushes with flat, green leaves. Insects hum loudly, the sound heavy in the warm air.

Once we're over the rise, we see the city.

An *outdoor* city, bursting and sparkling with lights, and the temple spire points tall above all the other buildings.

We're barefoot, and dripping-damp. But there's nothing we can do about that. We have to hope that the near dark will be enough to cover us. "We need to hurry," I say.

Night falls fast, but it isn't as absolute as night in Atlantia. Now and then, through the miasma of ruined air, I think I can pick out a star.

I can't help but stare at everything as we come closer—people, streets, shops—even though I don't want my gaze to invite any attention. I'm glad the swimming has removed all the siren makeup from my face, but I still feel that anyone could tell that I came from someplace else.

What did Bay think when she saw all this? What does True think now? I glance over at him, but in this light his eyes are as dark as the earth.

The Above has no gondolas, but it has other, faster, uglier ways of transport—wheeled carts spinning and racing so quickly that it's hard for me to know where I can walk and where I can't. Some of the carts are enormous. There are also many, many people walking and running everywhere, and they all seem to be in a hurry. The air is so thick and hot and moist that it has made everyone's hair bedraggled and their clothes cling with sweat, and others look as dirty and damp as we do. Still, I can't relax. *We have to get to the temple.* That is where the road ends, where Maire's instructions lead.

The voices of the people around us sound so strange, so flat after all the sirens calling, that I have a hard time understanding the words, though our language is the same. The cadence of their speaking sounds as choppy as the waves under the wind, and they have an accent I've never heard before.

Of course I've never heard it before. I've never been Above before.

The buildings are scarred and dirt- and dusk-colored, not the bright hues of Atlantia. Someone brushes against me accidentally and nods in apology but doesn't stop. I have never seen so many people moving so quickly. The Above teems with inhabitants.

I hear laughter coming from what smells like a restaurant, and shop doors stand open even though it is so late.

Atlantia is nothing compared to this. I am nothing compared to this.

And I feel light, knowing that I am nothing and that there is nothing above me but air. No water pressing down, no walls holding everything in and pushing everything back.

It is strange and unfamiliar, and I know that I can't survive here for long, but I love it. And I want to stay.

True and I become lost and found several times in the darkening streets. To get our bearings again, we find a place where the buildings aren't so close and look up to see the spire of the temple. I hurry, always conscious of the strange feeling of earth underfoot, sand between my toes, dust beneath my heels, and now and then the smooth roundness of a stone. True and I don't talk, afraid that someone will hear our accents and realize we don't belong Above, but we touch. His hand on my shoulder, me reaching back for him.

And then, without speaking, we stop at the same time.

Maire said I would know the temple, and I do, even though it's different from the one Below.

It's made of metal instead of stone, and it appears to be formed from chunks of other buildings welded together. I want to run my fingers along the rivets and see how well it all meets. And the whole building is covered in an oxidation of green, like it grew up out of the ground. I've heard of this before—pollution so bad that it can corrupt even metal, but in the moment it's beautiful.

True and I stand together, Above, in front of the temple, our clothes damp and our feet dirty. The door is not open, perhaps to keep out the air, but when I turn the handle, it moves easily. It's unlocked. It must be accessible at all hours, open to the people who need to pray, the way our temple is in the Below.

But I am afraid to enter.

Someone mutters and pushes past me. There are others who want to go inside, and I should move.

"Rio?" True asks.

"Bay," I say, remembering why I'm here, and I take a step inside.

The temple is fairly crowded, and no one seems to notice us come in.

I take a few more steps. It is so different and so much the same. The pews, the quietness, the softened voices and prayers. True and I walk past a woman crying and a priest comforting.

The gargoyle gods watch us. They don't adorn only the walls but also sit welded into place, like permanent worshippers, on some of the pews. Why, I wonder, and then in a moment I know, when I see their eaten faces, their pockmarked bodies, the way the air turned them green like they have been long underwater. The air. I had to weld our gods back into the trees for upkeep; the priests here brought their gods inside for shelter when the air was at its worst and have not yet taken them back out.

I stop in my tracks, utterly fascinated. High up, a seahorse curls its tail on a plinth, its head seemingly bowed in prayer while it supports the weight above. A whale with a bulbous head and startled eyes pushes out from the wall, and on the pew nearest me, a spiky-tailed shark shows its teeth. They are supposedly the same gods we have Below, with different forms, and they seem at once foreign and familiar. They would have had to make these after the advent of the sirens.

What would it be like, to make a religion? To fashion your own gods?

The pulpit is inlaid with shells from the Below, with a design similar to our waves that become trees. On their pulpit the trees turn and roll into clouds. It's beautiful. And I can't help but wonder if there are any voices trapped inside those shells. I close my hand around the one in my pocket.

As we approach the altar, I notice a large jar of water in the place where the jar of dirt sits in the temple in Atlantia.

And for a moment, I allow myself to imagine that this is another version of home, one where I find my twin and perhaps my mother, too, that she will come in to stand behind the pulpit to speak saving words to all of us, and she'll notice me and rush to take me in her arms and say, *All along we were here, Rio. We were waiting for you to come to the right place.*

I'm crying now without a sound. For the loss of my mother, and for Maire. I know she's gone, too. Somehow I can tell that her voice will never again be heard under the water or over the wind.

She is nowhere Above and nowhere Below.

And neither is my mother.

But my sister might be.

"Bay?" a man's voice says, close behind me, and my heart pounds with familiarity and fear. This used to happen all the time Below—someone has mistaken me for Bay. What can I say that won't give me away?

"Bay?" the man asks again, sounding puzzled.

I turn around. But he isn't talking to me. He's speaking to the real Bay, who has stopped in the middle of the aisle leading to the altar, staring at me as if she can't believe what she sees.

And I don't believe my eyes, either, though this is where I hoped I'd find her, though this is what I wanted more than anything else for so long, though almost everything I've done has been because I knew I had to see my sister again.

I see my sister again.

CHAPTER 26

I want to say something and I can't.

I'm afraid she'll leave the way she did the last time I saw her. Turn her back on me and walk away, again.

That she'll be angry with me for coming, because it isn't safe for me here.

But Bay throws her arms around me, and she's crying. I hold on so tight. She whispers into my ear, *"You're here. How?"*

It's such a long story. I don't even know where to begin. Priests stare at us and the gods sit among the people in the pews and my mother and Maire are dead. And the Above is not what I've been told it was all my life and I don't care, I love it anyway, and I can't live here. I'm a siren and no one wants me to live anywhere.

"Rio," Bay says, and I feel her smoothing down my hair, holding me close. I'm a mermaid girl, tears in my hair, salt on my skin, barely able to breathe under the heavy weight of what's happened and light with the relief of seeing my sister at last.

Bay leads True and me to a storage room at the back of the temple, a place full of boxes and books and odds and ends. She goes to a closet at the back of the room and pulls out some old robes for us to wear over our still-damp clothes from the Below. All the time I can't stop staring at my sister. It hasn't been long, but I can't believe how imperfectly I remembered her. I thought I remembered everything, but I didn't. I forgot how she moves when she wants to be quiet, how that looks. I forgot her profile when she's turned three-quarters away from me, how her ear from that angle is small and fine, like a shell. I realize that I didn't hold on to the exact color of her eyes.

She's cut her hair shorter, and her skin is tanned from the sun. Her arms look strong—I can see the muscles in them, even more defined than when she practiced in the lanes every day. There are dark shadows under her eyes, the kind that speak of weeks without enough sleep, rather than one single harrowed night.

Her voice still sounds gentle but also huskier—perhaps a result of breathing the air Above—and she's taken on their accent. Even so, I remembered the tone of it perfectly. It is the one thing I have remembered exactly right, I realize. Maire told the truth. I do know how to listen.

And then I finally say something.

"Maire," I say. I have to tell Bay what happened to Maire.

Bay flinches slightly at the sound of my flat voice. Did she forget already how ugly it sounds?

"It's not that," she whispers to me, as if she can read my mind. *"It's just that when I imagine you speaking, you're always using your real voice."*

"The sirens all came up," I say to Bay, "and the people Above killed them."

"No," Bay says, gripping my arm so hard that it hurts. *"No.* Are you sure?"

"I saw it happen," I say. "So did True." At that moment I realize that I haven't introduced True and Bay to each other, but before I can say anything else, someone opens the door.

It's a priest, wearing one of the sober brown robes, the same man who said Bay's name earlier out by the altar. He's a round little middle-aged man, unremarkable except for his kind expression and shock of unruly gray hair. And he's followed by Fen, the boy from the Below. Fen looks terrible—his eyes wild and tired, his hair a mess. He can't stop coughing. I take a step back in alarm.

"Don't be afraid," Fen says. "It's not contagious." He claps a mask over his face and breathes deeply. And then his eyes widen. "True," he says.

True grins, and the two of them embrace. Before True can draw back, Fen starts coughing again.

Bay glances over at Fen but then looks back at me. *"Who was killing the sirens?"*

Should I talk about this in front of Fen and the priest? Can they be trusted? Bay seems to think that they can.

"The people in the boats killed the sirens." It sounds stupid, and I shake my head in frustration. So much needs to be said, and quickly. "We all came up together on the transport. And when we arrived, people were waiting for us in boats. They never came ashore, but they started killing the sirens. True and I were the only ones who escaped, as far as I know. Maire helped us."

"Where is she?" Bay asked.

I can't answer.

"They killed *Maire*?" Bay asks, stunned, as if such a thing could never be true. I understand her. It seems impossible that Maire could have survived, but it also seems impossible that she could die.

"I think so," I tell Bay. "I didn't see."

"So you *left* them," Fen says.

It is exactly the wrong thing to say.

"*You* left us," I say to him. To Bay.

You left us.

"I'm sorry, Rio," Bay says. "We did. I did. I left." Her voice breaks.

Bay knows the question I'm going to ask. I can't help it. Even though I know the reason from the letter, I want to hear Bay tell me in person. Bay, who has dirt under her fingernails and short-cut hair and a patch of skin peeling on her nose, who has been living the life I intended for myself Above while I've been living out her time Below.

"Why did you leave?"

"I thought it was the best way to keep you safe," Bay says. There are tears in her eyes. "I made a mess of everything. I didn't know that the Above was going to kill the sirens and cut off Atlantia. Our mother didn't tell me."

"She didn't tell me, either," I say.

"We must go back to the island and see if there is anyone left to save," says the priest. He moves, and an emblem around his neck glints in the light. It's oxidized to a green color, not shiny like the one my mother wore, but the insignia is similar. It mirrors the image on the pulpit here in the temple Above—trees turning into clouds.

This is no priest. This is their Minister.

"It's all right, Rio," Bay says. "This is Ciro, the Minister." She leans closer and whispers to me. *"Don't worry. He's nothing like Nevio."*

How can she be sure? We knew Nevio for most of our lives and would never have believed him capable of murder. Bay has known this Minister for a few weeks. How can she be sure that we can trust him?

As far as I'm concerned, there is one Minister I trust and she is dead.

"Let me see what I can find out," Ciro says to Bay. "Stay here. Keep them hidden." He reaches up and touches the insignia around his neck. "May the gods be with us all," he says, and he moves quickly through the door.

"What does he mean, keep us hidden?" I ask Bay.

"The temple is the only place you might be safe," she says. "And even here, not for long. It's dangerous Above."

I know that. It's dangerous for me everywhere.

"You trust Ciro," I say. "Why?"

"Because he is the leader of the movement to save the Below," Bay says. "He believes that the Above should not let Atlantia die."

"Why would he care about any of us?" I ask.

"Because of the shells," Bay says.

Because of the shells. What does she mean?

"I didn't know anything about them until I came Above," Bay says. "But Ciro told me. And others, too. There have been shells coming up with the bodies for years—in the pockets of the dead, or tied around their necks like amulets. At first the cullers—the ones who take any valuables they can find from the corpses that make it through the mines—threw away the shells on the beach. You can find them everywhere up here—they're not worth much. But then, one day, someone picked one up. And heard a voice. A voice from the Below. Not a siren voice, commanding. Just a human voice, talking.

"The voice disappeared after it had been heard once," Bay says. "People thought that the first person was making things up. But then others started walking along the shore and picking up shells and listening, and sometimes they heard people speaking, too. The cullers began to realize that the shells with the voices in them must be the shells they found on the bodies from the Below. They started bringing those shells to Ciro instead of discarding them. The sounds of the voices broke his heart.

"For years there have been people up here listening. Not everyone Above wants us to die. People here believe the shells and the voices must be from the gods. No one knows how else such a miracle could have happened."

But I do.

Maire was the miracle.

She saved the voices.

I discovered long ago that some of the best voices can be heard in the prison walls. She told me that earlier. I wonder if those are some of the stories she sent up. People trapped, wanting to be free.

When Maire saved Bay's voice for me in that first shell, it must have been without Bay knowing. That explains why Bay was singing, not giving me a message. The secret of saved voices in shells was between Maire and Oceana, and then between Maire and me. She shared it first with her sister, and then with a siren.

Maire couldn't have known that Ciro would find the shells. She just hoped that someone would.

"The people here have heard our stories," Bay says. "They feel like they know us."

"But they still don't believe the sirens are human," True says. "They killed them."

"Some still hate the sirens," Bay says. "But there are many, like Ciro, who believe the sirens are human, too, and that getting rid of them is wrong."

"That's better than some of the people Below," I say. "Not many of them think that sirens are human."

"Rio," Bay says, and then she stops. What can she say? I've had to spend my life hiding my voice, and she's had to spend her life protecting me, and that's not what either of us would have chosen. We've both suffered because of what I am.

No. Not because of what I am. Because of the way people fear those who are different, when really we are so much the same.

"There's something I still don't understand," I say. "If siren voices are so powerful up here, how did the people Above resist the sirens on the island?"

"I don't know," Bay says.

I wish Bay and I didn't have to talk about all of this. I wish we didn't have to think of sirens and saving. I could tell her that True kissed me and that I was fast, so fast in the lanes. She could tell me how she feels about Fen and what she dreams of becoming without a siren sister to protect. But there's no time for that.

Will there ever be time for it again?

I sit down on the floor, suddenly weary. I put my head in my hands. It's getting harder to breathe, and I can't stop thinking of Maire.

I feel my sister's hand on my back.

"There *are* people who will help us," Bay says. "I've met many of them. They come to minister to those of us from Below who work in the labor camps."

"What do you mean about working in the labor camps?" I ask. Fen coughs in the background, and he sounds horrible. "Fen doesn't sound like he should be in a labor camp," I say. "He sounds sick."

That makes Fen laugh. "They don't care about that," he says. "They're not concerned about our health."

"They only let us keep coming up from the Below because we're free labor," Bay says.

"They think we're stupid," Fen says. "And they're right. We don't know the first thing about the way the world really is."

"They work us to death," Bay says. "We're allowed a free hour or two at night, and that's when we're supposed to come into town and take care of whatever needs we might have. We make a single coin a day. It's enough to buy only the smallest amount of food at the worst shops."

"You know your sister," Fen says, grinning at me. "Instead of getting anything to eat that first day, she headed straight for the temple."

"It was good we did," Bay says, "because we met Ciro. Now we come here every night."

No wonder she looks exhausted, if she works all day and then comes to the temple in the evening.

"I'm sure that the gods would forgive you if you missed a few prayers," I say.

Fen laughs again. "We don't just come for the gods," he says. "We come to show the people of the Above that we're like anyone else."

Fen starts coughing again, harder this time. It sounds terrible, dry and achy and bone-breaking. The air up here is still not clean, but he seems to be affected more than anyone else.

I glance over at Bay, at her tired eyes and her short hair, and I wonder if she cut it off because she couldn't braid it without me, or if she cut it off so she wouldn't have to remember me, or for a reason that had absolutely nothing to do with me.

"Please," she says to Fen. "Put it on."

I realize that she means the mask, which he holds at his side.

"I feel like I can't breathe at all when I'm wearing that thing."

"But it does help," she says. "Even if you can't tell. It buys you time."

"We're not sure of that," Fen says. But he puts on the mask.

"The air Above," I say, "is it doing this?"

"No," Fen says, his voice sounding like mine now, flat and neutralized through the mask. "I have water-lung. I had it before I came Above. The air isn't helping, but I'd be in trouble anyway. The mask helps me breathe."

My heart sinks for my sister. There's no cure for water-lung.

"How long have you known?" True asks, looking as stunned as I feel.

"I figured it out a few months before the celebration of the Divide," Fen says. "I could feel it happening."

"You didn't tell me," True says.

"I didn't tell anyone. They sell stuff in the deepmarket that can help you keep from coughing so that no one will know. It's not good for you, but I didn't care. If I was going to die anyway, what did it matter? That's when I started swimming in the night races, to keep my mind off things. And that's where I met Bay. When I found out she was going Above, I decided to come with her."

"We've learned since that there are doctors here who might be able to help Fen—they've gotten good at fixing people's lungs with all these years of pollution—but no one will waste any time on someone from the Below," Bay says.

"It's all right," Fen says. "We didn't know that when we came. I just hoped to be with you and see the Above before I died." He smiles at her and she smiles back immediately, lights up as hot and bright as the sun in an instant. She loves him.

And he's in love with her. I can tell from the things he says and from the way he looks at her.

She told him she was leaving.

But she didn't tell me.

Because she thought she had to protect me.

For a minute anger breaks over me as strong as waves against rocks. Anger at my mother and my sister, for loving me but always sheltering me. Anger at the people Below who want to contain the sirens and the people Above who want to kill them. And most of all, anger at the long-ago, greedy people who brought us to the point where the only way to survive was to Divide. Those people used up everything. They wasted the trees; they burned through the air. They didn't care, or if they did, they didn't care enough, and now we're the ones paying the price of their extravagance.

I think Bay might be angry, too.

She has also been trying to hold things in all her life. Trying not to upset me so that I wouldn't risk speaking too loudly, trying to build her own life around protecting me. It couldn't have been what she wanted, but she did it anyway. When our eyes meet, I know we are both angry at each other and that we love each other, just as it has always been and will always be.

"Maire wasn't supposed to die," Bay says, and her voice breaks. "She and I talked about it, before I left. She was supposed to keep you from coming here. She was supposed to use *her* voice to keep you safe."

Maire was supposed to use her own voice.

Instead she taught me about mine.

CHAPTER 27

$\mathcal{I}$t's morning when Ciro the Minister opens the door again and comes back inside the temple storage room. I know as soon as I see his face that he does not have good news for us. "I'm very sorry," he says. "My sources on the Council confirm that all the sirens are dead." In that moment I hate him, I hate his voice, the way it sounds, what he's saying.

"There were twenty-seven bodies retrieved from the island," Ciro tells us.

Twenty-seven. There were twenty-nine of us on the transport, but that number included True and me.

There's so much I want to say. But Maire said to wait. She kept telling me to wait.

Until when?

She said I would know.

"Are they *sure* that everyone died?" Bay asks.

"Yes," Ciro says, glancing over at True and me. Ciro must have deduced that we came with the sirens—how else would we have come to the surface?—but he doesn't say it out loud. "They seem quite certain that no one on the island survived."

Maire's voice worked, at least for a little while. She was the most powerful siren Atlantia has ever known. Why didn't she save herself to save the world? Why did she think I should do it instead?

"Why would the people slaughter the sirens this way?" I ask. "The sirens can't even live for long Above."

"Some people are still fearful," Ciro says. "They're afraid that the sirens might find a way to survive up here. They wanted the sirens eliminated permanently. They didn't want to take any chances."

"So they killed them," I say.

"How?" Bay asks. "I thought the siren song was more powerful Above. I thought there was no way to escape it."

"The Councils of the Above and the Below found a way," Ciro says. "Or, I should say, your Minister found a way."

I feel cold. "Nevio," I say. "Is he Above?"

Ciro nods. His expression and voice are hard to read. "He and some of the Council of the Below came up on a transport right before the sirens did. Apparently he, and the members of the Council he selected to come with him, are immune to the siren voices."

"It was them," True says, his voice soft as the sand. "They were the ones who killed the sirens."

Don't scream, I tell myself. *Don't speak. Wait. It's not time yet.*

It all makes sense now. Nevio didn't come up with us. We thought he was coming up after, but he came up before. And then, with the Council members, the ones who killed my mother, he murdered the rest of the sirens. I don't think he'd get his own hands dirty; he'd orchestrate it, the way he did my mother's killing. I can picture him sitting on one of the boats and giving the command to mow down the sirens.

Nevio knew I was coming Above. He knew True was coming, too. He should know there are two missing. Why hasn't he said anything?

Bay's fingers find mine and she squeezes my hand.

Because Maire won.

Maire saved us.

She hid True and me from Nevio so absolutely, so well, that he forgot we came up at all.

She told the people to listen to her, and they did. It was for a single moment, but that moment was long enough to save our lives.

She was more powerful than the Council members who believed themselves immune. More powerful than their masks. More powerful than any of the other sirens.

In the end, she was more powerful than Nevio.

Why didn't she save herself?

Why did she save us instead?

What did Maire mean when she said she cared enough about herself to want redemption?

Did she *have* to save us?

If she believed that, did that also mean she believed in the gods?

I know now with utter certainty that she believed in *me*.

"How could your Council agree to this?" Bay asks.

"They did not all agree to it," Ciro says. "I did not agree to it, and neither did many others. We were unaware of the plan to kill the sirens. There is a great rift among us." He takes a deep breath. "Nevio and the Council members who came up with him have been granted asylum here permanently. It is their reward for helping the Above rid themselves of the sirens forever."

I should have known that Nevio could never be satisfied with the Below. He wanted the Above, too.

He and I are alike in that way, but I never wanted to rule the Above. I wanted to see it. To be a part of it.

I need to talk to Bay. I know Nevio's secret. I know that he's a siren. And she doesn't.

"Tonight some of the Council plans to bring all the siren bodies here to the temple for a public viewing," Ciro says. "I believe they hope to stir up public support for the death of Atlantia."

"But maybe it won't work that way," Bay says. "Maybe if they see the sirens' bodies, they'll realize they're human, like everyone else."

"You can be sure the Council will make them appear as inhuman as possible," Fen says.

They won't even have to do that, I realize. The sirens did that themselves—the makeup, the clothes.

"There is more," Ciro says. "The Council has invited a special guest to give a sermon after the viewing. Nevio will speak."

Nevio. Of course. He can't wait to use his voice here.

The people of the Above were right to be afraid, I realize. *A siren has come along to control them, and this time they don't even know that he's doing it.*

Nevio is using his voice on the people of the Above, just as he did on the people Below. He saw that Atlantia was dying, and so he decided to save himself and those who put him in power, those who helped him kill my mother. But how does he think he can survive up here long-term? Doesn't he know that sirens die Above? Can't he feel what I feel? I've been here for a matter of hours, and already I know I'm losing strength.

"Can't you stop him from speaking?" True asks.

The Minister shakes his head. "I've tried. Our Council is broken. We are split into factions. Those who believe as I do are in the minority." His voice breaks. It is such a normal voice, the voice of a person—perhaps of a very good, very wise person—but that is all. "I do not know how much longer I will be allowed to retain my position as Minister. Some are already suggesting Nevio as a replacement."

Ciro cannot compete with Nevio.

True looks at me. Should we tell Ciro? I shake my head the smallest bit. How can we trust someone we haven't known for very long with such a secret? Would he even believe us? And what could he do?

And I've had another thought. If I turn in Nevio, will they kill him? They might. My voice has to be pure if I'm going to use it the way Maire intended. It can't have caused someone else's death. Even Nevio's.

"All the sirens are gone," Fen says, shaking his head as if he can't believe it. He doesn't know about Nevio, either, of course.

"We don't know that," I say. "Maire hoped there were more." I don't say the rest in front of Ciro, but I can tell that Bay knows what I mean. *More like me. Hidden sirens.* And there are potential sirens not yet born. I think of all those voices that might never have a chance to sing.

"I'm afraid we don't have much time to mourn," Ciro says. "We need to direct our attention to saving Atlantia. The Council majority has already begun debating how many people should be rescued from the Below. As it stands, anyone who hasn't had a siren in her bloodline is considered suspect, because one could still appear. Those like you"—he looks at Bay and me—"who have a siren in your lineage might be allowed to come up and be rehabilitated."

The Minister doesn't know that I'm a siren.

Bay told him about Maire but not about me.

She's still keeping me safe.

She says she trusts Ciro, but she hasn't told him everything. Something's kept her from doing it. And if that's the case, I'd better not tell him about Nevio.

Maire's words come back to me. *There are some things you only tell a sister. And some things you only ask of a sister.*

Ciro looks at Fen. "They've also decided that anyone who has lost a family member to water-lung or who is infected with it themselves won't be rescued."

"But that's most of Atlantia," Bay says. "You'd be hard put to find anyone who didn't have water-lung in their line somewhere. And if you also rule out all the lines that haven't had a siren appear, there will be hardly anyone left that your Council considers worth saving."

"I know," Ciro says. "They are letting fear control them."

"They are murderers," Bay says. "Your people are murderers."

"And so are ours," Fen points out.

He's right. The people of Atlantia have not fought for us. They have been afraid of us, too. They have forgotten to see sirens as human, only as lonely miracles, and in the end they are the ones who killed us when we came Above.

"But someone has to go Below," Bay says, her face pale. "Someone has to tell the people there what Nevio and the Council have done to the sirens. And that the Council is leaving Atlantia to die."

"Going Below won't accomplish anything." I have to work hard to contain the bitterness in my voice. "We don't know that the people there will believe you. And even if so, what can they do?"

"Rio's right," Fen says. "There's no reason to risk yourself for them." He's trying to protect her. And he sounds as angry as I feel.

"There's *every* reason," Bay says. She knows I won't survive without Atlantia, but she can't say that in front of Ciro or he'll know what I am. She takes a deep breath. "The people living Below now have never known the full truth."

"If you go down and tell it to them, what does that change?" Fen asks. "The Council up here will still condemn most of Atlantia to death."

"Maire really believed there could be more sirens?" Bay asks.

"Yes," I say. "Hidden ones." *There might be more people like me.*

Of course there might be more like Nevio, too.

"Maybe, if there are any sirens left Below, and they knew that they were safe to speak, they could cry out to the gods to help us," True says. "Or maybe they will be heard Above somehow. They are miracles, after all."

"We *need* to tell the people," Bay says. "Whether they die or live, they need to know the truth. They need to send their voices, siren or not, up to the gods and to the people Above to beg for their lives. They need to agree to change, too." Bay pauses. "But it can't be a siren who tells them."

She's right. I know it. I know she was born for this. She has always loved Atlantia; she has always heard the city breathing. Thinking of the greater good comes naturally to her. She could have been the next Minister if she hadn't always been so busy protecting me. "How are you going to get Below?" I ask, and Bay turns to look at me in surprise. And then she smiles.

"They are sending one more transport down tonight," Ciro says. "There are a few Council members of the Below who have been granted asylum who were not in the initial group. I may be able to get you on board that transport, hidden somewhere. I have a favor I can call in. But we must be certain we want to spend it on this."

"Can you think of anything else we might do?" Bay asks.

Ciro pauses for a moment, then shakes his head. "I will ask those here to speak for the people Below. But perhaps the gods cannot answer our prayers until both the Above and the Below plead together."

We are all silent for a moment. The temple storage room smells like stone and books and old cloth, just like the temple Below.

"Then I will go," Bay says. "You believe you can arrange it?"

"Yes," says Ciro the Minister. "I am sure I can get you to the Below. But I don't know that I will be able to bring you back."

"I understand," she says.

"And I can't guarantee your safety in the Below," Ciro says. "How do you think your Council will react when they see you?"

"I'll do my best to avoid them," Bay says. "I'll try to slip out of the transport and go straight to the temple, as fast as I can. There are people there who will help me."

"What about the peacekeepers?" Fen asks. "And the other citizens of Atlantia? No one has ever come back who chose the Above. You don't know what they'll do. They might be angry or afraid when they realize you've returned."

"Maybe if they see me," Bay says, "they'll think of her. Of our mother."

"I'm coming, too," Fen says.

"No," Bay says. "You know what the change in pressure did to your lungs on the way up. You can't risk that again."

"I'll be fine."

"No," Bay says. "You won't."

Something passes across True's face, his kind, laughing face that has always known the sun before he even set foot on the sands of the Above.

True should go back, too.

He knows it and I know it.

If he goes, he'll tell the people what he can do. Perhaps he'll find out that there are more like him. It's possible. The citizens of Atlantia have been hiding our real selves from one another. If there could be more people like me, there could be others like True.

Would those Below be more willing to let the sirens live among them if they knew there were some who could tell when the sirens spoke lies or truth?

And True has always known that he loved the Below. He has always known that he belonged there.

He and I rode in that gondola together through the fog, but we have always had our own journeys, and I have known that from the beginning. I've felt it somehow.

Perhaps that is why I was so afraid to love him.

"It's the best way for you to help save us," I say.

True's jaw is clenched and I see tears in his eyes.

"We made it Above, together," I say, and though I don't use my real voice, I know he hears it, as he always has. In front of everyone, he lifts my hand to his lips and kisses my palm.

"I'll go with you," he says to Bay.

"What?" Fen asks, surprised.

"We have to go *now*," Ciro says. "There isn't much time before they'll send the transport down."

Bay looks at me, and for a moment the question passes between us—should I go, too? We don't know how long I can last up here. And if she and True both go back, then everyone I love will be Below.

I see the realization on Bay's face the minute I feel it in my own heart. I feel us coming closer, the time and space of our separation dwindling the more minutes we spend together. We have been apart, but we are one again now, the same thoughts, the same purpose.

And we both know that I have to stay here.

Maire sacrificed everything to bring me Above. It was so I could do something here, not so I could go back Below. Not yet. I haven't yet done what I came to do.

I came to speak.

"Tonight," I say to Ciro the Minister. "In the temple. When Nevio speaks. I need to try to say something to the people."

Ciro nods. "I will help you," he says. "I will make sure that we get you to the pulpit." And I wonder if he has guessed what I am, though none of us have said it out loud.

"No," Bay says. "Then Nevio will know you're here. It's too dangerous."

"It's dangerous for you, too," I say. "But we will be speaking at the same time, or close to it." Maire said I would know when it was time, and I can tell that it's coming. Can Bay feel it, too?

She puts her hand to her mouth, and her eyes well with tears. She does.

She knows I could die up here, and I know she could die down there.

And I know I will mean it more, I will ask for Atlantia with *all* my heart and voice, when the lives of everyone I love depend on what I say. That way, the people Above can hear my love for True and Bay—my missing them—in my voice. And hopefully, though she's not a siren, the people Below will be able to hear Bay's love for Fen and me.

To save our city, we have to leave the ones we love.

To save our city, we have to love each other *more* than ourselves.

Which is how much, I now know, Maire loved my mother. And it's how much Bay loves me.

She came up here to try to save me. Now we are both going to have to try to finish what our mother and our aunt began— the saving of the sirens, of Atlantia itself.

I pull my sister close and she wraps her arms around me tight. "At least you know why I'm going this time," she says, and I smile but I'm very close to tears. I do know why, but as it turns out, that does not make it easier.

CHAPTER 28

$\mathcal{F}$en and I risk a moment outside to watch them go. The enclosed back courtyard of the temple opens out onto a busy street, and once they are gone—Bay and True and Ciro, three figures swallowed up quickly in the massive city of the Above—Fen and I linger in the courtyard for a moment. Once we're back inside, we will have to hide and wait, and neither of us is made for that. Even though illness has taken its toll on Fen, he still has a restlessness, an aliveness about him. I would have liked to see him race when he was well. I think he would have been fast and reckless and good.

I wonder what he would have thought of me.

I can't keep from glancing up at the sun—hot and round and white at this hour of the day, hard to look at but wonderful to feel. It's not lost on me how strange and marvelous this is—my seeing the sun, feeling it on my face.

"What are you thinking?" Fen asks.

"That I'm lucky to see the sun," I say.

"Don't look directly at it," Fen says. "It can burn your eyes."

And right then I feel something, some pressure on my heart and mind, and it's not just sorrow. Fen's face is the last thing I see before the world goes black inside my head.

I can't see, but I'm still here, and the sun is still hot.

"Hold on," Fen says. I feel his hands on my wrists, gentle, steadying me. Fen smells like sweat and dirt. I want True. "Can you walk?" Fen asks.

"Yes," I say.

"Hold on," Fen says again. His voice sounds far away. I feel him guiding me, and then the heat of the sun is gone, and my feet hit the familiar-feeling surface of the temple floor. We are back inside.

"Keep walking," Fen says. "I'll help you."

I hear the surface change to the wooden floor of the room where we were hiding before, and I hear a door close, and then it gets dark all the way through me.

"Rio," Fen says, but his voice is not one that can call me back.

Light appears in the corner of my vision. Soon the rest of the interior of the storage room comes into view—the closet, the dusty books on shelves.

"How long was I down?" I ask Fen, who sits near me, holding one of my hands.

"A while," he says. "It's afternoon now." He lets go of my hand. "The Above isn't good for you."

"Not for you, either," I say.

Fen starts to cough. It's my turn to put a steadying hand on him.

"I wish you were Bay," he says to me, between coughs.

"I wish you were True," I say, and that makes Fen laugh and cough harder.

"Can you convince the people Above?" Fen asks, his voice raspy. "Can you do this?"

I remember what Maire told me, just before she saved me. *The only chance of success is to trust in your own power.*

"Yes," I say. "I can."

We hear someone at the door to the storage room. Could it be Ciro? Already?

I glance at the door and see that Fen locked it, the way Ciro told us to before he left. The handle is moving. It's someone with a key. It could be Ciro, but if it's him, why hasn't he said anything?

Without a word Fen and I both head for the closet at the back of the room. I go inside first. Fen pulls it shut and locks it from the inside, and we hide behind the heavy robes. Even if they find a way to open the closet door, it's deep enough and dark enough that they might not see us.

"I don't have a key to the closet in here," someone says, the cultured tone of his accent reminding me of Ciro, though it is certainly not him. The door to the storage room opens, and I hold my breath. "But perhaps this room itself will work for what you need?"

"Yes," another man says, and I stiffen.

It's Nevio.

Fen puts his hand on my arm. He thinks I'm going to pass out again, but I'm not. In fact I feel perfectly clear, the best I've felt since I was in the water coming to shore. Because I hear other noises. Gentle rustlings. Plaintive cries.

The temple bats are here.

Nevio must have brought them up with him when he came. But why? Is he kinder than I thought? Even though he killed all the sirens, did he have mercy for Atlantia's second miracle?

"This will be enough space until we have more permanent quarters for them," Nevio says, his voice rich and gorgeous, even more sonorous than it was Below. "I appreciate your allowing them to come live here. The temple will feel the most like home to them. Their caretaker is coming up on the next transport, and he will see to their upkeep and feeding. But for now this room will be sufficient."

"Do they have trouble living away from Atlantia?" the other person asks. I wonder if he's a member of the Council of the Above. "I know the sirens couldn't last for long up here."

"No," Nevio says pleasantly. "The bats did not originate Below, as the sirens did. The bats are creatures of the Above that managed to stow away and survive the trip to Atlantia long ago."

"So they're not miracles?" the Council member asks.

"Of course not," says Nevio. "The bats are simply creatures that were meant to be Above and were trapped somewhere else, much like myself and the rest of the Council of the Below."

One of the bats cries out.

"In fact," Nevio says, "the bats do very well up here. Before we made you the gift of the sirens, we sent up some of the bats for your scientists to study. They determined that these little animals can survive—even thrive—up here, though they apparently have a bit of a penchant for flying over the water at night."

"But we must not let them do that," the Council member says, trying to assert his authority. "We have to keep them caged. We can't have creatures that once lived Below flying around freely in the Above."

"I agree completely," Nevio says. Is there an edge to his voice, or do I imagine it? But I am heartened to hear that the Council Above intends to oversee Nevio and the others.

Of course, Nevio may have other plans.

As soon as we hear them leave, I lunge for the closet door, pushing it open. Fen hisses at me to come back, but I have to see the bats. They tremble in their cages, but Nevio's right. They seem healthy enough—bright eyes and clear breathing. It's the cages that make them afraid.

"They're not supposed to be locked up like this," I say. "Especially not when night comes. That's when they're meant to fly free."

"Why do you think he saved them?" Fen asks.

"I have no idea," I say. I lean toward the cage, and some of the bats chatter their way closer to me. If I didn't know better, I'd say they remember me. "But I know it's for some selfish reason of his own. Not because he actually cares about them."

"Nevio is rotten, all right," Fen agrees.

Should I trust Fen? Should I tell him that Nevio is a siren? True would tell Fen. True would trust him.

So I do.

Fen's eyes widen in surprise but not for long. "I should have known," he says. "It explains everything."

"I know," I say. "I can't believe it took me so long to realize what he is."

"But if he's a siren, how does he plan to survive up here?"

"I don't know," I say. "He's a different kind of siren than we've ever seen before. Maybe the Above doesn't affect him."

"He's the people of the Above's worst nightmare," Fen says. "When you speak tonight, you have to tell them what he is."

"But if I do that," I say, "they'll think they were right about the sirens. That the sirens can't be trusted, that they should all die. I'll never convince the people of the Above to let Atlantia live that way."

"You're right," Fen says. "I didn't think of that." He bends down to look more closely at the bats, and they eye him balefully, which makes him laugh. "They like you," he says, pointing to my hand, which I've rested on the cage. They don't seem to mind, and they are calming down.

"I think I might be familiar to them," I say. "I used to clean the temple trees, where they loved to roost. But the temple trees have no leaves anymore. They've all fallen."

"They have?" Fen asks. "What else has changed?" I hear homesickness in his voice, and longing.

"Atlantia is breaking," I say. And then I realize we didn't even have time to tell Fen and Bay about the deepmarket. "The deepmarket drowned," I say. "There was a breach."

"No," Fen says, sounding horrified. "How many died?"

"Hundreds of people," I say. "And the bats were starting to die, too." I take a deep breath. I think the bats are calming me.

"So what are you going to do tonight?" Fen asks. "How are you going to get around Nevio? What are you going to say?"

"I don't know."

"You have to think of something," Fen says, growing agitated. "This is Bay's life you're asking for. And True's."

"Did Bay tell you? What I am?"

"She said that you had a secret," Fen says, "and that it was yours to tell. But I think I've figured it out."

He's smart. I can see why he caught her eye, why he has a hold on her heart.

"You're a siren," he says very quietly.

"Yes," I say.

And then Fen leans forward, coughing again, this time sounding even worse than before. Someone is going to hear us. He has to stop. I take my hand away from where I've been resting it on the bats' cage and put it on Fen's back. Soon he's quiet and his breathing settles.

"I'll wear the mask from now on," he says. "I promise. It's just—I hate it. I feel like I'm drowning when I have it on."

"I understand perfectly," I say.

He looks at me. "I guess you do."

He pulls the mask over his face and we settle back inside the closet to wait, closing the door.

"I heard there was another civilization that lasted as long as we have," Fen says after a while, softly. "They separated their people, too, around the same time we had the Divide. Some stayed on land, and the others went into the sky. Maybe those people are up there, watching us now. Maybe they're waiting for this to all play out, and then they'll come down and take what's left."

"People up in the sky? That sounds like the gods."

"I don't believe in the gods."

"Bay does."

"I know," he says. "Do you?"

"I don't know," I say.

Then we hear someone open the door to the storage room.

"Do you have the key to the closet?" a voice asks, and Fen and I both stiffen in recognition.

It's Nevio again.

"Yes," someone says. He's not the same person who came with Nevio before, but I can tell from this man's accent that he is also from the Above. "I think it's this one. It was in his pocket."

"Excellent," Nevio says.

I hear them jimmying with the lock on the closet door. Fen and I pull the robes in front of us and make ourselves as small as we can in the back, but I worry it's not enough. Are we about to be caught?

"This isn't a permanent solution," the other voice warns, and Nevio laughs. He seems a little farther away. I can hear one of the bats shrieking and the cage opening. What is he doing?

"I know," he says. "You only have to give me long enough to speak. Then we'll have someone come back and get rid of him."

"Where will you take him?" the other man asks.

"We can dump him in the ocean," Nevio says. "That seems appropriate. He seemed to have a fascination with its abominations."

The other person laughs. "Everything has gone very smoothly."

"Yes," Nevio agrees. "But I wish we knew what he was doing down near the water."

"Don't worry about it," the other man says. "It's as you said. He was fascinated by the ocean. He walked down by the shore all the time, gathering up shells and watching the waves."

The key engages in the lock, and the closet door opens.

I hold my breath. Fen is quiet as can be and I send up a silent prayer to my mother and the gods that he won't cough right now.

And then I stop praying and have to try not to scream, because someone is being pushed into the closet, someone slack and heavy and dead, and he lands in front of us, on us, and then the door swings shut, they lock it again, and the body is still on me, and I know exactly who it is. I saw his face in that moment of light.

Ciro.

"Might as well dump this in there as well, for now," Nevio says.

And then the door opens again, and they throw something else in—another body, this one tiny, but just as lifeless as Ciro's.

It's one of the temple bats.

It's so dark, and I scrabble for the closet door as soon as I hear Nevio and the other man leave the storage room. I find the inside lock and twist it, pushing the door open, and the bats all stare at me with wide eyes.

"I'm sorry," I say to them, to Ciro. "I'm so sorry."

I should have told Ciro what Nevio was. I should have trusted Ciro. But I didn't, and now he's dead. After everything he did to help us.

He's dead because of me.

"Rio," Fen says. "It's all right."

I shake my head. "How can it be all right?" I look at Ciro, his wild hair and his poor, dead face. I put my hand on his chest, but I feel no rise and fall, no heartbeat. I can't see a wound, but the lack of life in him, the emptiness of his eyes, is grotesque. Is this how it was for my mother? Did Nevio himself administer the poison this time, or did he once again get someone to do the dirty work?

"It's all right," Fen says again, pulling off his mask so he can speak to me face-to-face, "because True and Bay got Below. Did you hear Nevio? He doesn't know what Ciro was doing at the water. Ciro must have already helped Bay and True leave on the transport. Remember? *Nevio didn't see Bay and True.* He saw Ciro, alone. We still have a chance. You still have to speak."

279

Ciro is dead.

The sirens are dead.

Maire is dead; my mother is dead.

We're all going to die.

How is Fen staying so clear about all this?

And then I remember. He is already dying. He's been dying for months.

But Bay and True—they have to live. I have to do what I can to make that happen. And I want to live, too.

Maire said I would know when it was time.

It's time.

I have to go out in the temple. I have to speak.

I put my hand on Ciro's eyes to close them. He was willing to help me. But I have to do it alone. I touch the bats' cage as I stand up.

"You're right," I say to Fen.

He stands up, too. "I'll come with you. You shouldn't have to do this alone."

"I won't be alone," I say. I feel like Bay will be with me. And my mother. And her sister.

And there is something else I need Fen to do.

"Please," I say. "Let them go."

His face changes. For the first time, I see him break. "I can't," he says.

I realize that he thinks I mean Bay, and True. And I understand.

"The bats," I say, pointing to the cages. "Can you find a way to let them go?"

Fen nods. Relief washes over me. The bats are not meant to be locked up like this. They need to be free. I will speak better if they are free.

"Thank you," I say to Fen. "I'll see you again." And then, before I creep out into the hall of the temple, I touch Fen's shoulder in farewell. Even though I'm not who he wants and he's not who I want, we understand each other. I will do what I can to save what's left.

CHAPTER 29

*P*riests and guards line the halls. Many of them; one of
me. But I remember Maire at the floodgates, and on the small
island.

You don't see me, I say to the priests and the guards, as I walk
among them down the narrow hall, our robes almost brushing,
their faces so near that I know the colors of their eyes.

And they *don't* see me.

It is a strange feeling to walk among the people of the
Above and have them look past me and through me. In a way,
however, it is like speaking in the Below without my real voice.
In a way, it feels familiar.

The temple is full, and Nevio stands at the pulpit. Where
are the sirens? Ciro said the Council planned to bring their
bodies to the temple for a public viewing. Then I see black
boxes set up in the side aisles, and a note of foreboding rings in
my heart. The boxes weren't there when I came in last night.

I count them. Twenty-seven.

I stay to the side, pulling up the hood of my brown robe.
The temple is full of people—they even stand in the aisles,
in the nave—and if I keep out of the main aisle, and move
slowly, I don't think anyone will notice me. I don't want to use

my voice again, not yet, but I have to see the sirens' bodies. I have to know.

"People of the Above," Nevio says, "we are glad and grateful to be back among you. We have yearned for this moment for so long."

His voice sounds perfect here. His tones seem familiar and comfortable, right, and what he says is a flawless combination of coercion and command. Even now, even knowing what he is, I can't tell when he speaks the truth. There is often some of it mixed in with his lies.

I walk until I reach the nearest box. It is raised above the ground but low enough for me to see inside.

And there is a siren.

She died screaming.

It is hard to look.

Nevio keeps speaking. Has he seen me yet? I don't think so. I keep walking, my head low. People let me pass without noticing. Was my single command enough to hold them all for this long?

Or is it Nevio's voice that has them held?

"The sirens are gone," he says. "The day has come at last when the Above need no longer fear anything from the Below."

And then, at the end of the nave, there she is. They have tucked her away, and at first I find this strange, because then fewer people can see her, and I thought the point of bringing the bodies here was for people to see the sirens dead. But then I understand why they didn't put her body near the front.

Because Maire's face is at peace.

She looks beautiful in a way that is something like the sea, something like the sun. It is difficult to turn away, though it hurts so much to see her like this. I touch the edge of her robe and move toward the center aisle of the nave. It is time to be seen. It is time to be heard.

"We knew this day would come," Nevio says, his voice rolling over the pulpit, down the aisle. He opens his arms. "It is time for the Above to rid yourselves of the burden of the Below once and for all. It is *your* time."

I step out into the center aisle. Nevio looks up and our eyes meet, with the gods watching all around. And I realize that he has come to believe his own lies. He believes that he shapes the world as he speaks.

People turn to see what Nevio sees. Does he know who I am? Does he remember now that I came Above?

"Who is that?" someone asks.

I push back the hood of my robe. People move out of my way to let me pass. My feet on the marble sound like my mother's did when she went up in the near silence before a service. The jar of water still sits on the altar, and light shines through the windows Above.

"I am Rio Conwy," I say, and for a moment I can say nothing more.

Lies and truth have been spoken in this temple, and now my name is there with all the rest of it.

I see hatred and recognition in Nevio's eyes. He remembers now that I came Above, and he must also realize who made him forget. Maire. She was more powerful than Nevio in that moment, and in many others.

I am not afraid.

I know how to do this. Maire showed me, every step, from the first day in the deepmarket to the last day on the island shore. She even showed me what to say.

I turn my back on Nevio and face the people of the Above. I speak. I ask.

"Listen."

I feel it coming to me, going from me—all my siren power in that single word, everything I have saved, spent.

I want it to be this way. I want them to listen, but I want to speak to them as a person. Someone like them. Then maybe they will understand.

I want to be heard.

I can use my real voice now, stripped-down, still strong. I am as human as each of them, and they will hear that, if they can do what I asked and *listen*. I won't command them to do anything. That would be wrong. And that would not hold. They have to *want* to save us.

I know what Bay is saying at this moment, Below. What we are saying, together. I know her mind, and she knows my voice. We are water, the same; the river and the bay.

I hear my voice in the temple, and Bay's voice in my head, and Maire and Oceana, too. They speak with me, two dead and one living, all wanting the same miracle, for Atlantia to be saved.

"The people of Atlantia need you," I say. "And you need us. We need to help each other."

The gargoyle gods look down. I have seen their counterparts all my life. I know their sharp teeth and their stone gazes. I can almost see through Bay's eyes, what she sees now in the temple Below.

"For those who live Above, the gods look like the creatures of the Below. For the people Below, they are the animals that walked Above. But they are the same gods. Whether we made them or discovered them, they are the same. And we are the same. We are all human, Above and Below. Even the sirens. They are different, but difference does not have to mean death. It can mean life. Ours, and yours."

The temple is nearly silent. Even Nevio stays quiet, listening. But he is smiling. He thinks I have made a mistake. He knows I spent it all on that word—*Listen.* I asked them to listen, and they do, even Nevio. But he thinks that as soon as I am done speaking and the power of that word is broken, he will be able to come in and finish me, make short work of all I've said. Because he won't hesitate to use his voice on them. He won't balk at telling them what to do.

Don't think of him. Think of your mother and your aunt and your sister. Think of the boy Bay loves. Think of the boy you love.

"It will be the most difficult thing we have ever done," I say. "We will have to care about those in the other world as much as we care about those who are among us. For me this is easy, because my sister is there. She is not with me."

And when I say the words, they become true. I no longer feel Bay with me.

Is she gone? *What has happened Below?*

In that moment I falter, thinking of her, and the power of my voice is spent.

Nevio makes his move. "This is not the order of things," he says, leaning over the pulpit. "The Below had their time to be the world of the privileged, to make decisions about who lived and where. Now it is your time. And remember, the Below spawned the sirens. Those abnormal, mutated creatures. This girl is one of them."

"The sirens are human," I say. "No better or worse than any other humans. Nevio knows this. He is a siren, too."

Murmurs and cries break out in the crowd.

I didn't want to tell them. But they should know.

Nevio's face registers a brief moment of shock, and then he smiles again. "She is from the Below," he says, "and she is wrong. Ignorant. The Below is ignorant. But you, the people of the Above, are not. You are ready to be free. Free of supporting those Below, free of worrying about the past. It is time to move forward, without the fetters of Atlantia encumbering you, holding you back."

He is so powerful that it feels like there is a voice inside me responding to him, wanting to obey and believe what he says.

But it feels foreign. It feels wrong, like he has placed something there and then called to it. Not like it is part of me. When Maire spoke that last time, on the island, it did not feel foreign. It felt like she was singing a song I knew, one that was part of me, not put there by anyone else. She gave voice to something essential, something belonging to everyone alive.

Some people push for the exit. Where do they think they will go?

Some people kneel down to pray. Who do they think will hear?

I see Fen trying to get to me, his mask pulled over his face.

The peacekeepers of the Above are coming for me now. In the melee someone knocks the jar of water from the altar.

The glass shatters. For a moment, the silence is absolute.

Nevio and I draw in our breath at the same time, but before we say anything, someone at the back calls out, his voice desperate and anguished, ringing down along the nave and under the stained glass.

"The idea that we could do this," he says. "That we could save everyone. That we could overcome the problems of the past. It seems too good to be true."

"It *is* too good to be true," Nevio says.

Until now I felt strong, but my body is losing its battle with the Above. I feel fatigue coming over me, darkness asking me to sink into it and rest.

Nevio sees the weakness. His eyes are bright with power, and his voice is still strong. How does he manage to avoid the exhaustion?

I look up to the gods for help and something alive stares down.

One of the bats from the Below. Fen has let them out. I see them, one by one, flying in to perch on the gods of the Above the way they did in the Below. I feel strength coming back to me, just from looking at them.

I feel better when the bats are near. They are from the Below. And I calm them, too. We help one another.

I remember the little body thrown in after Ciro's, and suddenly I know.

This is how Nevio plans to survive. He takes the strength from the bats. He uses them up to stay Above.

I won't do that.

But the water on the altar is from the Below. And it can't be killed. The water can't be hurt.

I look back to where Maire's body rests.

She was the most powerful siren I've ever known.

And then I swear I hear her.

No, Maire says. *You are.*

I walk up to the place in front of the pulpit where the jar broke and put my hands in the water on the ground. I hear people gasp. Then I show them my wet palms. "We shouldn't be afraid to touch the Below," I say. "Haven't you missed it, deep inside? Don't you wonder what is down there?"

Some of them nod—only a few—but hope starts in my heart.

"Atlantia," I say, "is a city unlike any other. Your ancestors helped build it. You have helped keep it alive. Wouldn't you like to see it?"

And then I tell them about the city, the temple, the plazas, the wishing pools. I tell them about the trees, about the way the city breathes. I tell them about the songs of the sirens, the sea gardens, the racing lanes, about the gods, the gondolas. I tell them about the deepmarket, the drowning.

"And then there are the people of Atlantia," I say, and my voice breaks, thinking of True and Bay, of all the others. "We need to hurry," I tell the crowd. I feel stronger, but I can tell that it will not last; it cannot hold. The water can't help for long. "If we don't save Atlantia, then it will die. The city. The people. Please."

"We would have to trust that any sirens left would use their power for good," someone says.

"We would have to trust you to do the same," I say. "We are human. We are no better or worse than you." I remember that there are people like True now, people who developed traits in response to the sirens. "You shape us; we shape you," I say. "I believe it is what the gods intended. For us to change and teach each other."

And I realize: *I know the third miracle. It's Maire and what she did.* And it wasn't only her grand act of sacrifice, her superb display of power on the island. It was the way she saved voices and sent up shells for years, each one a personal, critical expression of faith and hope and humanity. "You have heard some of us."

"Yes," someone says. "We have."

I hear the sound of a hundred tiny wings, the soft cries of small miracles. The bats leave their perches on the gods and fly above us. *"Oh,"* the people say in unison.

As the bats pass by the windows, their blue wings outstretched, it is as beautiful as the ocean.

I am crying and I am strong.

I see Fen in the crowd. I smile at him. He did what I asked. He let them free.

Then one of the bats comes down, closer, closer. It settles on my shoulder.

And then another.

And another.

They soar right past Nevio and land on me. Their claws hurt a little, but I know I seem like home to them. I know they recognize Atlantia in me.

I am bristling with miracles. I wear them like a robe.

Nevio speaks, but the people no longer listen. They stare at me. Will they let Atlantia live?

Will the people Below listen to Bay? Will they accept the truth? Do they understand that they have to change, too?

"Thank you," I say to the bats. "But you can go. It's all right."

I won't use my voice to make people do what I want.

And I won't take from the bats in order to stay here.

The bats fly up, and I feel their strength leave me. My knees buckle.

Peacekeepers close in on me. Nevio's voice rings in my ears, but I clap my hands over them, tight as a shell around a sea creature. I hear my own breathing, steady as my sister's.

CHAPTER 30

*Y*ou see, Maire says. *I was right. You are the only one who could do this.*

"Because of my voice," I say.

And because of the work you did that had nothing to do with your voice, Maire says. *You made yourself strong enough to swim in the lanes, which meant you could get to the shore from the island. You cared for the bats for years, so they would come to you without your having to call. You were brave enough to speak in the temple Above, and when you did, the people felt like they could believe you. They knew that you spoke the truth.*

I open my eyes.

I know the voice I heard was Maire's—whether in my mind or saved somehow, I'm not certain.

I know that the face looking down at me is Fen's. I know that the soft sounds around me are the temple bats. And I know almost instantly where I am.

I'm on the transport, going Below. I can tell. I feel the Above vanishing behind us, the place where I spent a single day in all my life. The sun is in the past for me for now; the water feels deeper than it did before.

"We had to get you back down," Fen says. "You wouldn't do

what Nevio did and take the life from the bats. We used all the seawater in the temple to get you here, and then some. People went down to the shore and brought water back for you."

I can feel that, too. I've been drenched, and the salt is left on my skin. I smile. If I'd chosen the Above that day in the temple, I would have had a sprinkling of the sea and now I am covered in it.

Fen and I are not alone. Priests and Council members of the Above sit and speak in groups, and bats settle on the armrests of chairs and fly about the transport. Their presence indicates to me that we are not being sent down to die.

"It worked," I say.

"It worked," Fen agrees. "For now."

The Above is going to let us live. For now.

I feel my strength coming back the farther down we go.

"You shouldn't be coming Below," I say to Fen. "Isn't the changing pressure bad for your lungs?"

"Yes," he says. "But I have to see Bay. I have to find out what happened to her."

But I think I already know. I think that my sister was able to reach them, to help them understand. I think that those who were hidden might have finally dared to reveal themselves. I think voices from the Below, siren voices and regular voices, cried out to the gods for help and to one another to change. I think the Below might have been calling out in the very moment the bats came to cover me.

One of the bats stretches out its wings. In this light they are the same blue as the sirens' robes.

"They followed us to the transport," Fen says. "Some settled in the trees and stayed Above, but these ones flew on board. We thought it best to let them go where they wanted."

One of the priests in his brown robes edges closer. "I don't mean to interrupt," he says. "But can you—will you—tell us about the Below again?" He is young. His voice sounds eager, like he's thought about this all his life. Maybe he had a brother or a sister who indulged his dreaming of another world, the way Bay always did for me.

"It's beautiful," I say, "and broken."

I tell him again what I said in the temple Above, about the city and the people, and as I do, he weeps.

I have brought him to tears, and for a moment that scares me. Did I manipulate him unintentionally? But I have not tried to persuade him. I've tried to tell him the truth.

And I realize something else.

My voice is gone. It is no longer the voice of a siren. But it is powerful, strong, and *mine*.

"You think we can learn to live together?" the priest asks.

"I do," I say.

He nods to me and goes back to his seat. I hear him telling the priest next to him what I have said, and I think, *That's good. Let them convince one another.*

"Your siren voice," Fen says. "What do you think happened?"

"I think," I say, "that I gave it to the Above."

"You don't sound sorry," Fen says.

"I'm not," I say.

Because I am strong. I was born with a siren voice—it was a gift that I chose to give up to save my city—but I still have all the power I earned for myself.

And I can speak. I will never stop speaking.

I think Maire knew that this would happen. I think she understood, and she didn't tell me because she thought I might not be willing to give up my voice. I believe that in the end she did love me, but she loved the sirens more. She loved the city more. She wanted it all saved. And she was right.

It was worth it, what I lost, if it gained the lives of those who live in Atlantia.

The door of the transport slides open. A mass of people waits for us, and the city breathes.

I wonder if they can smell the sun on our skin or see the stars in our eyes?

This time it is not hard to find her. She's right at the front of the crowd, looking for me.

"Bay," I say. "I came back."

EPILOGUE

The sirens' island is quiet.

The salty winter air feels cool, and in this season the sky's colors are softer, pink and blue. When I take off my shoes and walk on the sand with my bare feet, it feels grainy and separate, instead of a smooth warm whole.

Bay waits on the island. She wraps her arms around me and pulls me close. The waves hit the shore over and over. I feel my sister's heart pounding against mine and I close my eyes and listen.

When we pull apart, I sit down on the sand and Bay sits next to me.

Most of the transports now surface at the shore of the main island. But when I come Above, Bay and I like to meet here, even though it is where Maire died.

That may seem strange to some but not to us. The island is beautiful. More than any other place, even more than the temple, it feels like a bridge between the Above and the Below. The bats that stayed Above never went back to the temple. Instead they make their homes in the caves near the sea. Sometimes, at dusk, they come out and roost in the silver-mossed trees, and I see their blue wings.

And the island feels like sacred ground.

Every shell in hand could hold her voice. Every stone under foot could be where she stood. Every whisper of wind or hush of water might be a message, or nothing at all. Nothing more or less than wind and waves and shells and stones.

I love it here. If I could, I'd build a house out of driftwood for Fen and Bay and True and me. I would set the trident god from Elinor over the lintel of the house. The bats might come to rest on him.

I wish I could stay Above.

And Bay wishes she could be Below. But neither of us can live where we'd like, and we can't be together. Bay needs to be with Fen, and Above is best for him now that their doctors will treat him. And for now the Below is better for me. I still can't last up here as long as I want—a matter of days, not weeks or years, thought it gets easier each time I surface.

And of course True lives Below. Together, we work on a crew rebuilding the deepmarket. We piece Atlantia back together with fire and metal. Yesterday, we raced side by side in one of the lanes, and when our bodies touched, I remembered when we came Above. When we climbed out of the water, True kissed me in front of everyone and ignored their cheers and catcalls. "Why me?" he asked.

"I've been listening a long time," I said. "No one sounds as right as you."

When I was growing up, I often felt trapped by the constraints of my voice, the concerns of my family, the confines of my city.

Sitting with my sister's arm around me, breathing the air of the Above while the sky of the Below laps at our feet, I know I am no longer trapped.

I am protected, shaped and built by what is outside, what they made of me, but also by what is inside, what I made of myself.

"Bay," I say, speaking to her for the first time, and I see her face change, grow still but not surprised. The wind touches her hair, blows sand along our skin.

"Rio," she says. "Your voice."

I smile. She hears it, too.

My siren voice is coming back.

I thought it was gone, and for weeks that was true. But then I felt it again, on the day some of the hidden siren children gathered in the temple to sing, and it seemed right that my voice would return, the way it felt right when it left. I spent it all and so was given it to share again. It made me think of my mother. Oceana gave what she had to save others, to protect and teach them. And somehow, that never diminished her. Somehow, that made her strong.

I thought I was the last siren in Atlantia, but now I am the first. Someone has to teach the younger sirens, those who have at last revealed themselves. Someone has to tell them the stories once hidden in Atlantia's walls.

"We ended up like Oceana and Maire, after all," I say to Bay. "Two sisters who have to live apart."

"I'm proud to be like them," Bay says.

So am I. They kept faith with each other. Neither of them tried to destroy the other, though they could have, the way the sisters in that siren story did.

It is easy to see my mother and her sister in every small thing, to feel them in the open places in my soul. I think they watch us. I think they love us still.

Bay wraps both arms around me and I feel her tears on my skin. We are not lost mermaids with seaweed hair and coins for eyes, but human girls, alive and found.

We are sisters, and we did not drown.

$\mathcal{A}$CKNOWLEDGMENTS

This is a story about family, and I am grateful for mine:

My husband, Scott, and our four wonderful children;

My mother, Arlene Van Dyke Braithwaite, a strong and creative woman;

My aunt, Elaine Braithwaite Jolley, who has none of the dark of Rio's aunt Maire and all of the good;

My father, Robert Todd Braithwaite, my brother, Nic, and my sisters, Hope and Elaine;

My cousins, Elizabeth Jolley, Caitlin Jolley, and Andrea Jolley Hatch;

And my beloved grandmother, Alice Todd Braithwaite, who passed away during the writing of this novel. When I was six, she gave me my very own drawer in her desk and told me, "You can write your stories and keep them here, and I will never read any of them unless you tell me that I can." I wish she could read this one.

I am also extremely grateful for my professional family:

My agent, Jodi Reamer, who makes me laugh and work until I cry;

My editor, Julie Strauss-Gabel, who is tremendously smart and asks the right questions;

My publicist, Shanta Newlin, the best in the business—unflappable, unstoppable, smart, and fun;

Don Weisberg, the godfather of all my books and my career at Penguin Young Readers;

The entire team at Penguin Young Readers, including Eileen Kreit, Anna Jarzab, Theresa Evangelista, Melissa Faulner, Jen Loja, Felicia Frazier, Rosanne Lauer, Lisa Kelly, Emily Romero, Erin Berger, Erin Toller, Carmela Iaria, Venessa Carson, and Nicole White;

Alec Shane and Cecilia de la Campa at Writers House;

And the staff at The King's English, whose love for readers and books and life in general is intoxicating and contagious.

I am also grateful for others I consider family:

Mylee Edwards, Mikayla Kirkby, and Vanessa Kirkby, who have loved and watched over my children with great patience, and who are each amazing women;

The young women in my neighborhood and church congregation, who are strong, smart, good, and beautiful—it is my privilege to work with you;

Wonderful friends—some fellow writers, some not—who make me laugh and lift me up, who truly know me and from whom I learn so much;

And always, *always,* I am grateful for my wonderful readers.

© Erin Summerill

$\mathcal{A}$LLY $\mathcal{C}$ONDIE

is the author of the critically acclaimed Matched trilogy, a #1 *New York Times* and international bestseller. The series has been published in more than 30 languages. A former English teacher, Ally lives with her husband and four children outside of Salt Lake City, Utah. She loves reading, writing, running, and listening to her husband play guitar.

Allycondie.com
Twitter: @allycondie

IN THE SOCIETY, OFFICIALS DECIDE.
WHO YOU **LOVE**.
WHERE YOU **WORK**.
WHEN YOU **DIE**.

Discover **Ally Condie's** internationally bestselling **Matched** trilogy:

"This futuristic fable of love and free will asks: Can there be freedom without choice? The tale of Cassia's journey from acceptance to rebellion will draw you in and leave you wanting more."
—**CASSANDRA CLARE**, author of The Infernal Devices and The Mortal Instruments series

"The hottest YA title to hit bookstores since *The Hunger Games*."
—*Entertainment Weekly*

"[A] superb dystopian romance." —*The Wall Street Journal*

"Ally Condie's debut features impressive writing that's bound to captivate young minds." —*Los Angeles Times*

"Love triangle + struggle against the powers that be = perfect escape."
—**MTV.COM**

★ "A fierce, unforgettable page-turner." —*Kirkus*, starred review

"Distinct . . . authentic . . . poetic." —*School Library Journal*